THE
LAUNCH

AMY TACKETT

Official Playlist

Songs to pair with your reading experience:

"River" — Bishop Briggs

"Poppin' Champagne" — All Time Low

"Your Way's Better" — Forrest Frank

"Ohio Is for Lovers" — Hawthorne Heights

"Up" — Forrest Frank

"Sk8er Boi" — Avril Lavigne

"One and Only" — Adele

"Congratulations" — Post Malone

"I Forgot That You Existed" — Taylor Swift

"Thriller" — Michael Jackson

"I Just Wanna Live" — Good Charlotte

"Centuries" — Fall Out Boy

"What Was I Made For?" — Billie Eilish

"Hard Fought Hallelujah" — Brandon Lake

"You're Gonna Go Far, Kid" — The Offspring

"Graves Into Gardens" — Brandon Lake

"Marry Me" — Train

AUTHOR'S NOTE

Dear reader,

This book is a sequel to *The Gala* and meant to be read in order. If you haven't read that book yet, I would strongly suggest starting there. If you have read *The Gala*, then you know that book blurs the line between thriller and horror. Similarly, *The Launch* is a unique blend of psychological thriller, horror, and (*surprise!*) contemporary romance. It also contains Christian representation, but please know, I do not classify this book as traditional Christian fiction. It is a very dark, gruesome story with foul language, and you may want to quit reading at times due to the nature of the content, but my hope is that you stick with Cole and the gang until the very end.

If you would like to review the content warnings before continuing, please visit my website. I have omitted them here to avoid spoilers, but as with all my books, this warning should not be taken lightly. My brain became *so very unhinged* while writing this.

With all my (demented) love,
Amy

To everyone who turned the page.

The light shines in the darkness, and the darkness has not overcome it.

—John 1:5

In the beginning was the reporter, and the reporter
was with me, and the reporter was me.

At least, that's how I saw it.

—Cole Sloane, The Great Chase

FRIDAY

LUNA

"COLE GETS OUT OF prison today."

Holy shiz, Luna thought. *Did I just say that out loud?*

This was all too surreal. Perhaps it was actually a dream, and she was going to wake up any second and realize she'd blurred the lines between fiction and reality yet again.

That was always a possibility with her.

Luna shifted the car into park and let out a deep breath, switching her cell phone from her right ear to her left.

Her best friend, Nyla, gasped. "Are you going to pick him up?"

Luna chewed the corner of her bottom lip, her eyes set on the prison before her. "Mhm. I'm here now."

Nyla made another theatrical sound over the phone, and Luna winced. She'd met Ny a year after The Gala at one of Jaxson's school events. The two instantly clicked, and Luna told her everything one night over one too many glasses of wine. How she'd fallen for Cole while he was still legally married. How she'd tried to ignore it and just be the friend he so desperately needed as they played Zanella's mind games. How he'd almost kissed her at River's grave before drunkenly spiraling out of control, nearly killing them both.

She'd told Nyla everything that happened with Cole before The Gala—and after. Which, to be fair, really wasn't much, considering he'd been behind bars.

They couldn't exactly move with the fluidity most couples did when they discovered there was something more in the air beyond conventional friendship. Nope. Gentle touches, hugs that lingered, and magnetic currents that pulled two bodies together were not an option within the confined walls of Materville Correctional Institute.

Instead, Cole and Luna were sentenced to five years of monthly letter writing, occasional phone calls, and weekly visits with *adult supervision at all times*. She cringed at the thought, detesting the dirty jokes the guards made at the end of their visits.

And yet, despite it all, Luna still felt magically drawn to Cole. She felt it every time she saw him. Every time she walked in and saw Cole's messy brown waves, scruffy jaw, and bulging prison muscles hiding under his orange jumpsuit, her heart thumped fervently inside her chest.

Which was honestly *so annoying*, now that she thought about it, because they really were *just friends*. Like, seriously, he was locked away for avenging his daughter's death—technically also called manslaughter—all while she was adjusting to her new life as a single mom of a teenage boy. A romantic relationship just didn't make sense, given their circumstances.

No matter how nice he looked in those—

Gah! Stop it!

The Lord would surely smite her if she finished that thought.

Like you care at this point.

"What're you going to say?" Nyla asked, reminding Luna she was still on the phone.

Luna shook her head, pinching the bridge of her nose. "Um, I don't know. Probably hi?" Had she mentioned Ny was as inquisitive as her journalist coworkers at the paper? Apparently, doulas are just as nosey as reporters.

"Oh my gosh, he's probably going to walk out and be all like, 'Hey, Lu,' with his scruffy prison voice."

Luna rubbed her temples and glanced back at the gate. Why had she told Nyla about Cole again? "I've told you, we're just friends. That's it. Cole's been in prison for five years, Ny—for manslaughter."

"Yeah, and that's hot," she quipped, making Luna snort.

Oh my gosh, Luna thought. *What am I even doing here?*

She cleared her throat and flipped down her sun visor, peeking at her reflection in the mirror. It'd been half a decade since she'd seen Cole outside these walls, half a decade since Graham Zanella waltzed into her life and introduced her to the son she never knew she had. Half a decade since she'd had a moment to breathe, to think—to *want* something for herself. She may have pined for Cole Sloane once upon a time, but now she didn't have time to think about whether his conviction and scruffy jail voice were hot.

No time at all.

Her focus was on her son, Jaxson.

And yet, maybe a touch of lipstick wouldn't hurt. She put the phone on speaker and set it down before pulling a neutral peach shade out of her bag. "I'm sure he has more important things than a relationship to consider, Ny."

"Oh, please," her best friend said. "He's been locked up with nothing but men for the last five years. I wouldn't be surprised if he popped a boner the second your skin touches."

"Nyla!" Luna's eyes widened, and her jaw dropped. "Please, you know I'm not like that. *We're* not like that. Cole and I, I told you, we're just—"

"Friends," Ny finished for her. "Yeah, yeah. I know. We'll see what you say in a couple of weeks."

Luna rolled her eyes and flipped the visor back up, her phone lighting up on her lap. She picked it up and frowned. "Oh, crap. I have to go. Jax's school is calling."

Ny's voice was mocking. "Fine. Whatever, but we all know you're Cole's little jailbait—"

"Bye!" Luna cut her off with a high-pitched tone and switched over to accept the next call. "Hello, this is Luna Monroe."

"Hi, Ms. Monroe. This is Kathy calling from Suttonville High. I just wanted to let you know we've had a little incident with Jaxson."

Oh no.

Luna felt her heart drop.

Not again.

She took a deep breath and put on a fake smile. "What happened?"

Kathy briefly paused before informing her Jaxson had been in a "slight altercation" with another student. Luna's chest tightened at the thought of another person bullying her kid.

"Is he okay?"

"Yes," Kathy said, "he's fine. But I do think you should come down here. His interpreter said he's having issues with his hearing aids again."

Luna felt like cursing, like screaming a whole slew of legitimate curse words. Jax had been bullied at his previous schools, and his temper was quick to get away from him. Luna had already replaced two sets of hearing aids in the time they'd been together, each one costing a small fortune thanks to the subpar health insurance *The Suttonville Chronicles* provided.

She took a deep breath and prayed they wouldn't have to buy new ones. "I'll be right there."

"Thank you, miss. I'll let Jaxson know."

Kathy ended the call without saying goodbye, and the optimistic outlook Luna had previously felt for the new school year dissipated in her chest.

"Jax, baby," she whispered, shaking her head. She was supposed to be protecting him, providing him with warmth, love, comfort—not allowing him to be bullied for his disability. Luna hung her head in shame, once again at a loss for words.

Five years later, and she still didn't have the slightest clue what she was doing.

A single tear formed in the corner of her eye, but a tap on her window made her jump.

The tear never fell.

Instead, she screamed, knocked over her lukewarm coffee, and looked up into the familiar face of the man she knew best.

"Hey, Lu."

COLE

COLE'S THROAT FELT RAW as he uttered her name.

She looked beautiful—all five foot one of her—as she sat there, starstruck and effortless.

It set his insides on fire.

"Cole." She smiled back at him and flung her car door open, slamming the window's top corner straight into Cole's right eye.

Fuck.

Cole screamed and doubled over, holding his eye as stars burst into his vision.

"Ohmygosh, Cole! I am *so* sorry." Luna cradled his face in her hands. The touch sent an entirely new sensation through him. "Are you okay? Let me see."

He'd just walked out of prison, ready to reenter society and the general population—all without a clue as to what he was going to do—and was greeted with a black eye. It should've scared him, angered him. Should've acted as a warning, perhaps a bad omen, letting him know things were about to go so very wrong.

But none of that happened. Because Luna was touching him.

Although reluctant to end the moment, Cole stood up slowly, trying to hide his wince from the pain. "Damn, Lu." His voice was gravelly and thick. "What a way to welcome me home."

He waited as she lifted her gaze from the bruise forming under his lower eyelid, stilling when her eyes locked onto his. Those beautiful, varying shades of blue would be his demise. He could feel it from that one look alone.

It made him grin.

"I wouldn't have it any other way," he added.

Luna's cheeks flushed. "I'm sorry," she said again, covering her face quickly with both hands before wrapping her arms around Cole's neck. "I'm such a klutz."

"My klutz," he said, pulling her in tighter.

Fuck, he'd missed this.

All too quickly, she pulled away and scrunched her nose. "I think that's going to leave a nasty shiner. I'm *so* sorry again."

Cole waved a hand and used the other to sift through his messy brown waves. "No worries. It'll add to my street cred."

He smiled at her again, and the blush deepened in her cheeks. He'd thought about this moment for so long. What it would be like to finally touch her again, to have the freedom to take his time and explore what this new era of their relationship looked like. He used to regret trying to kiss her that night at his daughter's grave, remembering how unhealthy he'd been at the time, how unfair it was to put Luna into that position, but now, he couldn't remember why.

All he knew was that his insides were swelling—with want, need, desire, *love*—like a giant wave that was too big for its own good, ready to break and curl inward on itself at any moment. Whether that break would be his ultimate demise or the baptism his soul so desperately needed, he didn't know.

"Okay," she said, blinking rapidly and clearing her throat. "I've got to run to Jax's school, but I want to hear everything on the drive. Let's go, Sling Blade."

Cole snorted, resisting the urge to roll his eyes. Sling Blade was his prison nickname, much to his dismay. "I still don't know why they called me that."

"Oh, I can one-hundred-percent see it." Luna spoke quickly before carefully opening her door and sliding into her seat. Cole frowned, sad he hadn't thought to open it for her.

"You, Cole Sloane," Luna continued as he stepped over to his side, "are a man of few words."

Cole pursed his lips, slid into his seat, and buckled his seat belt, the two quickly falling into their natural banter. "What do you mean? I'm a reporter-turned-author—I have so many words."

"Yeah." Luna threw the car into reverse and backed out of her parking spot. "But that's on paper. In person, you do actually grunt a lot."

"Mmm."

Luna snorted. "Okay, you did that on purpose."

Cole only grinned before offering another Karl Childers impression, and Luna smiled, sending his mind spiraling. Her blonde hair was longer than it used to be but still messy and wavy as it fell out of her signature claw clip. She always looked stunning with her hair pulled back like that. Cole didn't know why, but something about it made him feral.

She talked a mile a minute as they eased onto the road, attempting to catch Cole up on Jax's misadventures at school and some work drama, but Cole found it increasingly difficult to pay attention to what she was saying. More than anything, all he wanted to do was command her to pull over, unbuckle himself, and haul his large body across the small planes of the car before grabbing her face and burying her words with his lips. He wanted to taste her, touch her, feel her in all the ways he could—all the ways she would let him.

But he couldn't do that, not yet.

No matter how badly he wanted to.

"Are you excited for the launch party next week?"

Luna's question caught him off guard.

"Hm?"

"Your launch party," she repeated. "Are you getting excited?"

Oh.

The wave inside him finally broke, sending him crashing as his body tumbled beneath it.

Cole sighed and looked down, picking at a piece of loose skin on his thumb. He wasn't sure how to answer her truthfully. She was referring to the launch party for his tell-all memoir about what happened with Graham Zanella, the lethal spawn of a human who coined himself an artist. Cole had spent years chasing and obsessing over him, until it reached a boiling point when his fifteen-year-old daughter, River, committed suicide.

At least that's what Cole thought, or rather, what he was led to believe for two haunting years until Z came back into his life, inviting him to an insane art gala where the truth was finally revealed: that Graham Zanella had coaxed his daughter into killing herself. Had convinced her to pick up the knife and talked her through it until the very end.

When Cole found out, he killed the man.

And then he went to prison, where he wrote a book.

Call it unconventional, but it was the best form of therapy money couldn't buy.

"Excited but nervous," he finally said after a minute. "Ready to get it over with."

"Over with?" Luna cast him a sideways glance, and Cole mulled over his words before responding.

"I don't know." He turned to look out the window, the red and gold autumn hues blurring by. "I mean, I'm happy to have the story out in the world finally, but the idea of being in a large crowd . . . at a party . . ."

The words hung between them, much like the swirling leaves outside. The party was scheduled for Halloween night at a local indie bookstore; it had been for years. Cole's agent, Dani, had sold his manuscript in a bidding war nearly four years ago, on the condition they wait until Cole's release to go to print.

"This is *your* book, Cole," Dani had said one day when visiting him, her stiletto nail pointed directly at his chest. "We can't celebrate without you. It wouldn't be right."

Cole remembered nodding his head, reluctantly agreeing to her suggestion, which he suspected had more to do with maximizing sales and less to do with his feelings in the matter. Publishing was a business, not an art form to these people. Cole couldn't very well smile for a photo-op and sign books in prison after all.

It wasn't until this moment that he realized the launch party would be the first time he'd be in a crowd, a non-incarcerated crowd, since The Gala.

"A party does feel like a lot." Luna's voice was soft.

Cole swallowed and let out a deep breath. "Yeah."

The silence resumed, but only for a moment.

"It's too bad we can't change the whole thing—scale it back to a smaller setting. If only someone had considered all this sooner . . ." she trailed off, and Cole detected a hint of mischief in her voice. Almost as if—

"Lu?" He raised an eyebrow. "What're you getting at?"

But she shook her head, puckering her lips nonchalantly. "I don't have the slightest idea what you mean."

Cole started to question her again, but as soon as she pulled into the school's parking lot, both of their phones chimed with a group text from their favorite British-Australian rock star.

Sol: *You out of the slammer yet, mate?*

Luna squealed. "Here," she said, hitting the call button and shoving her phone into Cole's hands. "You talk to him. I have a bully to deal with."

LUNA

Smoothing out her coffee-stained blouse, Luna exited the car and made her way into the principal's office, where Jaxson was sitting front and center. Her heart melted at the sight of her baby boy, now fourteen, and the messy strawberry-blond curls that he'd loosely styled to cover his scars.

"Jax," she signed, *"are you okay?"*

Her son nodded and looked away.

"What happened? Kathleen said there was an incident and your hearing aids aren't working?" She laid a hand on his knee and watched as he held out the turquoise-blue aids in his palm.

"Here. I don't want them anyway. Stupid things never work." Jaxson pushed them into her hand and turned away, arms crossed.

Luna sighed, anger and defeat circling inside her as she wondered how she'd possibly fix this.

God, she silently prayed, *please . . .*

And then she stopped, because she didn't quite know what to say. Didn't know what she was really asking of the big man upstairs at this point because, honestly, her prayers hadn't been doing much of anything lately.

Her body involuntarily winced at the admission, but it was true. She still believed in God, of course, but sometimes, things felt . . . hopeless.

And it made her start to wonder about things that her pastor would surely not approve of.

"Miss Monroe?" The sound of Jax's interpreter, Florence, snapped Luna out of her numbing, downward spiral.

"Flo, what happened?" she immediately blurted.

The middle-aged woman tugged at her striped cardigan and flicked her green eyes to Jaxson before responding. "Charlie Henson was mocking him during math class. So, when it was Jaxson's turn to go to the board and solve a problem, he wrote one plus two equals Charlie's brain cells."

Luna rolled in her lips and closed her eyes, taking a deep breath. Her internal thoughts were torn between *that's my boy* and *oh, Jaxson.*

Flo went on. "Charlie was embarrassed, as you can imagine, and he shoved Jaxson into a locker after class."

Luna gasped, placing a hand on her chest.

She would kill that little weasel. Stomp his guts out and throw him to the curb.

Or maybe you'll have Cole do it for you.

Her eyes widened at the intrusive thought.

Oh my gosh, stop!

She shook her head and cleared her throat. "Is he okay? Did he get hurt?"

Florence cocked her head to the side, her expression unreadable. "He's okay. He's a tough little guy, but I wonder if you've put any more thought into enrolling him in the Ohio School for the Deaf?"

Another wave of insecurity crashed through Luna. "Not really," she said, smiling sheepishly. "That's all the way in Columbus, and you know I work here at the paper."

"They have on-campus living options for students," Flo retorted quickly.

"Uh, yeah," Luna started. "I don't know. I missed out on so much of his childhood already . . . but I'll think about it, okay? Thanks, Flo." She spun back around, pushing down the thought like a balloon underwater, knowing fully well it would pop up again before she was ready.

"Come on, Jax," she signed. *"Let's get out of here."*

School wasn't over for another few hours, but on days like this, Luna felt it was best for Jaxson to get out and have a mental health break.

"Ice cream?" She looked back at him as she stepped outside of the school, holding the door open.

She watched as Jax nodded but didn't say anything back, and her heart cracked at the silence.

"Hey," she tried again. *"I have a surprise for you."*

That caught his interest. *"What?"*

Luna smiled, already knowing he'd be ecstatic to see Cole. Once Jax had coped with the events from The Gala, he had begged to go with Luna every time she visited the prison. The boys bonded more easily than she could've ever dreamed, and Cole picked up ASL rather quickly.

"Cole's in the car."

She watched as a smile similar to her own lit up on her son's face. *"Wait, what?"*

"He got released today. He's in the car—I went and picked him up."

Jax's blue eyes turned a shade warmer, and he took off in an instant. *"Come on!"*

Luna laughed as she watched him dart to the car, his once-boyish features giving way to those of the young man he'd become. She clutched her chest as she often did when she wondered about the other set of genetics he'd inherited—*whose* genetics he'd inherited.

After Zanella had revealed that Luna's egg donation had resulted in Jax's birth—and that his surrogate and adoptive moms abandoned him due to his condition—she'd tried to convince the fertility clinic to release the name of the sperm donor, but they'd insisted their hands were tied. She didn't have the funds to pursue further legal action after the war she had with the state to get legal custody of him, so she'd had to make peace with the fact that she may never know, that Jaxson may never know, who his father was.

It wouldn't be so terrible if he looked more like Luna, but he had several physical attributes that did not match hers. His frame, with its long, gangly limbs, was nearing six foot three, and his ash-and-ginger-colored hair was more lush than ever, a stark contrast to her petite five-foot frame and fine sandy-blonde hair. Sometimes, she wondered if this had all been some impossible mix-up, like Zanella had lied to her and was continuing to orchestrate this whole production from beyond the grave, but then there were the moments when she knew, without a shadow of a doubt, that Jaxson was her son.

It was in the subtleness of his features. The way he hitched his lip to the side when he was thinking, and the way his smile melted into his face with ease. The kindness in his heart that settled so easily over the dark traumas of his past. He'd inherited her gentleness and her character, and for that, she was thankful. Her main prayer now was that Jax would also acquire her faith, accepting Jesus's love for him.

Perhaps witnessing her son come to Christ would strengthen Luna's beliefs again.

She straightened her still-stained blouse and followed her son back to the car where Cole was already squeezing Jaxson in a bear hug.

"What's up, man? I've missed you! Mom didn't tell me you were getting out today." Jax's hands moved with excited energy, his facial features aglow.

"We wanted it to be a surprise," Cole signed. *"I was going to be at your place when you got home, but this way is even better."*

Jaxson pumped his fist in the air, and Luna's heart swelled at the sight of her boys communicating.

"Mom, can we take Cole to the new donut place after ice cream?"

Cole and Luna laughed in unison.

"You don't have to ask me twice," she replied. *"Let's go."*

"So, what did Sol say?" Luna asked through a bite of her blueberry cake donut while Jaxson worked on his homework. She'd been dying to know but didn't want to interrupt Cole and Jax while they talked. Aside from Luna's dad, Jaxson didn't have any male figures in his life, so knowing he had Cole meant everything.

"Oh." Cole paused to lick his thumb and forefinger, a knowing grin on his face. "Like you don't already know."

Luna feigned innocence. "I don't have the slightest idea what you mean."

Cole cocked an eyebrow, his signature move making her feel giddy from the inside out. "Uh-huh."

Luna tugged in her bottom lip, grazing it with her teeth as she held back a squeal. "Okay, fiiiiine. Dani asked Sol and me what we thought about moving the party to Solstice's cabin so we could have something more low-key with a smaller crowd—to help you reacclimate and whatnot—and I said it was a great idea!"

She said it all in a rush, hoping it had been the right choice and that she hadn't made a total error in judgment.

Cole sat back in the red vinyl booth, patting his face with a napkin while a slow smile crept across his lips. "I love it. It is a great idea, Lu. Thank you."

The tension in her chest eased.

"Phew," she breathed. "Okay, thank God. I'm so glad to hear you say that." She plucked another donut from the baker's dozen they'd ordered, a maple spice latte one this time. "We leave tomorrow for the week."

"Wait, what?"

And boom goes the dynamite.

Luna shrugged. "Yup. Surprise. Sol and I thought it'd be good to help you readjust to civilian life for a few days, especially with it being the weekend before Halloween, a.k.a. your first Gala anniversary outside of the pokey."

What she really meant was she was worried about Cole having a PTSD trigger, but she didn't say that.

"We've got it all planned out. Me, you, Jax, Sol, and Greyson will go to Sol's cabin tomorrow evening and make a fun vacation out of it all." Convincing Greyson, the paper's social media manager who'd helped them during Zanella's twisted mind games, had been a little harder than Luna expected. He claimed he didn't want to be without cell signal, but she assured him Sol had boosters. In the end, he had rolled his eyes and agreed to go, claiming it was only for her, *Momma Lu,* when really she knew it was because he loved and missed Cole just as much as the rest of them. Grey just had a flare for the dramatics.

"A vacation?" The deadpan tone Luna had come to know and love escaped Cole's mouth.

"Yes, it'll be fun!" she said, her voice rising in pitch. "Don't be such a grump about it. We'll all just have a chill week away from the press, with a small, eloquent launch party in the middle of it for a bit of funsies. It'll be great."

She watched him stew it over as Jaxson peeked up from his homework.

"What're you guys talking about?"

Smiling, she replied, *"About how we're all gonna go to Solstice Blackwood's cabin tomorrow for a week-long vacation to celebrate Cole's release, both from prison and his book."*

Jax smiled back at her as his face lit up, and he turned to Cole. *"Really?"*

Luna tried to hide her satisfaction as she watched Cole's thoughts roll across his face.

He could never say no to Jax. He was like a different person around him, as if his natural instincts to father this fatherless child simply couldn't be contained.

And Jax was the same, too. He was drawn to Cole in a way that almost made her jealous, if only because she wished they could bond that easily. Luna had become his safe space over the years, and with that came boundary pushing, blaming, and a raw shard of glass that stabbed her identity as a mother every time he accused her of abandoning him.

But she knew he loved her.

And that was enough.

She could be okay with Cole taking on the fun role in her son's life.

More than okay with it, if she was being honest with herself.

"I guess when you put it like that," Cole signed, rolling his lips in, *"yes, really."*

This time, Luna really did squeal as Jax high-fived Cole.

This was going to be so good. For her, Jaxson, Cole—this would be good for everyone. Exactly what their souls needed in the midst of bullies and finances and just freaking *life*.

She was going to the woods for a week with all her boys.

What could possibly go wrong?

I remember it all so well.

The way his neck felt in my hands. The way his pulse ricocheted beneath his papery skin. The way I wanted to crush his windpipe until every last drop of air was gone.

I remember everything about that night.

—Cole Sloane, The Great Chase

COLE

Cole stepped into his house for the first time in five years, and it was intoxicating and terrifying all at the same time.

Because this was the place where it all began.

Where he and Rose built their first home, where River was born, where she grew up.

Where she died.

It was the place where Rose fell out of love with him and cheated on Cole with his brother, David. The place where he learned about their baby. *Clara.*

It was the place where it all happened.

And in the midst of it, he'd always had Emmett, his mastiff, best friend, and emotional support animal, right by his side.

But not today.

As Cole closed the front door and stood in the foyer, his gaze fell to Emmett's empty dog bed.

Em.

A lump formed in his throat. Mastiffs had notoriously short lives, so Cole knew this day would come. He just never expected to not be there when it did. When he was incarcerated, Luna had taken Emmett in like he was her own, claiming she needed him just as much as he needed her while she attempted to navigate life as a new mother. Hell, she'd even brought him to visit Cole in prison until he was too ill. Luna cared for him until the very end, assuring Cole that Emmett was happy and healthy in Heaven.

Cole didn't know if he believed that. Not because he didn't believe in Heaven, because he did, but he didn't know if dogs really went to Heaven. It was a nice thought, but when Cole asked the prison chaplain about it the next morning, he couldn't give Cole a clear answer.

"The scripture is very clear that God values animals," the man had said as they sat together in a makeshift altar. "Scriptures tell us many times that God believes animals to be good. He is also a God who promises perfect love and gifts in Heaven, so it could be a fair assumption to believe animals are in Heaven, too."

Cole had scrunched his eyes and furrowed his eyebrows. "But there's no absolute? No definitive scripture that says one way or the other?"

The pastor clicked his tongue before vaguely shaking his head. "I'm afraid not."

And that was why Cole still had issues with this religion. In his own time, he had come to believe God was real, but he had trouble fully accepting things that weren't absolute. His mind was logical, detail oriented, factual. He didn't operate on theories and blind belief.

It was why, much to Luna's dismay, he'd still not been baptized. He wanted to, really, truly, he did, but his heart wasn't ready for it. He still had so many questions.

He whispered a quiet "love you, bud" before glancing away from the empty dog bed. He was ready to shake off the blues and celebrate his newfound freedom, but Emmett's ghost wasn't the only one haunting Cole's past. As he turned toward the kitchen, his heart caught when he spotted the family photos lining the walls.

School photos of River.

Annual family pictures at the beach.

His wedding day.

A collective representation of a life he no longer knew.

A beam of light shone through the curtains, casting a glow on the bottom corner of River's seventh-grade school picture, highlighting a fine layer of dust. Cole walked toward it and carefully swiped his finger across the frame. They say a percentage of all dust is composed of dead skin cells; Cole wondered if any of them belonged to River.

His stomach grumbled, and he sighed, knowing better than to reopen this wound today. He blew the possible ashes into the sunlight's beam and made a wish.

The kitchen, too, was exactly as he'd left it. A modest, open-concept dining space with a white subway-tile backsplash and a porcelain farm sink, all coated with another fine layer of dust.

Cole brushed his fingertips along the granite countertops, sliding them over the smooth surface as the weight of the world fell off his shoulders. Because even though he still had hardships to face, he was now a free man. Free from the prison cell that had consumed the entirety of his vision twenty-four hours a day.

He no longer had to fear how he acted, how he carried himself, or what expression he plastered on his face. Nobody was waiting around the corner, surveying him with a shiv up their sleeve, deciding whom they would take as their next victim—how they would play God that day.

He rolled his shoulders, releasing another deep breath as memories of his time in jail flooded him. He wouldn't lie; it had been rough. Not as horrible as the movies made it out to be, but it sure wasn't a walk in the damn park either. Cole had witnessed many stabbings and caught several black eyes himself. He learned it was best to keep to himself, which proved to be easier once Sol was gone. He was grateful for Sol's company in prison, but the man's theatrical nature and celebrity status garnered more attention than Cole would've liked.

One particular memory made him shudder as it tried to resurface, but Cole shut it down before it had a chance to take hold of him—just like the prison therapist, Dr. Hart, instructed.

She was much better than the marriage counselor he and Rose had gone to, in Cole's humble opinion.

He pushed himself off the counter, smiling when a glint from an old whiskey bottle caught his eye. He'd been sober for five years, and surprisingly, he hadn't missed it like he thought he would. Sure, he craved an occasional drink while he'd been locked up, but not in the way he used to. Alcohol used to be his crutch, his coping mechanism in a world marred by grief. But after closing his fist around the throat of the man he hated most and watching him take his last dying breath, well . . . Cole didn't feel the need to reach for the bottle anymore.

Perhaps that was another reason why he didn't want, *didn't deserve*, to be baptized. To be washed by the blood of Christ for a sin he didn't regret committing, not even a little bit.

He rubbed at the peeling label on the Johnnie Walker bottle for a moment longer before setting it back down and reaching for what he'd actually missed most of all during these years: a decent cup of coffee.

His phone buzzed in his pocket, interrupting his plans.

Mom Calling.

An audible groan escaped his lips. He hadn't missed her incessantly nagging voice.

"Hey, Mom." Cole's throat was dry, and he cleared it in an attempt to sound friendlier. "How are you?"

"How am I? Cole, honey, how are *you*?"

The concern in his mother's voice was almost cause for *Cole* to be concerned. Janet Sloane was a lot of things, but a caring mother was not one of them. Their relationship had been minimal, strained at best, and he could count on one hand how many times she came to visit him in prison.

"I'm fine." Cole shifted the phone to hold it between his shoulder and neck so he could grab a mug from the cabinet. "Just got home."

His mother released a dramatic sigh. "Samuel . . . Samuel! It's Cole. He's *home.*"

Cole smirked at the way his mother said home, as if by doing so she could distance herself from the fact that her son had been incarcerated.

"Your father says that's wonderful, dear."

Cole poured a scoop of coffee grounds into a fresh filter. "I'm sure he did, Mom."

Janet huffed in moderate annoyance. "Cole, honey, you know we love you and would have been there for your release today, and for your party next week, if we could. Your father couldn't rebook the tickets with the cruise line, but please know we're so proud of you. We know you worked so hard for this."

A mix of emotions swelled in Cole's chest as he tried to pick out which of his mom's statements would cling to him most.

"Thanks, Mom. I appreciate it."

A beat of silence sat between them, and Cole went back to brewing his pot of coffee.

"Well, enough of that," Janet said. "I want to hear all about it when we get back—and your plans for work now that you're . . . *home.*"

There was the mother Cole knew and loved. "I don't know yet, Mom. The publisher said my preorder numbers have been great, so hopefully the book does well enough to sustain me while I figure out my next move."

It was a topic he'd had several years to marinate on, whether he would return to journalism or not. The pit in his stomach said no, but he had no idea what he would do if his royalties weren't enough to get him a second book deal. Perhaps he could get some freelance work to hold him over.

"I'll let you know when I find out."

The gurgle from the coffee maker sputtered in the background, and Cole heard an equally distracting echo of chatter on his mother's end. He took that as his cue and told her goodbye before swiftly hanging up. His mind wanted to spiral, but he forced himself to stop. Tomorrow's problems would worry about themselves.

Today, he was going to sit on his back porch in his grandma's old rocker and enjoy his long-awaited cup of coffee.

SATURDAY

LUNA

Luna glanced at her reflection in the rearview mirror, trying to calm her nerves.

"He's going to love it." Jaxson's hands found her gaze in the mirror. *"Relax."*

Luna started to argue, ready to explain all the million and one reasons why this might be a bad idea, but a loud bark interrupted her.

"What's the matter, Lemon girl?" Luna turned and scratched the dog's head. "Are you nervous to meet your new daddy, too?"

The dog whimpered, and Luna's heart melted.

"Don't listen to me, Lemmy Lou. I was being crazy before." She paused, laughing as the dog kissed her nose. "Jaxson's right. He's going to love you."

The golden retriever was a rescue Luna had saved from euthanasia at the local shelter three months ago. She'd scanned the center's website routinely since Emmett passed away, yearning to fix the hole his absence had left in everyone's heart. Originally, she'd wanted to wait until Cole was released so they could pick out a pup together, but when she saw the status of poor Lemmy, her heart couldn't take it. She'd driven down to the shelter immediately after work that day and filed the adoption paperwork.

Lemon was officially a Monroe.

Or a Sloane.

Luna hadn't quite figured out the logistics yet.

With a deep sigh, she looked at Jax. *"Come on. Let's go introduce them."*

"Right on." Jax smiled, the goofy wide-set perimeter of his mouth stretching across his entire face.

Luna grinned in return, but not without wondering, *Who gave him that face?*

Lemon yelped before clumsily falling to the ground as Jaxson opened his door. He'd sat in the back for the trip to Cole's house, keeping Lemon company since she didn't like long car rides. The drive from Luna's house to Cole's wasn't all that far, but with the pit stop they had to make for Jax's hearing aid repairs, they'd ended up being in the vehicle for nearly an hour by the time she'd pulled into Cole's driveway.

Her bundle of nerves returned, setting Luna on edge as she stepped out of her car and onto the smooth pavement that lined Cole's house. Mentally preparing herself to be around Cole again was one thing, but they were about to spend an entire week together, alone, in the woods. With her son present. She truly didn't know what to expect. It had seemed like a good idea at the time, but now she wasn't so sure.

"You shouldn't expect anything, Luna," she scolded herself under her breath. "You're just friends, remember?"

Keep telling yourself that.

Luna's eye twitched, and she sighed. It was so hard keeping up with herself.

She ran her hands through her hair as she hopped up the steps, flipping the strands back and forth, back and forth, until she forced herself to stand still and stop fidgeting.

She was being silly. This would be a good time.

Just her, and her son, catching up with America's most beloved convict and future best-selling author, reuniting for the first time in half a decade to celebrate his release from prison and the launch of his debut nonfiction novel.

Nothing bad could happen.

Right?

Right.

Luna balled her hand into a fist and slammed it against the door a little too aggressively. Lemon barked as she rolled around in the yard, stretching her muscles and enjoying the sunlight that cascaded around them.

A moment passed, and Luna felt her stomach grumble.

She tried knocking again. "Cole? Cole, it's Luna and Jax. And we're hungry!" She bit the inside of her lip, both her anxiety and need for food taking over. "Cole! I swear, if you make me wait one more minute, I might actually die of starvation!"

Luna bounced on the balls of her feet, waiting for a response. She was about to start pounding on the door again, demanding food immediately, when she heard a rustling from her left. She whipped her head around, but neither Lemon nor Jax seemed to have noticed anything, the two of them still playing together in the yard.

Probably your anxiety hearing things again.

She ignored her (rather rude) self remarks and turned back to the door, ready to tip it off its hinges if Cole didn't answer soon. But then she heard the noise again, and her heart sped up just the slightest bit.

What the—

"Cole?" She took a nervous step toward the side of the house. She didn't used to be paranoid, but after what happened at The Gala, she was hardwired to remain on high alert.

Taking another step, Luna felt the panic rise inside her chest with each passing breath, preparing herself for whatever, or whoever, might be lurking in the unwanted shadows.

"Cole, if that's you, you better come out right now before I bonk you in the head." Her voice was still calculated despite her growing hysteria.

A loud crash sounded, and Luna screamed. An animal scurried from behind a tipped-over trash can.

"Cheese and rice!" Luna breathed.

"What's going on? Why are you screaming? Are you okay?"

Oh, great. Cole had chosen this precise moment, as she recovered from a mild heart attack, to make his appearance and fire off twenty questions.

Luna turned back to reassure him she was fine, it was probably just a raccoon, but her words got caught in her throat. Cole was standing in the doorway wearing nothing but a towel draped around his waist, his bare skin covered in water droplets. Luna resisted the urge to stare at his somewhat (definitely) chiseled abs that were sprinkled with dark curly hairs, trickling straight from his belly button to his—

"Um, yes, yes, I'm fine." She cleared her throat, remembering her manners. "Is this why you've kept me waiting from my deluxe chocolate s'mores bar and strawberry champagne? A shower?" She didn't actually know if Solstice had these things, but a girl can dream.

Cole cocked his head to the side, and if Luna didn't know any better, she'd say he was amused.

"The showers in prison are awful," he said.

Luna swallowed. "Well, you best be saving some for the fishes, or the showers out here will suck, too."

Why did she say these things? Why did she say things at all? She should just keep her mouth shut and shield her eyes from this beast of a brutally beautiful, half-naked man standing in front of her.

A grin cracked across Cole's face. "Duly noted." He turned to wave at Jax, but his expression fell the moment his eyes locked on Lemon. "Who's that?"

Luna tried to think straight, not at all focusing on the water droplet that was currently sliding down Cole's left bicep. "Hm?"

"The dog," Cole said, his voice almost a whisper. "Who's the dog?"

"Oh." Luna cleared her throat again and plastered on a smile. "That is Lemon, or as I like to call her, Lemmy Lou."

Cole shot his gaze back to Luna, a question in his eyes. "Lemon," he said slowly. "Lemmy."

Luna bit back a smile, a blush threatening her cheeks. "Yes," she said, nodding. "That's our Lemon girl."

She saw the expression on Cole's face transform from questioning to shocked to, dare she say, pure joy?

And then she realized what she'd just said.

"I mean, she's yours. And ours. I got her for all of us, since Emmett, you know." She winced, seeing the quick flash of pain on Cole's face. "We can, like, trade weeks or something. Have shared custody, or whatever you want to call it. But, she's ours. She's yours. She's, she's—"

"Lemon," Cole said, interrupting her. "She's . . . Lemon. She's our Lemon."

Luna peeked at him through her fanned-out lashes, feeling shy and giddy in a way she didn't fully understand. But then, before she knew what was happening, before she could grasp the magnitude of the situation, Cole Sloane stalked over to her, picked her up, and wrapped his giant prison arms around her midsection, letting out a sound somewhere between a cry and a laugh as he spun her around.

"Thank you, Lu," he whispered, setting her down. "She's perfect. I love her already."

Luna would've thought she'd died and gone to Heaven at the feel of Cole's half-naked body pressed up against her, a towel the only thing separating her from seeing his—*you know*—if it weren't for the fact that her son was still standing *right there*.

She pushed herself off him, pretending she wasn't delirious, and waved her hands. "Oh, it was the least we could do. Emmett was family. Now, Lemon is, too."

Before walking back toward his door, Cole gave her one of his lazy, flirtatious smiles, the kind she somehow sensed was reserved only for her, the one she'd dreamt in her sleep. "Let me just get changed. Then I'll come out and meet her."

Luna nodded, attempting to shake off the heat rising in her cheeks. "Great, coolio. Yeah." Then, without thinking, she blurted, "I'm raiding your fridge."

She was going to need a vat of ice cream after that interaction.

COLE

"ALL RIGHT, YOU READY, Lu?"

Cole slammed the hatchback of his Jeep shut, Lemon and Jaxson already spread out and waiting in the backseat.

"Mhm." He heard his favorite blonde answer through a bite of ice cream, making him smile.

He still couldn't believe this woman had given him a dog.

But then again, that was who Luna was. The kindest, most caring soul in the world. She'd known how much Emmett meant to Cole, how much he'd grieved when the two-hundred-pound English mastiff passed last year. She knew that Emmett was the unsung hero of Cole's life and that, had it not been for him, Cole likely wouldn't have survived after River died.

He cleared his throat as his eyes burned.

I really hope all dogs go to Heaven.

Lemon barked from the backseat before promptly sticking her head out the window and licking Cole's face, as if to say, *I love you already, Dad.*

Cole laughed and gave the pup a large bear hug. "I love you, too, Lem."

"You excited for the party?" Jax peered over the dog's floppy ears.

"You know it," Cole replied immediately, trying to convey more enthusiasm than he felt.

than he felt.

It's not that he wasn't excited, exactly. He was proud of the work he'd produced, and a lot of his fears had been alleviated when he found out the party had been moved to Sol's cabin (*thank you, Dani*); but still, something about it twisted his stomach into knots. People had read and commented on his work every day when he was a reporter, and it never bothered him. But this memoir, this story—it was different. Vulnerable in a way that only other writers could understand as he laid his heart out on the page, finally free of the journalistic integrities that had prohibited him from ever having an opinion.

"The better question is," he started, refusing to let his anxiety dampen Jaxson's spirit, *"are you ready?"*

Jax stuck his tongue out and made a rock-and-roll sign. *"Always."*

Cole laughed before tapping his hands against the cool metal frame of the Jeep's door as Luna hopped into the passenger side. He couldn't help the feral grin that painted itself across his face as his eyes raked over her body. She was dressed in an old, emerald-green flannel, which he recognized from her prison visits, and a pair of black leggings that hugged her petite frame. Her hair was twisted up into a claw clip, and as he scrutinized her face, he doubted she had on any makeup.

Not that she needed it.

She was naturally beautiful, and he loved the way she looked climbing into his Jeep.

"Ready!" she squealed.

Cole snapped his attention back into focus.

"You comfy?" he signed to Jax before sliding into his seat.

"I'm fine. Let's go!"

Cole smiled at the boy-turned-man, who was all long limbs with an Ivy League haircut that lent itself to his strawberry-blond waves. His arm was casually draped around Lemon, and Cole felt a familiar pang in his chest as a flashback of River and Emmett sitting in the same spot came to mind.

"Let's go," Cole replied, a softness melting his chest. Then, he turned to Luna. "Music?"

Her eyes widened. "What? No news?" Her tone was mocking, a devious look on her face.

"Yeah, I don't know. I found I don't love listening to the news as much as I used to." He shrugged like it wasn't a big deal, but he and Luna both knew it was.

He could see her resisting the urge to say more, to pry, but in the end, she didn't.

"Fine." She leaned forward and cranked the dial on the radio. "But I'm deejaying."

It was a simple gesture, but Cole smiled, grateful in so many more ways than one.

Thank God he had her in his life instead of Rose.

What about Clara?

Cole winced, conflicting feelings warring inside him.

He had never met Clara, but he thought of the little girl daily. His *niece*. River's *sister*. His head and heart spun the way it always did when he thought of her. Because while Clara's name used to elicit feelings of pain and betrayal, that grief had morphed into something else along the way. Something strange and bizarre that perhaps felt a lot like love.

A tiny seedling had burrowed itself into the dark, dirty crevices of Cole's heart when it came to her, steadily growing into a bud of hope. He was hopeful for a chance to meet Clara and have a relationship with her. Hopeful for the time and space to watch her grow and experience the things River never did. Hopeful for a glimpse of his daughter's ghost in his niece's face.

He hoped for so many things.

But maintaining a relationship with his ex-wife wasn't one of them, and he couldn't possibly be in Clara's life without Rose present.

He sighed and passed another car before getting off the exit.

The drive to Solstice Blackwood's cabin was only about twenty minutes from Cole's house, but with the heaviness that weighed on Cole's chest, it felt like an eternity.

At long last, the sight of the tree line began to dull around him as he turned onto Sol's road, and Rhododendron Lake came into view. The cabin was tucked away on the east side of the small man-made lake, making it almost invisible at first, what with the dozens of pines that fanned across the grand entrance. Cole had forgotten how beautiful the cabin was. He hadn't been here since he, Sol, and Luna were getting ready for The Gala. An old, whacky seamstress named Belinda had been there, forcing him into a ridiculous Clark Kent costume. He shook his head at the memory, then rolled to a stop in the lengthy gravel driveway.

"Almost like nothing's changed," Luna said under her breath.

Except everything has.

Before he could get out any words, a roaring flame appeared in front of him, and he jumped, the sight triggering an old part of his brain as images of Jax, The Gala, and the library all ran through his mind. He noticed Luna wincing, too, and he reached for her hand, cupping it and offering a reassuring, gentle squeeze before turning to check on Jaxson.

"What is Sol doing?" Jax's question made Cole's eyebrows furrow. He whipped his head back to the flames, realizing a beat later that it was just a bonfire, and behind it, stood a familiar rock star who was staking a pole with a flying prison jumpsuit into the wild flames.

Cole chuckled, the anxiety that had threatened him retreating. *"What isn't Sol doing is the better question."*

LUNA

Luna could kill Sol.

Okay, not really, but when she saw those flames dancing in the wind, she felt like ripping his sloppy man bun off his head.

"Time and place, Solstice," she squeaked as she took a deep breath and rolled her shoulders back. "Time and place, my dude."

She shook off the eerie feeling and resisted the urge to run her fingers over her child's scars as they hopped out of Cole's Jeep together. Jax seemed largely unbothered by the ring of fire, but Luna's instinctual feeling to protect him flooded her all the same.

He's okay.

He's safe.

She cleared her throat, brushing a loose strand of hair from her face. "Solstice Blackwood, what are you doing?"

"I thought it was fitting, aye?" His dazzling teeth shone through the smog as he grinned. "Our boy's outta the slammer, both of us free men now."

"Where did you get that jumpsuit?" Cole asked as he heaved their luggage out of the back.

"It's Halloween, mate. They have these things everywhere."

Luna sighed as Cole snickered. Jax made a face when his mom interpreted what Sol had said.

"Deranged," he signed back, and Luna laughed.

"Did he just call me bonkers?" Sol demanded, dodging a flyaway ember.

"You'd know if you practiced your signing." Luna raised a brow. She'd taught him some, but he hadn't practiced as much as Cole.

Sol scoffed and came over to clap a hand on Jax's back. "I'm watching you," he spoke and signed before cracking another shit-eating grin and turning to Cole. "It's good to see you, mate. On the outside."

Cole and Sol hugged, clapping each other on the back the way men do. It'd been so long since Luna had seen them together, and her heart squeezed at the picture-perfect moment. She grabbed her camera out of her bag and threw the daisy-printed strap around her neck, quickly snapping a photo before anyone noticed.

"Grey here yet?" Cole asked, pulling away and sliding his duffel bag strap back onto his shoulder.

Sol shook his head. "Nah, said he won't be in until tomorrow. I think he has a date with a new bloke."

Cole and Luna exchanged a glance and raised their brows.

"Ooh la la," Luna teased.

"Yep. Told him you'd say that." Sol huffed a laugh and then swiveled on the balls of his feet toward the cabin. *"Come on, then. Let's have a beer."*

Luna rolled her eyes as Jax's face lit up. *"No. Don't even ask."*

"Come on, Mom," Jax begged. *"You're no fun."*

Luna winced at his comment but didn't back down. *"And you are fourteen. No sir.* Sol, what's wrong with you?" She voiced the last part, letting out an exasperated sigh when Sol snickered.

On second thought, maybe this was your worst idea ever.

Her inner critic was back. Lovely.

Go away, self.

She followed the men into the wooden home, ignoring her annoying brain and admiring the building's ornate beauty. The place had always been grand, but the additional furnishings Cole's publishing house sent over for the launch party made it exquisite.

She walked past the high-end chandelier and fancy Halloween decor in the foyer before entering the dining room, where PR photos now hung on the wall, one in particular standing out. Her hands traced the framed image of Cole's book cover, and she smiled as her own work stared back at her. The publisher had hired her to shoot the cover, and Luna had photographed the issue of *The Suttonville Chronicles* that featured Cole's mug shot on the front page. She smiled as she took in the tiny details the graphic designer had added, making the cover pop.

"*The Great Chase*." Cole's voice sounded behind her as he entered the room. "I'm still not sold on the title."

She turned to face him, that familiar warmth from earlier glowing again in her chest. "*The Inception and Death of a Reporter* was a bit long."

Cole sighed. "Yeah, I know. I guess you're right."

"I'm always right," Luna quipped with a smile, her breath hitching as Cole raised his hand and gently rested it on hers, his index finger tracing the letters on the image.

"Is that so, Lu?" he whispered into her ear.

She felt her heart muscles constrict, the cracked ventricles begging to be touched.

Jumping Jehoshaphat.

Her quest to remain just friends with this man was proving to be much harder than Luna thought. She feared this was going to be a very long week if he kept doing things that made her insides melt.

Don't act like you don't love it. This is what you fantasized about.

She squeezed her eyes shut, silently chastising herself. Because, yes, of course she had fantasized about him doing this *very thing* (and more) with his tongue and his lips and his breath and his whole dang mouth. He was Cole freaking Sloane, for crying out loud!

But that was precisely why they could not be together. Besides the fact that she had a teenage son to raise and a plethora of other responsibilities, Luna lost all sense of control around Cole. She was useless, like a puddle of marshmallow goop falling out of an overindulgent s'more.

Ugh. It almost made her miss him being in prison. When visiting him, she was confined to one side of the table with a guard quite literally hovering over her, ensuring she didn't break any rules. She was forced to comply. There was no risk of her slipping, of her forgetting what she'd learned after becoming a Christian in her late teenage years. No risk of feeling shame or regret the next morning.

Maybe that's what she needed to do now. Pretend she was visiting Cole in prison. Yes, invisible boundaries sounded like a *great* idea now that she thought about it.

Her faith may be questionable lately, but this was a line she still didn't want to cross. At least not yet.

Right?

COLE

Berries.

Luna still smelled like berries, even after all this time.

He'd fantasized about it a lot in prison, or at least as much as one can when sharing a jail cell with another man. He'd only caught a whiff of it once, in the Forest Fox Brewing Co. bathroom that night during The Gala Games. He'd been intoxicated beyond belief as she sat next to him in the small, confined space, but her scent stuck with him long after, even if it took him a while to admit it.

"Bottoms up, mate." Sol's voice cut through his thoughts, and Luna almost jumped out of her skin.

Dammit, Sol.

The singer always had impeccable timing.

"Thanks, man." Cole took the Sam Adams Oktoberfest and savored the feeling of the cold bottle against his skin. He'd wondered what this moment would feel like. If the alcohol would still taste the same. If he'd still enjoy it, or if the acquired taste had worn off. He'd been tempted to try the old whiskey at his house last night but decided to wait, decided for perhaps the first time in his life, not to drink alone.

Five years of sobriety, all coming to an end. "Cheers."

He raised the bottle in the air and then pressed the glass to his lips before a chilled blend of lager and spices danced across his tongue, slightly burning his throat on the way down.

Exactly like he'd remembered it.

He smiled and took another sip.

Jax came up behind Cole and looked at his mom with an edge of annoyance. *"I still think you should let me try one."*

"Absolutely not!" Luna yelled and signed, causing Cole to nearly spit out his beer.

Jax rolled his eyes and walked away, plopping down beside Lemon on the oversized leather sofa. The puppy was busy chewing on a bone but paused and wagged her tail when she saw Jax. Cole smiled and followed, eager to get some puppy kisses himself.

"Such a good girl, Lem." The retriever barked and licked his face all at once, causing another genuine laugh to escape Cole's lips.

"Quit flirting with my girl," Jax said.

"Your girl?" Cole asked. *"Don't you have one of those at school?"* He watched as Jaxson's face turned crimson, the same way Luna's did. *"What? Feeling shy now?"*

Jax stuck his tongue out but then shot a glance at Luna before adding, *"I'll tell you about her after Mom goes to bed."*

Raising his eyebrows in surprise, Cole nodded and then sat back to enjoy the first of what he hoped would be many beers with Jaxson, Lemon, and Luna.

And Sol.

Can't forget Sol.

THE FIREPIT GLOWED TO life as Solstice threw another log on it. The image of the flames haunted Cole, licking up his spine and making him shudder. He closed his eyes and took a deep breath, reminding himself that Jax was safe.

Luna was safe.

He was safe.

Shifting in the camp chair, he cleared his throat and took another sip of his third drink, letting it soothe the anxiety that threatened his chest.

Cole had been better as of late, much better in fact. He wasn't taking the antidepressants anymore, and the prison therapist had really helped. He received closure after The Gala, and now, he was ready to move on to the next phase of his life—whatever that was. The fear of the flames, the unforgettable scent of rotting flesh, those were just memories he had to let die, let wither away until they no longer infiltrated his lungs.

Thank God he had fresh air readily available again.

That and Luna.

He would definitely like to breathe in her air.

Her *hot* air.

"Cole!" Sol broke through Cole's thoughts. "Beer me, mate."

Smirking, Cole swigged the last of his beer and leaned forward to grab Sol and himself another from the cooler. They'd enjoyed hot dogs for dinner and were sitting around the campfire now, the men several drinks deep while Jaxson sketched in his notebook by the flickering firelight.

"Lu?" Cole looked at her empty hands, wondering why she hadn't indulged yet. "You sure you don't want a drink?"

She shook her head, wrapping her yoga blanket tighter around her chest. "No, I forgot I have to wake up early to edit photos from that wedding I shot last weekend. I don't want to be hung over."

"What?" Cole wrinkled his brow. "This is supposed to be a vacation. You're not working." He paused and looked at Jax, waiting to catch his attention. *"Hey, tell your mom she can't work on this trip."*

Jax laid his notebook down. *"Good luck with that. She works nonstop."*

Luna shifted in her chair, looking away. *"Do not."*

"Do too," Jax retorted.

Cole watched as she blew out a breath and rolled her eyes. *"You know what? I think it's late. You should be going to bed."*

"Bed?" Sol said, his voice hitting a high pitch. "Did she sign bed?" He looked at Cole for confirmation. "I only caught half of what you blokes said, but none of ya can go to bed yet. I was just about to tell ya my favorite ghost story."

"What?" Jax asked his mom.

Cole laughed as Luna sighed in frustration yet again before raising her hands to interpret.

"Ghost story!" Jax's eyes widened, a smile painting itself onto his face. *"I wanna hear."*

"Ghost stories are silly and not real," she signed and spoke aloud.

"Aww, come on, Lu," Cole said, his gaze locked on her petite frame as Lemon hopped up on her lap. The two looked like the most natural pairing in the world as they snuggled by the flames. *"It could be fun."*

Jaxson let out a deep, throaty yelp as he clapped his hands and sat up in his chair. *"It's story time."* He looked at Luna and added, *"His sign language sucks. Can you interpret?"*

Cole almost choked on his beer as Luna giggled. Sol's expression dropped. "What did he say?"

Cole, Luna, and Jax all shared a look and continued laughing until finally, Cole said, "Nothing. Let's hear this story. I'm all beers."

Luna snorted at his silly dad joke, and when she looked at him, he winked. He watched as she bit her bottom lip, and it took everything in him not to yank her from her seat and bite it himself.

Instead, he cleared his throat and stretched his hand out to hers, offering her a drink. "What do you say, Lu? Work can wait until next week, right? Have a beer with me."

After a pregnant pause, she cracked a grin and sat up slowly. Cole swore he could detect a faint pink hue on her cheeks.

"Fine," she said. "Beer me, bish."

Cole obeyed, then pulled his chair closer to hers. "That's my girl." He grinned yet again and then turned his attention to Sol. "All right. Hit us. Whatcha got?"

He wasn't a huge horror fan, had never really bought into ghost stories or the like. But tonight, the idea of sitting around the campfire together as Sol told some ridiculous tale in an attempt to scare them—well, it sounded like fun.

Harmless even.

LUNA

Ohmygosh.

Cole Sloane is sitting right beside me, looking all hot and bothered by this stupid fire, and my son is four feet away from me.

I don't think I can breathe.

Luna let out an accidental whimper as she adjusted herself in her seat, which caused a curious glance from Lemon.

Don't look at me like that, Lem!

Jax waved a hand at her, trying to grab her attention. Apparently Sol had already started talking.

"Sorry, Sol, can you start over?"

"Are you kidding me, mate? That almost hurts me feelings." Sol clutched a hand to his chest as he placed a leg on the cinder blocks surrounding the firepit.

Luna scoffed, trying to hide her frazzledness. "Sorry! Lem was . . . looking at me weird. I'm ready now."

From the corner of her eye, she noticed Cole raising a brow at her, but she refused to acknowledge it. She had to focus.

Because, again, *her son was right there!*

"As I was saying," Sol started, raising his voice before continuing. "This is the Legend of the Rhododendron Recluse."

Luna could sense Cole wiggling his eyebrows beside her, but she tried her best to ignore him as she signed for Jax.

Focus, Lu.

"Rumor has it there was once a man named Roger, who lived alone here by the lake in a cabin not unlike ours. He was an all right chap at first, but then things started to happen, and poor ole Roger got a bit clammy."

Despite the eerie nature of their setting, Luna felt her shoulders relax as she fell into her usual rhythm of interpreting for her son.

"After a few years of living here, Roger started to hear whispers in the night, and he swore they were coming from the lake. The voices would grow louder and louder, shriller and shriller, until Roger couldn't take it anymore, and he'd drop everything he was doing and march right down to this very lake."

Solstice walked theatrically around the campfire, pausing now to crouch down in front of the flames, his voice a whisper. Luna chanced a peek at Cole and internally squealed when he winked at her *again*.

Focus, Lu.

Stop calling yourself Lu! That's making it worse.

Sol stood again, and his voice rose like a crescendo, steering Luna from her thoughts. "Only, when he got there, when he'd reach the water's edges, brushing the tips of his toes against the ice-cold water, the voices would stop. But the echo of their whispers would continue to taunt him throughout the night, and he'd wonder yet again if he'd made it all up. If he was crazy.

"Then weeks passed with nothing, and Roger, the poor ole chap that he was, chalked it all up to too much alone time. Too much *solace*, if you will." The singer-turned-con paused again, a feral grin spreading across his face before he continued. "One night a couple months later, Roger was sitting on his front porch carving a plank of driftwood when he heard new voices, this time coming from the woods. He felt his spine begin to tingle, the hairs on his neck prickling and standing on end, as the voices edged closer. And just when he thought they would consume him, he realized they belonged to actual people."

Jaxson shuddered, and Luna nodded in agreement, a slight chill starting to creep up her spine.

"A group of hikers had landed on the old bloke's property," Sol went on, adjusting his man bun as he made another loop around the firepit. "Scared him so much, he almost shot one of 'em with his pistol, but as luck would have it, their lives were spared. Roger listened to them vent about their problems and their woes and how they'd gotten mixed up a bit in the woods, and he decided to be a good sport and let them camp in his yard."

Luna's fingers moved at lightning speed, her heart rate slowly picking up.

Ghosts aren't real, ghosts aren't real, she reminded herself.

Except the demons who shudder in the night.

She trembled and mumbled the name of Jesus under her breath, trying to soothe the anxiety that was bubbling in her chest.

"Roger went to bed that night just like any other night, but with a slight ounce of pride for the good deed he'd done, what with letting those mongrels sleep on his grass. Hell, he was a happy bloke for once, or at least, not a rueful one. Yes, yes, ole chap went to bed in a bloody good mood . . . until the voices returned."

Sol jumped on top of the beer cooler, sloshing some of his drink in the process.

"Roger was awakened in the middle of the night by the startling, invasive sound of a whisper. It sounded like it was right inside his ear, chilling its canal until his eardrum reached the point of rupture. Roger screamed, instinctually muffling the sounds with his pillow, until the voice wrapped itself around his brain, snaking its way inside his skull.

"The lead voice, the permanent one, summoned him to the lake, and this time, nobody stopped him when he toed off his shoes, stripped down to his bare bollocks, and walked straight into the murky water, gulping the tainted liquid until it filled his lungs beyond the point of repair, and he gasped underwater, silently screaming into the black abyss until his body stilled."

Luna continued to meditate on the name of Jesus as her heart rattled inside her rib cage, too enthralled in the story to do anything other than listen and relay it to Jax, even though she knew she shouldn't.

"Roger died in the lake that night, oh yes, but it wasn't the last time he roamed the earth."

"What's he talking about?" Jax asked.

"I'm afraid to know," Luna answered, and somewhere beside her, she heard Cole cracking another beer.

"On that particular night, after he drowned in the lake, Roger emerged, hours later, and murdered every hiker."

Luna gasped and dropped her hands, jumping when she felt Cole squeeze her knee.

"It's just a story, Lu," he said under his breath as his thumb made small circles on her leg.

"This part of the story changes up quite a bit depending on who's telling it, but from what I gather, Roger carried each one off into the night, attempting to muffle their screams while he bludgeoned them all to death with an ax before extracting their bones. Then, if the rumors are true, he sat down by the lake afterward and began to carve those very same bones, whittling their fingers and femurs into forks and knives as he watched the sun rise over the valley."

"Sol!" Cole and Luna scolded in unison as Jax's jaw dropped.

Solstice burped, falling back in the grass, and his laugh penetrated the air.

"What the fuck, dude." Cole leaned back in his seat and cracked his jaw. "Where did you hear that?"

"One of my buddies from the Remote Renegade circle told me."

Luna hadn't heard him mention the Remote Renegade circle in years. Despite calling this place Sol's cabin, she'd completely forgotten he wasn't the owner, but rather, one of many celebrities who used the cabin as a private escape. It made her wonder who else had been here, who else had access to the cabin at all times, and whether they'd be an issue for Cole's upcoming party. She made a mental note to ask Sol about it later.

Solstice propped himself up on his elbows. "He told me that story the first time I ever came here. Can't believe I hadn't told it to you sooner, now that I think about it. Roger's spirit supposedly still dwells here, haunting the lake."

Luna rolled her eyes and chugged her beer, shuddering at the bitter flavor. "I need a snack. That was disturbing."

She stood slowly, careful not to bother Lemon too much, and wrapped the blanket around her tiny frame.

"Luna," Sol said through slurred words, "you're the only woman I know who can hear a story about bone whittling and still think of food."

"Wait." Cole stood, seemingly coming to her defense. "I'll join you."

Oh, fudge.

Why was he following her, *alone*, into the cabin?

What did he think was going to happen?

Ohmygosh, what if he tries to—and what if I have to tell him—

No.

She shook her head, stopping the thought before it had a chance to bloom. He was probably just hungry, too. She was getting ahead of herself. Just because he'd winked at her a few times and whispered into her ear earlier did not mean he was about to break the silent barrier between them. That invisible line that said do not cross unless you're willing to let go and let everything change for a chance to risk it all.

Luna certainly wasn't ready for something like that. Not with her best friend.

She peeked over at Cole, but that was a very, *very* bad idea considering he was staring right at her with those big, puppy-dog brown eyes that she couldn't help but get lost in.

"On second thought, I think I need another drink first. 'Scuse me!" She brushed past Cole, accidentally knocking his beer out of his hand in the process.

Ugh, you klutz! she chided herself, her eyes going wide. "Shiznit, I am *so* sorry, Cole!"

Her face flushed with embarrassment, and she searched for something, anything, to sop up her mess. And maybe somewhere she could crawl into and hide for the next decade.

"Here," she finally said, shoving her blanket to him. "Let me help you—"

"Lu," he said, cutting her off. "It's okay. Let's go inside. I'll get changed, and we can have that snack—and another drink if you still want."

Okay, it was official now: She felt her heart literally beating outside of her chest.

Okay, maybe not literally, but it was a darn strong figurative statement.

She offered Cole an awkward smile and nodded, biting her bottom lip to keep from saying anything foolish.

As if that could stop you.

COLE

THAT DAMN BOTTOM LIP again.

Cole couldn't resist the pulse he felt in his jeans. He quickly grabbed her hand and led her inside the cabin, away from Sol and Jax. He held the cabin door open for her, and once they were both inside, Cole swore he could've cut the tension with a knife.

He'd tried once to tell Luna how he felt. And not in the drunken, misplaced way he had at the cemetery that night, but in a real *I've healed and I'm in love with you* type of way.

It was a Wednesday afternoon, their typical scheduled visit, about a year after his incarceration. He'd been shamelessly flirting with her like usual, but something about that day was different. It was one of the rare instances where she'd come alone instead of bringing Jax and Emmett. And she was wearing a *red* leather jacket, the same one she'd worn over her dress the night of The Gala.

He'd always had a thing for red.

Luna looked beautiful, more stunning than usual. And so, even though he was in jail, even though he was a convicted felon with an ex-wife and dead kid and would be locked up for several more years, he simply couldn't contain himself any longer.

"Lu," he'd said, interrupting her unusually long monologue about pineapple upside-down cake.

She stopped talking immediately, avoiding eye contact at first, then zeroing in on him when the silence stretched too thin for either of them.

Cole's throat ran dry when her lips parted, showcasing a deep red lipstick that matched her jacket. But no words came out. Instead, she simply closed her mouth and continued staring at Cole, her eyes blinking rapidly.

"Luna," he said, her full name on his lips. "You have no idea how badly I want to kiss you right now."

Her cheeks instantly flushed at his confession. "Um—"

Cole could sense her hesitancy, so he cut her off, not wanting to miss his chance. "You don't have to say it back. I know I'm in here, and you're out there. And you have Jaxson . . ." he trailed off, trying to find the right words. *If there were such a thing.* "I just—" He cleared his throat. "I just can't focus on anything but those damn red lips."

An odd, sheepish noise escaped her—something akin to a squeak.

It made Cole's heart stutter, heightening his senses.

"I'm sorry to distract you," she eventually said.

A feral grin stretched across his face. "You have nothing to apologize for."

And then Cole almost did something bold, something drastic. He almost spilled his other truth to her. *I love you, Luna.* The truth that would change everything between them, the line they couldn't uncross. *I'm in love with you.*

The words were right there, on the tip of his tongue, but then she said, "I have to pick up Jax."

And then those same words died on his tongue, forever haunting him.

Because of course she had to get Jax. Of course that was her priority. And of course she didn't want to be with Cole, not like this. Not while he was locked up for the foreseeable future.

Cole knew exactly what she wasn't saying. He didn't blame her for feeling that way.

He'd nodded, leaned back against his chair, and admired her for a moment longer before the bailiff signaled it was time to leave.

She returned the following week, and the week after, and so on and so forth, but she never wore the red lipstick again.

Cole inhaled a deep breath as he stared at her now, thankful he'd held his tongue all those years ago. The timing hadn't been right, and if he'd pushed it, tried to force it before they were ready, he may have missed this opportunity, right here, right now, to finally profess his love for her.

They were standing so close together, just inches inside the doorway. Luna's blonde hair glistened beneath the cabin's warm lighting, her eyes like two crystal clear pools. Cole wanted to touch her.

So he did.

He lifted a hand and grazed his thumb across her cheek, savoring the feel of her soft skin. He traced a small smattering of freckles, and she inhaled sharply. His heart rate sped up, and just as he was about to cup her cheek and pull her in for a kiss, she yelled, "Your shirt!"

"What?" He blinked rapidly, feeling dazed and confused.

"Your shirt," she repeated. "I spilled beer on your shirt. You need a new shirt, Cole."

I don't need any shirt, is what he wanted to say, but instead, he managed, "Okay." He offered a teasing smile before he tucked in his own bottom lip, making a tsking sound. "Be right back."

And even though his body was on fire, burning to finally be touched by this woman—*his* woman—he spun around on his heel and ran upstairs to the guest room. He quickly tugged off his Springhill University Alumni sweatshirt and replaced it with a T-shirt from *The Chronicles* before pounding back down the steps, eager to pick up where they'd left off. When his feet hit the landing, though, he saw that she was already buried in the refrigerator with a drink in hand.

"Whatcha fixing?" he asked, his voice throaty and deep.

Luna jumped, and he licked his lips, satisfied at the way her body reacted to him, even from ten feet away.

"Well"—her voice echoed from inside the cooler box—"I was originally thinking s'mores, but to be honest, I don't really want to go back out there after Sol told that story." She paused, closing the door with her hip, both hands now preoccupied. "So, I figured ice cream would do the trick."

Cole smirked. He'd always loved the way she ate without remorse. It reminded him of River—in a good way.

His eyes trailed back to her hand with the drink. "Didn't like my beer?"

She took a sip of the homemade cocktail and shrugged. "I once told you I like anything that bites. Beer wasn't doing the trick."

Cole felt something inside him twist, and he took a step toward her. "And is this"—he jabbed a finger at the drink—"doing it for you?" He took another step toward her, his gaze now locked on hers.

Luna slowly set down the cup, and Cole could've sworn he heard a light gasp escape her lips. It had been so long since he'd attempted to kiss her, taste her, touch her, all during that awful night at River's grave site. He'd promised himself that if he ever got the chance, he'd make it up to her in all the ways he could.

Her eyes remained glued to his, neither of them talking now, as they both drank in each other's presence. Cole took one last step, closing the remaining gap between them, and swiped a loose piece of hair out of her face.

"I've missed you, Lu," he whispered under a raspy breath, his gaze falling back to her mouth and then sliding up to her crisp blue eyes.

She swallowed. "I missed you, too."

His body tingled. That was all the confirmation he needed to swoop down and—

Bang!

Something that sounded like a gunshot popped outside, and Luna screamed, jumping back from him. "What was that?"

Cole's eyes were wild with desire and his skin flushed. "I don't know." He was content to assume the noise had come from a neighboring cabin on the other side of the woods, but then his mind turned to Jaxson.

And River.

"Fuck." Heart racing, he adjusted his stance and ran for the door. "You stay here. I'll check."

LUNA

"Like heck I am," Luna mumbled as she followed Cole outside.

Her Deaf son was out there, alone in the middle of the woods with a drunk rock star who knew very little ASL. What was she *thinking*? This was exactly why she couldn't date, especially not Cole Sloane. One moment alone with that man and she'd all but forgotten her responsibilities as a mother.

She was pathetic, the worst actually. And now her son may—

Bang!

She nearly jumped out of her skin as neon green lights exploded in the sky.

And then she breathed a sigh of relief before the anger set in.

Freaking fireworks? Really, Sol?!

"Solstice Blackwood!" She marched over to the fire. "What is wrong with you? Don't you know you're not supposed to let off fireworks when you're drunk? Where did you even get these? It's October, for crying out loud." Her voice rose with annoyance, but she was still relieved all the same.

"Ah, lighten up, love!" Sol looked at Cole before his face split into a grin. "No pun intended—ha! I crack myself up."

Luna watched as he swiped a fake tear from his eye, and she shook her head, wrapping an arm around Jax. *"Come on, I think it's time we got to bed."*

"Aw," Jaxson said. *"I want to light one."*

"No way. Come on, off you go." She waited for him to stand and then whistled for Lemon to follow, too. "Come on, girl. Bedtime." Then she paused, instinctually wondering if she'd overstepped since this was now Cole's dog.

Their dog, she couldn't help but think.

"Unless you want to keep her outside, Cole."

He shook his head. "By all means. Go ahead."

Lemon yawned before wiggling out of her blanket cocoon and hopping down from the camp chair to stretch. Luna could feel Cole's gaze on her; she ignored it. Jaxson was fine, but the bang from the fireworks reminded her just how easily she let Cole distract her.

And she couldn't afford to let that happen again.

She had a duty to protect Jax. Not just as his mother, but as the woman who'd caused him years of trauma. She may not have made the decision to drop him off on CPS's doorstep—like his surrogate mother and intended parent did once they realized he was Deaf—but it was still her fault.

She'd chosen to donate her eggs, to sell a piece of her DNA for money, like she was some kind of sick and twisted human trafficker. She was disgusted with herself, knowing that if she hadn't, then Jaxson would've never been born into those horrific circumstances. Never would've endured feelings of hopelessness and abandonment.

Never would've tried to kill himself by lighting his head on fire at Graham Zanella's *art* gala.

If she had just been a mother the natural way God intended, then she could've saved her baby boy from so much pain and sorrow. Which was why she'd vowed to do whatever she could to make it up to him, to protect him and love him the way a mother should.

That was her primary focus.

Not Cole Sloane.

She straightened her posture and waved good night to the boys. "See you all in the morning."

"Night, Lu," Cole called after her.

Ugh. If he could just stop using that nickname, that would be dandy.

SUNDAY

LUNA

THE NEXT MORNING, LUNA rose bright and early, despite the whiff of a headache she felt brushing at the edge of her forehead. She'd never technically agreed to not work on this trip, so if she woke up early before the others and got it out of the way, it was fine, right?

Right.

She threw on an old, oversized flannel over her cropped sleep tank and gray joggers before twisting her hair into a claw clip. Then, she responded to a text from Nyla, grabbed her laptop, and headed downstairs to brew a pot of coffee. The wedding she shot last weekend had been beautiful, and she was excited to see how the images turned out. She still worked full-time for the paper, but with Jaxson's extra expenses, she'd been taking on more freelance work as of late. It was a lot to keep up with, but she could use the distraction, especially right now.

"Morning," a familiar husky voice said, making her jump as soon as her feet hit the kitchen floor.

Fudgesticks!

Why was he awake this early?

"Morning, Cole." She wrapped the flannel around her body a little tighter, suddenly feeling shy.

"Coffee's on," he said with a nod before lifting a cup to his lips.

Luna couldn't help but blush at the sound of his sleepy morning voice. "Thanks." A bashful smile formed on her lips.

Are you twelve or thirty-three?

Is there much difference, really?

She tuned out her inner dialogue and reached for a mug from the cupboard.

"You sleep good?"

She nodded, careful not to slosh any of the hot liquid as she poured herself a cup of coffee. "Yeah, actually. That mattress was lovely."

Cole smiled behind his cup before saying, "So was mine."

Oh my lanta, he's smizing at me.

Luna didn't even know that was still a thing until this very moment.

Focus. You need to work.

She took a sip of the hot, black liquid and sat opposite Cole at the kitchen island.

There, this is safe.

A whole island between us, if you will.

Satisfied with herself, she set the mug down and opened her laptop.

"I thought we agreed no work." Cole stared at her, his messy bed head trying to steal the show from the sexy grimace on his face. "Lu?"

Luna blinked, trying to remember what he just said. "Um, it's not really work. Just looking at some pretty pictures. You know how I be."

Nice.

Cole chuckled. "Fine. I have a few things to do before the launch party Wednesday, so I guess I can't get on you too much."

"Oh, yeah," Luna said, sitting back in her chair and grabbing a muffin from under the cake dome. "What's on your agenda?"

From the stairs, she heard a shuffle, followed by the sound of Lemon's paws padding down the steps. Cole noticed, too, and his face lit up. He greeted the dog before answering her, scratching Lemon's ears and giving her a treat. Luna had to stop herself from blushing because *dang it* if everything about this man wasn't attractive.

"Not sure yet. Dani texted me last night saying we needed to go over the details, so we scheduled a call for this morning." Cole took a sip of his coffee and bent over to play with Lemon some more before casually adding, "She wants me to invite Rose and David."

Luna stopped typing, her fingers suspended in midair. "I'm sorry, what?"

Cole nodded, scratching his beard stubble. "Yeah. Says it'll be good press if they can leak a couple photos of us talking."

Luna's mind raced as she let the gravity of Cole's words sink in. When he first told her that his ex-wife, Rose, had cheated on him with his brother, David, she'd been at a loss for words. And then when Cole added the minute detail that they'd also conceived a baby, she'd nearly fainted.

"That's redonkulous," she said, eyes wide.

"I know." Cole looked at her, rubbing the back of his neck. "There's more."

Oh no.

Luna's heart skipped a beat as she waited for Cole to confirm her next thought.

"They want Clara to come, too."

Frik frak apple snack.

"You cannot be serious."

"Dead," Cole retorted.

Luna stared at him in disbelief, her jaw likely sweeping muffin crumbs from the floor it was hanging so low. Cole had never met Clara, the love child of Rose and David.

A heaviness weighed on her heart as she searched for the right words.

After a beat of silence, she finally landed on, "How do you feel about that?"

Cole finished off his cup of coffee and stood to pour another. "I think I'm excited. I mean, she's my niece . . . River's sibling. I feel like I should know her. I *want* to know her. I was just thinking about this on the drive in yesterday."

Luna nodded, processing his words.

"And," Cole continued, "it's not her fault, about Rose and David, y'know? She's just an innocent, happy-go-lucky kid who barely knows she has an uncle."

A familiar, warm presence melted over Luna as she felt the Holy Spirit invading the space. "I think that's very noble of you, Cole."

Noble, and attractive.

Cole smiled softly, a distant look in his eyes. "Yeah, well, I'll let you get to work. I'm gonna go outside and call Dani before the rest of the house wakes up. I think Sol mentioned something about a hike, so he might actually be up at a decent hour."

Luna snorted, a serene feeling blooming in her chest. "Can't wait to see how that goes."

COLE

"Bloody hell, mate."

Cole rolled his eyes as Solstice groaned. They'd been hiking in the neighboring woods for the past hour, and the rock star had sweated and complained the entire time.

"Why did you even suggest this if you were going to whine the whole time?" Luna chimed in, asking exactly what Cole had been thinking.

"To detox, o'course," Sol said matter-of-factly. "I've gotta keep my skin nice and fresh for the tour next month."

"You could just not drink," Cole offered, stepping over a fallen branch as they descended the hill leading back toward the cabin.

"That's not funny, mate." Sol paused and placed his hand on his hips, a serious look on his face. "Spent enough time being sober in the slammer. Worst three years of my life."

"As your previous roommate, I take offense to that," Cole said with a smirk.

Sol adjusted his purple bandana and started moving again, this time cutting Cole off and sliding down the remaining trail. "You know what I meant. Speaking of, a beer sounds great." He turned to look back at Jaxson and signed *beer* with a wink.

Luna didn't miss a beat. "He's fourteen, Solstice! Absolutely not," she signed and spoke.

"You're no fun, Mom." Jax feigned a sad look. Cole watched as Luna rolled her eyes, but he also wondered if maybe the comment stung a little. He remembered the struggles of not being "cool" enough anymore when River was that age.

"Drop it, Jax. You're not drinking."

Jax slumped his shoulders and pushed past his mom, making his way to the cabin.

"Hey," Cole said, reaching his hand out to Luna's. "It's just a phase. He doesn't mean it."

He watched the way she scrunched her nose, her cheeks slightly flushed.

"I know," she said, her voice uneven. "It's fine. I'm fine."

Cole wanted to press for more, but instead, he gripped her hand tighter and pulled her to a stop, wrapping his arms around her. He took a deep inhale, cherishing the warm feel of her body against his and the berry scent that emanated from her hair and tickled his nose.

He lowered his mouth to her ear and whispered, "It's okay if you're not fine."

He felt her stiffen and then relax, leaning into his embrace and wrapping her arms around his midsection.

They fit perfectly together, like two human puzzle pieces made for each other.

He held on to her for another minute and thought about tipping his mouth back to her ear. He thought about opening said mouth and brushing it against the soft tissue of her earlobe, running his tongue along the outer edge, all while resisting the urge to bite her, taste her, make her moan.

But none of that happened.

Because just as he was about to part his lips, a piercing scream hit the air.

LUNA

Luna felt her skin crawl as she jumped out of Cole's embrace and turned toward the cabin.

"What was that?" she asked in a rush, her feet already moving.

Cole was right behind her. "I don't know."

Together, the pair moved swiftly over the remaining terrain until they'd reached the French doors leading into the cabin.

"What the devil are these?"

Relief flooded Luna's chest at the sight of her friend and coworker, Greyson. "Grey," she breathed. "You scared me."

Eyes wide, Greyson turned to her from the kitchen. "Uh, I think you should be scared, hun. You wanna tell me why there are fucking *bones* in the silverware drawer?"

And just like that, the panic resuscitated her lungs.

"What do you mean?" Cole demanded, stalking toward Greyson.

"I just opened this damn drawer to get a spoon, and there are *bones* inside it." His signature Southern drawl was seeping out as his voice crept an octave higher.

Luna grabbed at her chest, her fingers fidgeting with her cross necklace. "Surely they're not real." They couldn't be. That wasn't a reality she was willing to accept. Luna twisted around, looking for Sol. "Sol! I think the PR crew misplaced some Halloween decor."

She heard a crash from the second floor—along with a few choice words from America's heartthrob—before Solstice descended the stairs. "Oi, what are you all yelling about?"

Greyson answered for them. "Solstice, there are *bones* in your cutlery drawer."

Sol looked at Greyson, an eyebrow raised. "Bones?"

Luna watched as Grey let out an exasperated sigh and pinched the bridge of his nose. "How many times do I have to say this?" he mumbled. "There are *bones* right here. Just look!"

With his brow still cocked, Sol sauntered over to the kitchen and pulled out the drawer in question. Luna watched as he gave Greyson a smirk and then looked down, peeking at the contents inside.

Sol's face dropped, and Luna's heart rate started pounding again.

"Sol?" She took a cautious step toward him, eyes wide. "I'm assuming the publisher just put these here as a Halloween joke or something?" The words tasted funny in her mouth, but she swallowed them just the same. "Those aren't real . . . right?"

Silence rang in her ears as she waited for the singer to say something—anything that would deny her suspicions. Because if what Greyson found was real, then that would mean they were all in danger.

Grave danger.

Sol cleared his throat and let out a hearty sound. "I don't know, love." He stuck his hand inside the drawer before pulling it back out in one swift motion, a large white femur on display. "This looks pretty fucking real to me."

COLE

Cole felt the familiar pit in his stomach as he watched Sol wave the giant bone around.

It could still be a fake—this could all be some elaborate prank by Sol or Grey, or both.

But something in Cole's gut told him otherwise.

"I don't fucking believe it," Sol muttered. "I thought those stories were just made up."

"What stories?" Greyson demanded.

"Wait," Luna chimed in, shaking her head. "You can't seriously be suggesting—"

"The Rhododendron Recluse," Sol said, cutting her off.

Cole stepped closer, ignoring Grey's exaggerated groan. He hovered over the drawer now, his body tense as he observed the cream-colored marrow sticks that glared back at him.

"There are more in here," he said, cutting through the incessant bickering in the room.

"Yes," Grey said, "that's what I've been trying to tell you, Grandpa. There are fucking *bones* in the drawer. *Bones*, as in plural."

Cole cut his eyes to Luna, who looked white as a ghost.

"Do you think they're real?" she whispered.

"Course they're bloody real!" Sol answered. "Don't you remember the story, love? The Rhododendron Recluse whittled human bones into eating utensils. I told you some people think his spirit still dwells here, haunting that fucking lake."

Grey's jaw dropped. "Solstice Blackwood, what are you talking about?"

Cole returned his attention back to the drawer while Sol recounted a brief version of last night's ghost story. There were five bones in total, each one in a different state of decay. Cole took a deep breath and picked up one that was sharpened to a point, resembling a knife. He had seen bones in prison—femurs and tibias that stuck out of men's legs after someone had attacked them. The sight had caused Cole phantom pains the few times he'd witnessed it, and now, he felt that same nonexistent crunch in the marrow of his own bones.

"They're real," he said, his voice raspy.

Luna whimpered. "Okay, so they're real, but that doesn't mean they're *real* real."

"English, please, Momma Lu." Greyson crossed his arms.

"I mean," Luna continued, "they could be animal bones, right? Like even if they're real, that doesn't mean they're *human* . . ." Her voice trailed off to a whisper, even as she emphasized the last word.

Wanting to offer Luna some sort of comfort, something that would calm her fears and settle her nerves, Cole looked to Sol, then Greyson.

But he had nothing.

And apparently neither did the other two men in the room.

Luna noticed it, too. "Where's Jax?" she asked with a sharp inhale.

"Went to take a nap with the dog," Sol answered. "Said the hike wore him out."

She took off without another word, and Cole immediately sensed her panic. He felt the same way, a dagger of fear piercing through his own chest.

Without thinking, he dropped the bone-knife and followed Luna up the stairs. His instinctual reaction was to call for Jaxson, but he cursed himself, remembering that would be of no use.

At the top of the second-floor landing, Luna barged into Jaxson's room, flicking the lights on and off several times as Cole trailed in behind her.

Oh, thank God.

A heavy sigh left his lips when his gaze landed on Jaxson, who was rubbing his eyes and staring at them in disbelief. Lemon wagged her tail from her spot on the foot of the bed.

"I'm trying to sleep!"

Luna gasped, throwing her arms around him. Jax pushed her off. *"What gives?"*

"I'm just glad you're okay."

Jax looked at Cole. *"What's going on with her?"*

He started to raise his hands, but Luna stood back up, cutting him off. *"Nothing, sorry. That ghost story just got in my head last night, and I wanted to make sure you were okay."*

Cole raised an eyebrow but didn't say anything.

Jax rolled his eyes and threw a pillow at him and Luna. *"You guys are so weird. I'm going back to bed."*

Throwing his hands up in mock surrender, Cole exited through the bedroom door, waiting for Luna in the hallway.

"You wanna tell me what that was about?" he asked once they were both outside the room.

She let out a deep breath and bent over, placing her hands on her knees. "I just didn't want to scare him."

Cole huffed a sarcastic laugh. "A little late for that I think."

Her eyes snapped to his, and he instantly regretted his words when he saw the worry visible in her features. "Not funny," she said.

He glanced away, an uncomfortable feeling settling inside him. "Sorry, Lu."

She took a deep breath before rolling her back and shoulders up into a standing position, much like the yoga instructor used to do in Rose's home-workout videos. Cole grimaced and cleared his throat, willing the thorn in his side to fall away.

"We should check the rest of the cabin." Luna looked at him as she spoke, an unwritten understanding passing between them.

Cole nodded. "You go back downstairs with Sol and Grey. I'll check here—make sure everything's all clear. I'm sure it's just a Halloween prank of some sort, though . . ."

He knew that didn't make sense, but he had said it anyway, desperate to calm Luna's frazzled nerves. He knew the pain of losing a child all too well, and even though Jax wasn't biologically his, he felt like a son to Cole.

Luna agreed, a solemn expression on her face, and quickly padded down the stairs.

Cole spent the next ten minutes carefully inspecting every inch of the top floor, leaving no space untouched. When he was finished, he found no evidence that anyone else had been at the cabin.

So then, where did the bones come from?

LUNA

This was bad.

This was very bad. Luna knew it in her soul. Even though none of them had found evidence of foul play, she could sense that something was off.

"I'm telling ya," Sol said after everyone had finished canvassing the cabin, "it's that bloody ghost. Roger is having a bit of fun, placing some of his old carvings in here for us to find."

Luna crossed her arms over her chest and sat down at the kitchen island. "Sol, ghosts aren't real." She shook her head, annoyed with his incessant tirades. "I don't believe this is some voodoo spirit haunting us!"

Why not? her inner self questioned. *You believe in demons. Jesus himself preached about them. Why are you so apt to believe they don't exist here?*

Luna's entire body convulsed. Because yes, she did believe in demons, technically. They were in the Bible, but they weren't like this. Demonic spirits were evil entities that latched onto vulnerable souls—usually people who didn't believe in God or Jesus—not little old men who haunted forests and carved cutlery out of bones.

Right?!

Her internal thoughts began to spiral, but she shut them down as a more rational—albeit no less frightening—scenario entered her mind. "What if there's someone out there."

Cole crossed his arms. "Nobody's out there, Lu. We're safe."

"But you don't know that!" she countered.

"What, you think there's some stalker out there?" Greyson asked.

Luna chewed the inside of her cheek as a pattern of goose bumps skittered across her forearms. "I mean, there could be?" She tried to rationalize why someone would be after them. "Sol, do you have any weird super fans?"

Sol laughed, the sound throaty and loud. "Do I have any super fans—have you met me, love? Course I do."

"Now's really not the time for an ego trip, Solstice." Grey shot daggers at Sol from his blanket cocoon on the couch.

Their childlike bickering made it hard to think. "I think we should call the police," Luna said. "Just to be safe."

There was a certain finality in her words.

Or so she thought.

"We can't call the fucking cops!" Sol threw his hands up, his gesture more dramatic than normal.

Luna's eyes grew wide. "But Sol, we could be in *danger*. What if you have some crazy stalker out there who's watching us, waiting to kill us all in our sleep?" She jabbed a finger at him. "You've read the tabloids same as I have—it's not a crazy assumption."

The more she went on, the more she believed it.

"First of all, I would welcome the opportunity to shag an obsessed fan right about now. If that's the case, I hope she comes out right now. Perhaps I'll go see if I can find her, play a little kinky game of hide and seek while we're at it." He paused to shove a fist full of Cheez-Its in his mouth. "And second of all, in case you've forgotten, sweetheart, Cole here just got out of prison two days ago, and I myself am an ex-con. You seriously think the coppers are gonna believe we just *found* some random bones? They'd bring us both in for questioning, guarantee it."

Luna opened her mouth, wanting to argue but not knowing what to say.

She hadn't thought of that.

For a moment, they all stood in collective silence.

Until Greyson broke it. "I thought this was supposed to be a relaxing vacation with a splash of party prep mixed in. What the hell have you all gotten me into now?" His hand was on his hip and his tone accusatory.

Luna grabbed at her rose-gold cross necklace , searching for a familiar sense of comfort but finding that it was lacking.

"I don't think there's a need to call the police, Lu." Cole placed a hand on her shoulder, his touch gentle. "We searched everywhere. There's no one here."

She wanted to believe him, but a sense of unease still pooled in her stomach. "Then how do you explain the cutlery, Cole?"

"I told you—" Sol started.

Luna raised a hand, cutting him off.

"Don't you dare say this is the ghost of the *Rhododendron Recluse*." Her tone came out snippier than she expected, but she didn't care.

"I'm just saying," Sol continued anyway, "what are the odds I tell you blokes that story last night, and then this happens today?"

He stared at them all with one eyebrow cocked. When no one answered, Luna huffed and rubbed her palms across her face. It wasn't a logical explanation, she knew that, but for some reason beyond her control, she couldn't quite shake the theory.

Because perhaps there was a tiny inkling of truth buried somewhere beneath the absurdity of it all.

"Wait," Cole said, pulling her from her thoughts. "Sol, who was the last person that stayed here before you? Like from your celebrity circle thing."

Sol snagged a beer from the fridge. "Come on, mate, don't be rude. We have a name." Cole rolled his eyes. "Fine, fine, whatever. I think Wrenner Wrenner Chicken Dinner was here last."

Luna's head snapped up. "Wrenner Scott was here?"

"Yeah, left about two weeks ago I reckon," Sol answered.

Cole raised his brows, then pointed at Luna with his thumb and forefinger. "He could've left them here. Guy's kind of a freak."

"Kind of?" Greyson challenged, rolling one of his many blankets over his head. "That man drinks his own piss on stage and bites the heads off of bats." He cringed. "I better not find something gross in my bed tonight."

Luna sat back on her stool, mulling over the information. It wasn't a horrible theory. Probable even. Wrenner Scott was a mongrel on stage, so something as grotesque as having human bones for silverware likely wasn't outside of his demented augmentation of reality.

"That's not a bad point," she said, flicking her eyes to the staircase when she heard movement. She still wasn't fully convinced, but she didn't want to discuss this with Jax present. "I think I hear Jax coming. Can we reconvene about this later?"

"Why?" Sol asked. "It's not like he can hear—"

Cole punched him in the arm, cutting him off.

"Well, you didn't have to fucking do that, mate!"

Luna rolled her eyes before shaking her head and looking at Cole.

"Everything's going to be fine," he whispered. "I'm sure Wrenner just left these here. Nobody's after us, and there's no ghost haunting the halls."

He squeezed her knee once for reassurance, and she offered him a small fake smile to show her appreciation.

But she still didn't like this. Not one little bit.

My obsession began just like everyone else's.

Slow at first, and then entirely at once. It became an all-consuming disease that plagued my every thought. *Graham Zanella*. The world's most infamous underground artist, known to instigate controversial performance art across the East Coast. He was every investigative reporter's dream, and because I was the best, or rather, determined to be the best, I had decided he was *mine*. Nobody else would conquer this feat, no one other than Cole Sloane was worthy of such a story.

I suppose you could say I'd developed a God complex, which, of course, back-fired.

—Cole Sloane, *The Great Chase*

COLE

Cole didn't sleep well that night. Although he had tried to convince Luna things were fine, he wasn't entirely convinced himself.

But he supposed prison would do that to a man.

Always having to be on high alert, remembering not to drop the soap or look at someone the wrong way—it all impacted his mental health. The therapist there had helped him overcome many of his old traumas, but, unfortunately, she couldn't stave off the new fears and anxieties that were inflicted upon him due to circumstance. Cole no longer had night terrors, crippling depression, or panic attacks, but he did have a fear of the unknown.

Was someone lurking around the corner waiting to jump him? Had he overheard the wrong part of a conversation that now made him liable? Had he pissed off the wrong person on the inside who also had an ally on the outside?

These were all fears that raced through Cole's mind as he tossed and turned and tried to make sense of what was happening.

It was probably Wrenner, he told himself. *Wrenner Scott is a freak of nature.*

Not that Cole had ever met him, but he'd heard the stories.

After what felt like hours, he finally gave up and slipped out of bed to grab a drink of water. If there was one thing he'd missed in prison, it was the freedom to leave the four walls of his room whenever he pleased.

He quietly tiptoed into the hallway, careful not to wake anyone, and padded down the wooden staircase until he reached the landing.

And that's when he realized he wasn't alone. *"What are you still doing up?"*

He watched as Jaxson waved and stuffed a spoonful of peanut butter in his mouth. *"Couldn't sleep."*

Cole sighed. *"Me neither."*

He glanced at the clock on the microwave and internally groaned when he saw 1:41 a.m. staring back at him.

"Why did Mom freak out on me today?"

Cole's eyes went wide, Jaxson's question surprising him.

"I'm not dumb," he continued. *"She's a spaz but usually not that spazzy."*

Cole smirked and scratched the back of his head while the heater kicked on, its hum offering a backdrop to their silence. He had no clue what to say.

On one hand, it wasn't his place to tell Jaxson anything his mother didn't want him to know. But on the other . . . Jaxson deserved to know. And he was right, he wasn't dumb. He was a smart, perceptive kid. He'd figure it out one way or another.

"Fine," Cole said, conceding to what he believed was right. *"Earlier today, we found some bones in the kitchen drawer. It's probably nothing, but your mom got a little worried about you is all. She wanted to make sure you were okay."*

Jax's eyes went wide. *"Bones?"*

Cole nodded and then helped himself to a spoonful of peanut butter as well. He'd barely eaten dinner, and now his stomach was in knots.

"It's the weekend before Halloween," Jax started. *"And rock stars live here. Probably nothing serious?"* He locked eyes with Cole as he signed, and Cole felt the child's need for confirmation in his words.

"Probably nothing serious," he replied.

Jax nodded fervently, his strawberry-blond ringlets flying everywhere.

And then he asked the question that made Cole's heart rate spike.

"You killed him, right?"

Cole set down his spoon and met Jax's gaze. In an instant, he felt it all come back—the rush of adrenaline as he chased Zanella through the library's haunted maze, the sight of the flames as they licked up Jaxson's head and then threatened his own, the scent of burning flesh.

And then the vile anger that rose in him as he realized Zanella had played a role in his daughter's death. The nasty way Z, or Harley, had looked at him when he finally revealed his true identity as Cole's former roommate, and then the building crescendo of neurotransmitters that flooded his veins as he and Z teetered on the line of life or death before Cole squeezed the former out of Graham Zanella and watched him take his last breath.

It had been exhilarating.

"Yes," he finally said. *"I killed him. He won't ever hurt us again."*

Jax nodded, and Cole smiled to himself, letting his shoulders relax. Then, the pair sat together and enjoyed their snack in a comfortable silence.

MONDAY

COLE

Cole wasn't much of an outdoorsman, but he had to admit the fresh air on this side of the lake felt good.

They'd decided to try a different hiking trail this morning, the whole gang needing a break from reality after yesterday's chaos. It wasn't as steep as the one they'd done before, but the exercise was good all the same.

"I am ready to stick my feet into a warm bubble bath." Greyson wiped the sweat from his brow and stopped to take a drink of water. "This is too much dirt and sweat for me."

Lemon wagged her tail and barked, demanding her own sip.

"You could've stayed back at the cabin." Luna bent down to pour Lemon some water in a travel-size dog bowl.

Greyson shook his head and threw back another drink. "Nope. I want to look my absolute best for this party Wednesday."

Cole didn't have the heart to tell him that one hike wouldn't suddenly sculpt his body into a fitter, toner version of himself. Not that Greyson was overweight, necessarily, but he definitely rocked a dad bod.

"You guys are so slow." Jax had wandered ahead of them but was on his way back now after realizing they'd stopped.

"Blame him," Sol said, which elicited a chuckle from Jax and Luna.

Grey didn't miss a beat. "What did you say, Solstice?"

Cole tuned out their banter and took Lemon's leash from Luna. His calves were anxious to keep going, to work up a sweat the old-fashioned way as opposed to in the prison gym he'd been stuck with. Up ahead, he spotted what he thought was a small clearing, so he took the lead, allowing Lemon to weave the way for them through the group.

Except, just as Cole began climbing the small mountain, Lemon veered in the other direction.

"Lem, girl," he said, trying to rein her in. "This way, sweetie."

But Lemon wasn't listening. Instead, she started whining and pulling Cole, insisting she follow him off the path. She wasn't anywhere near Emmett's size, but Cole was surprised at her strength. He gave in after a moment of hesitation and followed her through the small maze of pine needles and rocks.

"Hey, where are you going?" Sol called from behind.

"Don't know," Cole yelled back over his shoulder. "Lemon's caught scent of something."

The dog continued to lead him further into the woods, and Cole almost lost his footing a few times.

"Lemon, girl, where are we—"

His words were cut off by his own shock.

What the hell?

"Are you guys coming back, or should we follow you?" The question came from Luna, but Cole couldn't answer. His words were stuck in his throat, like a fly trapped in molasses.

He blinked once, then twice, squeezing his eyes shut tight and hoping the scene before him would disappear when he opened them again, like this was all some bad mirage.

But it wasn't.

Because of course it wasn't.

Cole sighed, then began surveying his surroundings. To his right, he clocked two one-person tents, and to his left, one large one. Except, they weren't just tents. They were mutilated, blood-splattered tents that had been completely destroyed in every way. It looked like a crime scene, one you'd see on *NCIS*.

That wasn't the worst of it, though.

In the middle of the extinguished firepit lay a dead animal.

And it smelled.

Horribly bad.

"Cole, what—" Luna's words were cut off by a gasp.

"What are you being so dramatic about, Momma Lu?" Grey asked as he came up behind her.

Sol muttered something unintelligible, but Cole's brain couldn't fully process what the others were saying. His analytical mind was still surveying every piece of the scene, committing it to memory. Because whatever happened here had been recent. Blood had seeped into the ash all around the animal, staining the ground a dark red hue. As he inspected it closer, he figured the creature was in the early stages of decomposition. It still had all its fur, its face was still intact. In fact—

Cole took another step forward, crouching in front of the dead creature and searching for the source of the wound. If this had been a fight with another animal, it would've been beaten up, perhaps its body ripped open. But this guy didn't have any signs of that.

He only had a single gunshot wound.

"What is that?" Luna asked, her voice small and sheepish.

Cole squinted, trailing his eyes back up to the creature's ears, then down to its tail. "Bobcat, I think."

"I would say bloody hell, but that's a bit too on the nose, innit?" Sol said as he came up behind Cole, crouching down, too.

"Someone shot it." Cole's voice was low and gruff, barely loud enough for anyone but Sol to hear.

Or so he thought.

"That's illegal!" Luna quipped. "They're endangered in Ohio."

Sol scoffed. "Yeah, well, I'm guessing this lot didn't give a mummy's tit about that." He stood to inspect the tents. "It probably started attacking them, and someone shot it, causing the blood to splatter everywhere before it fell here and died."

"Who are you, Dexter Morgan?" Grey asked.

Sol cocked his head. "Who?"

"Oh my lanta, the man doesn't even know who America's favorite serial killer is, yet he's acting like a blood-spatter analyst."

"That stinks." Jaxson covered his nose with his shirt, having finally caught up with the group. *"What happened?"*

Luna signed to him, quickly recounting their findings, which wasn't much.

"Gnarly," he responded when Luna finished.

That was one way to put it.

"I don't think this has been here that long," Cole said after a moment. He stood back up and pulled Lemon by her collar. He didn't want to alarm them, but he was certain this must've happened sometime in the last few days. "Did anyone hear anything that could've been a gunshot since we've been here?"

He looked at Luna, then Greyson, then Sol. When no one responded, he cursed under his breath.

"What?" Sol asked, no trace of concern in his voice. "Probably happened before you all arrived. We all know I'm not the most reliable narrator. Probably happened while I was drunk off my arse."

"Or when you let off fireworks," Luna countered, a hint of disdain lacing her words.

She had meant it as an insult toward Sol, but Cole considered it for a moment. He supposed this could've happened right when Sol was having his little fire show Saturday night. The timing did align, but—

Another thought edged into the crevices of his mind. One he desperately wanted to ignore but didn't think he could. "What if someone staged this?" he asked.

"What do you mean?" Lu crossed her arms, confusion apparent in her gaze. "Why would someone do that?"

Why *would* someone do that? He had no idea, to be honest. It didn't make a whole lot of sense now that he'd said it out loud. It just . . . didn't look quite right. Didn't add up in his brain yet.

He was probably just being paranoid.

"I don't know," he said, waving his hand. "Forget I mentioned it."

Greyson quirked a brow. "Weren't there campers in your ghost story, Sol?"

"Oi, you're right, mate." Sol sucked in his bottom lip and furrowed his brow. "Didn't even think of that."

Cole didn't quite see the connection. "That's different, Grey."

Luna agreed. "Yeah, that story involved murdering people, not animals." A loose piece of hair fell in her face. She took out her claw clip and twisted her hair back up again. "Although this is almost equally as terrible. Poor thing."

Lemon tugged on her leash, wanting to sniff the dead bobcat again, but Cole pulled her back.

"Hey, Jax," he signed. *"Can you take her for a little walk? I don't want her getting into this bloody mess anymore than she already has."*

Jax nodded and took the leash before disappearing into the neighboring tree line.

"Dunno, lads," Sol said, taking the lead on the conversation. "First, silverware carved from bones, then a gruesome camp scene with a dead animal. All legends have variations. Maybe Roger had a pet cat."

Cole didn't like where this was going.

"Would you stop with that?" he demanded. "There are no ghosts here haunting us. It's just a dead animal some campers shot in self-defense, I'm sure."

Sol walked past him to the edge of the cliff. "Then why do you suppose they were set up right here, in this exact spot?"

Cole's brain spun. "What do you mean?"

Sol turned back to him and jabbed a thumb over his shoulder. Cole waited for him to speak, but when the rock star just continued to stare, eyebrows raised, Cole sighed and stepped around the deceased creature before joining Sol at his side.

And when he did, his heart beat a little faster.

Because the ledge had a direct view of Sol's cabin.

They could see everything from here.

LUNA

If Luna were the type to freak out, she'd totally be freaking out right now.

Which she was, because she was *totally* the type to freak out.

She began pacing around the outer edge of the bloodbath, covering her mouth with her shirt as the stench of the poor deceased creature intensified.

"Well, looks like Roger was having a little peep show." Sol could never be serious, not for one minute of his life.

"That's grotesque," Greyson said.

"Compared to the rotting carcass beside you, mate?"

Luna couldn't take their bickering.

"I knew it," she said. "I stinking knew it. Somebody was literally camped out watching us. Probably one of your deranged fans, Solstice! We need to call the police. Or better yet, maybe we should just get the heck out of here. This has bad news written all over it, Cole. Ugh, no pun intended."

She was speaking a mile a minute, slurring her words together and probably not making any sense, but she didn't care. She knew something was wrong after they'd discovered human remains in the silverware drawer yesterday, and now, her suspicions were confirmed. Someone was watching them.

Or haunting you.

Shut up, self! We do not *believe that.*

Do we?

"Oi, I don't have a stalker," Sol said. "I was just messing with you before."

"I'm sorry, what?" Luna did a double-take. "Just messing with me?"

Sol waved a hand. "I mean, sure, I've had some unhinged DMs and fan mail before, but nothing that serious. Plus, my fans think I'm in Aruba for some off-the-grid hippie festival."

"Aruba?" Greyson asked.

"Yeah." Sol nodded. "I've got loads of fake alibis. You never know when you'll need one."

Luna shook her head at the ridiculousness of it all. If someone wasn't targeting Sol, then who else—or *what* else—was behind this?

"Then how do you explain *this*?" When no one answered, she looked at Cole, her damaged and expectant heart waiting for him to say something, anything that would fix this.

"It could be a coincidence . . ." His words trailed off, and Luna felt her heart squeeze as she waited for him to explain this craziness away. Because that's how his mind worked. Cole was logical, analytical, methodical. It's what made him a great reporter.

"Yeah, and I'm the Queen of England," Solstice countered, tucking his unruly hair into his bandana. "I'm telling ya, I know you don't want to hear it, but this has creepy ghost haunting written all over it."

Luna rubbed her fingers over her eyes, trying to make sense of it. She did not want to entertain the idea of this being a ghost, or rather, society's version of what they thought was a ghost. It was completely absurd and frightened her more than she cared to admit. But if what Sol was saying was true, then even if he did have a crazy stalker, they'd be off on some wild goose chase in Aruba. And who else would be watching them? Sneaking bones into their cabin and slaughtering poor, innocent animals at a campsite near by?

Was it worth considering that perhaps the most illogical answer was actually the most logical of all?

"Maybe," Luna started, her voice weak, not wanting to say it but also not able to avoid the topic. "Maybe we invoked something by telling that story Saturday night." The words tumbled out all too quickly, and she suddenly wished she could take them back.

Cole's eyes snapped to hers. "I thought you didn't believe in ghosts."

Luna diverted her gaze and instead focused her attention on the poor, sweet bobcat. "I don't. At least, not in the traditional sense." She paused, chewing her bottom lip and wondering if they'd think she was crazy. "I believe demons exist—because they're in the Bible—but I don't believe in old campfire stories and legends and myths. Like, I don't think Bigfoot or the Rhododendron Recluse are out there, waiting to get us, but . . ."

"But what?" Cole pushed.

She took a deep breath and said the words that had been quietly gnawing at her since yesterday. "But I do think there can be spiritual truth to those stories sometimes. Like, the origin of ghost stories and legends and myths likely came from someone encountering a demonic presence."

Cole's brow was fifty shades of furrowed at this point. "So, what are you saying?"

"I'm saying," Luna continued as the shame encompassed her, "there is a chance that whatever demon attached itself to Roger, or whoever, years ago, may return if called upon. The Bible tells us that our words have power, and well, if we were up late, talking about this thing and believing its presence were possible, then we could've made our hearts susceptible to it."

What she didn't say was that *she* had made her heart susceptible to it by allowing a seed of doubt to grow in her. Luna should have known better than to let that happen, known that the devil would take any and every opportunity to burrow himself into the hearts of believers. But she'd ignored it, thrown caution to the wind by cracking herself open and making herself vulnerable to him in a way she hadn't since before she came to Christ.

Was it possible that, in her quest to forgive the Lord for what had happened to Jaxson, she'd allowed her heart to harden so much that something evil had taken root? Something that had grown and festered, lying dormant until it had the chance to blossom into something dark and sinister?

Did I cause this, Jesus?

"Why would a ghost, or a demon, put a gunshot wound into an innocent animal, though?" Cole asked, stopping Luna from her internal spiral. "Even if what you're saying is true, that part still doesn't make sense in this scenario." He turned back around to face the scene. "Ghosts don't shoot guns. A human did this."

She considered his words as a calming presence enveloped her.

"Yes, it's a little weird," he continued, "that the spot the hikers picked has a direct view of the cabin, but"—he turned, motioning his arms in a large circle—"in case you haven't noticed, this is also a very nice, flat piece of land. It would make sense to set up camp here for a night if they wanted to be on even ground while sleeping. Plus, it's far enough from the trail that passersby wouldn't bother them but also close enough that they could find their way back easily."

Luna took a deep breath, the rhythm of her heart slowing as the Holy Spirit began to comfort her through Cole's words.

"My guess?" Cole cocked his head to the side and studied the area. "Some folks found a flat spot they liked, decided to set up camp for the night. Someone awoke to the animal, freaked out, and shot it in self-defense. Probably ran off right after. The tents were ruined, so they left them."

Okay, Luna thought. She liked what he was saying.

"I like Cole's theory better than Sol's," Greyson stated matter-of-factly, to which Solstice muttered something ridiculous under his breath.

"I think we're all just on edge after yesterday." Cole walked to Luna and grabbed her hand, offering it a gentle squeeze. "I'm sure we're all just getting ahead of ourselves."

She smiled at him, appreciative, but then leaves crunched in the background, and she realized Jaxson and Lemon had wandered back.

"Hey, sweetie," she said, instantly dropping Cole's hand and wiping at her eyes. *"Lem girl getting tired on you?"*

Jax shrugged, noncommittal. He'd been uncharacteristically quiet today.

"Hey," she said, stopping him. *"Is everything okay?"*

She stared at his crystal-blue eyes as his strawberry-blond waves rustled in the gentle breeze, and she was caught off guard again by his adultlike features.

"Depends. Are you gonna tell me what you all are saying, or are you going to lie to me again?"

The color drained from her face. *"What are you talking about?"*

Jax rolled his eyes before throwing his arms up. *"I know you lied to me yesterday. Cole told me about the bone silverware."*

Luna felt like she'd been punched in the gut. *"What? Cole had no right—"*

"Don't be mad at him," Jax continued. *"I knew you were lying, so I asked him to tell me the truth. You think I can't handle anything, but I'm not a little kid. I've been through enough shit that a little scare doesn't bother me."*

Luna stared at him in awe, her mouth agape. She felt anger. Anger and betrayal and embarrassment and hurt. But most of all, she felt terrible for how she'd made Jaxson feel.

"Whatever." Jax threw Lemon's leash at her. *"I'm going back to the cabin. See you there."*

For a moment, they all stood together, awkward in their silence, until Greyson and Sol shuffled around her to follow Jax, leaving her alone with Cole.

A minute passed.

"Lu?" Cole tried.

She took a few deep breaths, contemplating what to say. She didn't want to be crude, but she didn't want to be dishonest, either. "I just . . . need a minute."

Without giving Cole a chance to respond, she passed him Lemon's leash, curled her oversized flannel tight around her petite frame, and started the long trek down the mountain.

COLE

Cole's journey back to the cabin was long and lonely, even with Lemon at his side.

He'd hoped Luna would be ready to talk by the time he got back, but considering she wasn't even there when he arrived, he took that as a no. He made it approximately thirty minutes before he could no longer stand it and decided to look for her.

Unsure of which way she'd gone, Cole restocked his backpack and threw in an extra jacket and a lightweight blanket. It was nearing five, which meant the sun was going to set soon. This worried him for more reasons than one.

It wasn't like Luna to walk away from a conversation. Then again, Cole hadn't spent this much time around her in over half a decade, so who's to say this wasn't her new norm?

He shook his head, that thought bothering him more than the last. He hated that she'd had to deal with the aftermath of The Gala on her own. Cole would've been there in a heartbeat if he could've. Because Luna was everything to Cole. And now she was upset, and it was partially his fault.

He took a gulp of fresh air as he stepped out onto the squishy, lush terrain with Lemon back at his side. She'd taken to him quicker than expected, like she instinctively knew he was her new dad. It made Cole's heart soften as he remembered Emmett clinging to him in a similar fashion.

Lem and Em.

If only they could've met.

Cole's lips twitched upward, but then he shook his head and refocused his attention on the task at hand: finding Luna.

Thankfully, it didn't take long.

He'd half expected her to walk all the way to the little mom-and-pop diner they'd passed on the way in, but he found her sitting on the dock, her feet dangling over the lake.

Lu.

He walked toward her now, his throat becoming increasingly dry as he thought about what he'd say. She had a right to be angry with him, but Jaxson also had a right to know what was going on. Cole wouldn't have felt comfortable lying to him.

Lemon followed closely by his side until her paws hit the dock, and then she was off. Cole laughed at first, dropping her leash and letting her run to Luna, but as Lem neared the edge, he noticed Luna wasn't turning around.

And Lemon wasn't stopping.

Oh no.

His face drew into a concerned expression, and he cupped his hands around his mouth. "Luna!"

But it was already too late.

Luna's tiny body turned around, and he watched with anguish as Lemon tackled her, licking her face for all of two seconds, before Luna screamed and they both toppled over, falling into the lake.

Shit.

"Luna!" Cole threw off his backpack and flew down the dock, racing to save his girls. He didn't know what temperature the lake was, but given it was almost November in Ohio, he knew the water likely wasn't refreshing.

A shrill cry broke through the air, and Cole pounded his feet harder against the wooden dock until he reached the end, swooping into the lake with a swan dive. His body jolted at the cold shock, his earlier assessment now confirmed, and he broke through the surface, quickly catching his breath. He swiveled around, spotting the two blondes under the pier. Lemon was clutching to Luna for dear life, causing Luna to bob up and down underneath the water.

"Hang on, Lu!"

Cole took a deep breath and dove back under, swimming until he reached their writhing bodies.

"Here!" he said, taking Lemon off Luna and pushing her to the shore. He turned back to Luna and scooped her in his arms. "I've got you."

He swam them both to the edge of the lake before standing and carrying her cold body the rest of the way. He could feel the goose bumps all over her arms, her body writhing as she coughed.

Once he'd reached a dry patch of land, he sat her down gently and moved faster than a predator chasing its prey to retrieve his backpack from the dock.

"Here." He kneeled back down beside her a minute later as he pulled out the emergency blanket he'd stashed away.

"Thank you," Luna said with a hoarse voice as Cole wrapped the warm fabric around her cold body.

"Are you okay?" He held her gaze, searching for signs of something, anything that might indicate she wasn't.

Luna nodded. "I'm okay." And then, "Lemon."

Cole squeezed her arm and then snapped his head to the right, looking for the pup. Goldens were good swimmers by nature, so he hadn't been too concerned when he shoved her to the edge of the lake. But now, as he looked around and didn't see her, an alarming thought began to creep into his brain.

"Lemon!" He stood when he spotted a yellow tail wagging from behind one of the dock pilings. He let out an exaggerated breath and called for the dog again, this time gaining her attention. "Come here, girl!"

Relief washing over him, he sat back down beside Luna and wrapped his broad arms around her in an attempt to warm her up. As he did so, the scent of her wet hair invaded his nostrils, and he internally cursed.

Even after falling into a dirty lake, she still smelled like berries.

LUNA

Luna's teeth may be chattering, but her insides felt all hot and bothered as Cole wrapped his buff prison arms around her—all worries from earlier forgotten.

Seriously, how much had he worked out in jail? Because she did *not* remember his body being this hard and massive before.

Like that ever stopped you from looking.

She silently chided herself and willed her body to level out from this game of icy hot she was playing.

Finally, after several minutes of shivering—for multiple reasons—Luna's movements stilled, and she breathed a sigh of relief.

"I can't believe that just happened."

She turned to look at Cole, embarrassment flooding her features as she was sure he would notice her flushed skin—only to see his heated gaze.

Oh, barnacles.

Had he been feeling what she was feeling, too?

Somehow, she involuntarily snagged her tooth on her bottom lip as he stared at her, and if she wasn't mistaken, she could've sworn she saw his nostrils flare at that exact second.

The past two days had been so overwhelming that Luna wanted nothing more than to let herself go—to enjoy this moment and this *man* and let the worries of it all melt away.

But even though her body and heart were telling her one thing, her brain was still screaming about how wildly inappropriate it was for her to be sharing such intimate moments with a man she wasn't married to, and all in the same vicinity as her son.

She held his gaze for as long as she could, but when she saw his eyes drop to her mouth, she nearly knocked him down as she scrambled to stand, the now wet blanket falling to the wayside.

"Lem! Come here, girl. Let me dry you off." Her voice was shaky, which she desperately hoped Cole would attribute to the unplanned swim she just took mere days before Halloween.

The dog playfully trotted over, her tongue hanging lazily out of her mouth, and Luna busied herself by running the blanket over Lemon's fur.

"Ugh," she groaned, realizing it wasn't much help. "I think she'll need a bath."

"I'll give her one," Cole said, standing entirely too close yet so far away all at the same time.

Luna exhaled, her breath resembling a cloud of smoke as the cold air mixed with her carbon dioxide. She had been so warm a minute ago . . .

"Here." Cole's voice broke through her thoughts. He reached into the bag for something else.

She laughed when she saw what it was. "I don't think that jacket's going to help me. I have to get out of these clothes."

She looked at Cole, not realizing the way that would sound as the words fell out of her mouth.

A subtle, sly grin appeared on Cole's face, making her cheeks flush again. "You can at least take your top off and put this on. That'll help some until we get back."

She felt her face fall at his comment, and she had to scramble to put her jaw back into place.

Cole laughed, a flirtatious look in his eyes. "I'll turn around."

She waited as he did so, but suddenly, she didn't feel cold anymore. The way this man could affect her physiology was beyond her.

Dang chemicals.

Slowly, she peeled off her flannel and then her T-shirt, pausing before unhooking her bra. "No peeking."

"I wouldn't dare," Cole responded, yet something in his voice suggested otherwise.

Luna took a huge gulp and then snapped her bra off, slid the straps down her arms, and yanked Cole's thin black jacket on.

"Okay," she said after zipping it up. "You can look now."

Cole turned too quickly for Luna's liking. He was staring at her again, with those dark, broody eyes and prison muscles that wouldn't stop bulging out of his shirt no matter how much Luna willed them to.

She crossed her arms over her chest self-consciously and looked away.

This time, Cole seemed to take the hint and stepped back, scratching Lemon's ears. "I'm sorry about telling Jax."

The shift in gears gave Luna whiplash, but her heart softened all the same. "It's okay," she said, toying with a damp piece of hair. "He was right. You were both right. He deserved to know. I shouldn't have kept it from him."

Her shoulders relaxed at the admission, the tension between them momentarily clearing up as she focused on her son.

"He's a strong kid, Lu. He can handle it." Cole picked up the wet blanket and his backpack before adding, "Come on. Let's get you ladies cleaned up."

Luna offered a soft smile and nodded. "And some food, please."

Cole laughed, and she followed him back to the definitely-not-haunted, definitely-not-being-watched cabin.

Everything was going to be fine.

COLE

Even after a chilly walk back to the cabin and a multitude of subject changes, Cole still couldn't shake the outline of Luna's nipples from his thoughts.

They'd been on full display through the thin fabric of his jacket, and he'd wanted nothing more than to rip her clothes off and take her right then and there. But he didn't. Because, for whatever reason, she'd been holding back. Every time they'd had what he considered a moment, they'd either been interrupted or Luna had stopped it from going further.

This thought frustrated Cole, partially because he'd spent the past five years fantasizing about her, but also because this caused another fear to surface.

What if she didn't want him in the way he wanted her?

What if all this time, he'd been misinterpreting the signs, and she actually wasn't interested in him? Perhaps when she'd politely rejected him that day in prison all those years ago, maybe it was because she truly wasn't interested and not at all because of all those other reasons he'd rationalized. Understood.

His heart couldn't bear the thought.

And neither could his pants.

The sexual tension had been slowly building between them for so long that Cole considered having a date with his hand just to relieve some of the pressure, but he'd been waiting, hoping, to share that euphoric moment with her.

His Lu.

Surely the feeling was mutual.

It had to be.

Then why is she avoiding me?

Cole silently groaned as he sat back in his chair at the dinner table. Maybe it was Jax's school situation. She hadn't said much else about the bullying incident, but he knew that must weigh heavily on her. It didn't take a genius to connect those dots. Combine that with the weird incidents they'd had since being here, and it suddenly made perfect sense why their relationship wasn't at the forefront of her mind.

Luna was a mom. A damn good one. Cole should be more patient, more understanding.

"All right, kids," Greyson said, interrupting his thoughts. "We have cheese, extra cheese, pepperoni, pepperoni and sausage, and vegetarian." He was slicing through the last of the frozen pizzas, his Southern drawl becoming more apparent as the night—and the drinks—went on.

Cole heard Luna snort at Grey's words, and he had to shift in his seat.

Why did everything about this woman drive him mad?

"You're the second youngest here, Grey," Luna said, taking a slice of each onto her plate.

His response was instant and snappy. "Yeah, I know. Someone tell me how it makes sense then that I'm the most adult one here."

Jaxson looked at Luna and raised his hands. *"Is he the one who likes old men?"*

Luna made eye contact with Cole, and he couldn't help but crack a smile with her as she burst into laughter.

"Yes," she said, speaking and signing in tandem. "Greyson does like old men."

Cole watched as Grey's cheeks flamed and his eyes narrowed. "You tell that boy he'd be lucky to attract such fine wealth like I do. Raymond is gonna be my sugar daddy one day and let me quit the paper."

Cole rubbed an eye and shook his head, another laugh escaping him. He didn't care who Greyson dated. He just thought he might be happier with a man who didn't need Viagra to get himself going. "Whatever makes you tick, man."

Luna took a large bite of the extra cheesy pizza and said through a full mouth, "I can't believe you haven't already quit *The Chronicles*."

Now it was Greyson's turn to snort. "I could say the same about you."

Luna rolled her eyes. "Yeah, well, I have a family to support, and it's not like stable photography gigs with benefits are just floating around out there."

Cole was surprised by their conversation. He had quit the paper for obvious reasons—see: incarceration—but he wasn't aware Greyson and Luna wanted to leave.

"Why do you guys say that?" he asked, licking pizza grease off his thumb and reaching for the cold neck of his beer bottle.

Grey chortled. "You try working for Nate after your whole saga went down. He's still on a power trip, even five years later."

Fair, Cole thought. His former boss was definitely an acquired taste.

"Yeah," Luna said, using one hand to sign and the other to hold her pizza. "All he wants is clout. Talks about you all the time still. It's kind of annoying, really." She snapped her mouth shut, her eyes widening. "Not that I'm annoyed hearing about you, it's just that when you have to listen to the same man spout out the same nonsense, day after day, when he clearly had no role in catching Z, it kind of makes my ears bleed."

She didn't sign the last part.

"It really is quite obnoxious," Greyson said. "I've been looking for work elsewhere, but most newsrooms are giving their social jobs to fresh graduates so they can pay them less. I'm not trying to take a pay cut just to do the same job, so I'm stuck dealing with Daddy Nate for now."

Cole nodded, rolling his tongue over his teeth. Nate wasn't his favorite person, but he had been Cole's mentor in the beginning. He always said he *saw something* in Cole, latching onto him like a Venus flytrap capturing its prey. Cole realized too late that Nate only wanted him to do well so the paper would do well. Nate was a newspaper man first and foremost, cut from the same cloth as J. Jonah Jameson, the editor-in-chief from Spider-Man. Kinda funny when he thought about it now, considering Nate's obsession with Zanella.

"Nate is who he is," Cole said, shrugging. "Can't change a man like that. Better to just work with him and ignore it if you like everything else about the job."

"Like hell!" Sol said, a mouth full of cheese. "He's an arse. I say leave, the both of ya."

"I thought you liked your job?" Jax asked Luna.

"I do," she assured him. *"Our boss is just frustrating sometimes. You'll have that with any job, though."*

Cole felt bad watching their conversation, knowing fully well she'd only said that to comfort Jax.

"I still call bullshit." Sol chugged the last of his beer and stood to grab another before directing a question at Cole. "You're not going back to work for that bastard are you?"

Cole shook his empty bottle in the air. "Grab me one, too, please." He wiped his face with a napkin and contemplated his next words. "I don't know, honestly. If my book does well, I may get a contract for another manuscript, but I don't know if that's the route I want to take." He paused, tapping his thumb against his thigh. "I actually think I might want to do something for River."

Luna set her fourth slice of pizza down. "Like a charity?"

Cole shrugged. "I don't know yet. Maybe. Or perhaps set up a scholarship at Springhill in her name. I haven't figured it out yet. Actually . . ." He waved his hands at Jax to get his attention. *"What do kids your age want these days? What's considered cool?"*

Jax cocked his head to the side, a questioning look on his face. *"Parties are always cool."*

Cole's lip curled to the side. *"Not exactly what I had in mind."*

"You could throw a gala," Sol said, throwing his two cents into the mix. *"That'd be a sick turn of events."*

Cole rolled his eyes. *"Never mind."*

"I think that's a great idea, Cole," Luna said, her eyes kind. "I'm sure you'll figure out something."

She smiled warmly at him, and something inside him hummed, a warmness coating his veins. Because Cole believed her. He may not have it all figured out just yet, but he trusted that God did.

He smiled at the thought.

Look at you being a little believer, he could practically hear Luna saying.

LUNA

JUST CHILL.

This is no big deal.

So what if you're watching a scary movie right beside Cole Sloane while you're all alone in the woods in a cabin that may or may not be haunted or stalked?

It's fine.

And it would be—fine.

At least that's what Luna hoped.

After Jaxson went to bed, they'd decided to watch the new *Halloween* movie. Michael Myers had already been unalived thirteen times prior to this remake, but somehow, the franchise had managed to bring him back yet again.

In hindsight, Luna had no idea why she agreed to this. She despised scary movies. The very idea of them made her skin crawl, yet here she was, seated in the middle of the long leather sectional with Greyson to her right and Cole and Lemon to her left, all while Sol lounged in the oversized matching chair. It was nearing eleven, and while Luna would usually be on the verge of passing out at this hour, she was wide awake as the opening scene played out, someone's guts already splayed across the screen.

She had resisted drinking much on this trip, but tonight, she had a giant glass of red wine poured, right next to her bowl of Kroger-brand movie-theater butter popcorn. Apparently, slasher films called for the classics.

Nyla would die if she knew what Luna was doing right now. She made a mental note to text her an update in the morning and then tried to focus her attention on the movie.

Somewhere around the third or fourth time the classic theme song played, signaling the monster's slow walk—Luna never understood how he always managed to catch up to his victims despite never running—Luna felt her eyelids begin to droop.

"Here." Cole's voice cut through to her, her eyes popping wide open. "You can lie down if you're tired."

She watched as he fluffed a pillow on his lap and gestured for her to move. Normally, she would definitely, probably, *maybe*, object, but she'd managed to put down two oversized glasses of merlot during the first half of the movie, so her decision-making abilities weren't up to speed on the matters of her heart versus her head.

And so she lay down, hiccuping and giggling in the process.

"You're so snuggly, Cole," she said, wrapping a blanket around herself.

She felt his hand rest on her back before he slowly started rubbing circles.

It felt nice.

So nice that Luna felt herself drifting lazily off to sleep without a care in the world. Her body started to go numb as her mind wandered away from the blood and guts. Away from the chaos and finances and bullies and human remains and haunted lakes and hot prison men and *every single thing* that'd been weighing her down so much that she sometimes felt like she was drowning.

Except . . . wait a minute.

Was she drowning? Was she underwater?

No, her mind must be trapped in a hypnagogic state—the moment where your brain skirts between consciousness and unconsciousness. Yes, she was confident that's what this was. She'd experienced this sensation before, her body always jerking awake at the last possible second before she dove off a cliff or fell down a waterfall.

Except, this time, her body didn't jerk. And her lungs filled with more and more water as the seconds ticked by, with no sudden gasp of oxygen to save her.

It was at this very moment Luna realized she was not asleep.

She was not on the couch.

She was not even inside the cabin.

She was in the lake.

Her eyes tried to flutter open, but they stung against the dirty water, and she closed them again. She flailed her arms and legs around, desperate to break through the surface and breathe fresh air, but no matter how hard she kicked, her foot never hit the bottom of the lake, never ricocheted her to the top, giving her the boost of adrenaline she needed to soar through the suffocating bubbles and into the moonlight.

She screamed, her voice trapped as more water rushed into her lungs. Her world was fading quickly now, from dark to light, then dark again. Visions of human skeletons and animal carcasses flashed through her mind, the bones and tufts of fur swirling through the pitch-black swamp.

Then a burst of color, red, swirled into her vision. At first dark and maroon, then bright and bloody as the streams of color mingled with the water before blossoming into something else entirely.

Something that looked a lot like petals.

Flower petals.

Luna screamed as the deadly rhododendrons encompassed her, staining her heart and her lungs.

Jesus, help.

She was out of air and out of time.

COLE

F OR THE SECOND TIME in less than twenty-four hours, Cole jumped into the lake.

He had left Luna asleep on the couch when the movie ended, but after another few hours of tossing and turning, he retreated back to the kitchen for a glass of water.

Only this time, no one was there to greet him.

Not even Luna's sleeping body.

In an instant, he knew something was horribly, horribly wrong. His eyes flashed to the door, and seeing it standing wide open, he lunged outside. Without thinking, his feet moved by muscle memory, subconsciously leading him to the lake.

When he arrived, he saw Luna's blanket and a stained wineglass lying on the lakeshore, and his pulse spiked as his body broke out into a cold sweat.

He didn't think before reacting; he only knew one thing.

He had to save Luna, if it was the last thing he did.

Now, his body submerged in the cold body of water, he moved on instinct as he navigated the small but dangerous man-made lake. His heartbeat raced as he searched for her, the oxygen in his lungs quickly depleting. He didn't have much time. Luna had drunk almost her entire bottle of wine, which meant she was likely still intoxicated below these waters, and drowning could occur in minutes, if not seconds.

He was starting to panic, like seriously panic, when something flashed out of the corner of his eye. It was dark underwater, so he couldn't see much, but he moved on a hunch, hoping, praying, it was Luna.

His body came into contact with something, and he all but screamed when he felt a strand of her hair float through his fingers.

Quickly, Cole wrapped his arms around her and kicked with all his strength, until finally, they broke the surface. He took in a sharp breath, his anxiety still booming in his chest when he realized Luna did not do the same.

"Come on, Lu!"

He raced to the shore, standing when it was shallow enough, and ran to the lake's edge before falling to his knees and checking her pulse. It was faint but viable, and he threw all of himself into checking her airway for obstructions, administering CPR, and conducting chest compressions.

"Dammit, Luna! Stay with me."

Sweat rolled off his forehead despite the cold, and he worked his arms in a rhythmic motion as he fought to bring her back to life.

He could not, *would not*, lose another woman he loved.

One, two, three.

He continued to pulsate his hands against her chest, until finally, in an act of desperation, he pounded his fist against her sternum, and at last, Luna coughed and spewed water everywhere.

"Oh, thank God," Cole breathed as relief flooded him. Luna rolled to her side and continued to cough and spew water. "It's okay. You're okay now," he said as he patted her back. "You're safe, Luna."

As the coughing fit slowed, he pulled her into his arms and stroked her hair while she cried.

"Shh-shh," he whispered. "It's okay. I'm here. I've got you. You're okay, Lu. You're safe."

He echoed the words on repeat until her body calmed down enough to stop shaking, planting the occasional kiss on her forehead in the process. His mind reeled as he tried to fathom what had just happened.

How had she ended up out there?

How long had she been underwater?

Would she have any brain damage from the time she was unconscious?

The thoughts steamrolled through his brain, but he refused to let any of them form on his lips, his only job now being to comfort the woman in his arms.

Finally, after what felt like forever and no time at all, Luna's cries slowed, and she looked up at him.

"What happened, Lu?" Cole croaked, his own eyes misty.

She shook her head and looked away again before answering. "I don't know. One minute I was closing my eyes on your lap while we watched that ridiculous movie, and the next thing I knew, I was drowning." She shuddered before continuing. "I thought I was dreaming, or at least, halfway dreaming. You know when you're not fully asleep but not fully awake yet? That's what it felt like. Until I couldn't breathe and finally realized what was happening."

Cole's heart ached as the revelation of her words sunk in. "Do you think," he started, clearing his throat, "that you were sleepwalking?"

He knew it was a desperate attempt to explain away what he was really thinking, but he was too scared to put that unimaginable thought into concrete words.

Luna looked up at him again, her eyes red and glassy. "No, Cole. I don't think I was sleepwalking."

His heart thudded, ready to take off as he searched the grounds for whomever this predator was that threw her body in the lake.

"I think," Luna said, steadying him like a buoy, "that Sol may be right."

LUNA

Her body felt rigid, tense, as she spoke the words.

Yet she felt in her gut they were true.

How else could she explain what she'd just seen?

Her brain began to panic, stumbling over the possibilities. She'd been so conflicted the past two days, but right now, as she sat on the muddy shore of this decrepit lake, the visions of the bloody, swirling petals still floating in her mind, one thought became increasingly clear:

Something demonic was happening.

And she didn't know what the hamburglar to do about it.

The light wrinkles in Cole's forehead deepened as he stared at her, considering her words. "You think this is a demon doing all this?" She nodded slowly. "Not a person? Like, maybe one of Sol's fans who's stalking him, or"—he swallowed—"I don't know, someone else?"

A new wave of goose bumps erupted over Luna's skin. "I—"

Words failed her as she tried to articulate everything she was feeling. If he'd asked her yesterday or this morning if she thought it was a person, she'd say yes. Heck, she did say yes! When they found the bones, that had been her first thought—that someone was after them. Then, when they found the campsite, her fears were escalated, ramped up by Sol's words and the possibilities of evil spirits, but once she'd cleared her head, meditated on a bit of prayer, she'd talked herself into believing it was all a coincidence.

Everything could be explained away.

But now, after being in that lake, her screams trapped beneath the water as her lungs cried out for air, the bones and animals and rhododendrons screeching in her head, Luna's soul felt unwell, her spirit restless.

"I don't know how to explain it," she said, her voice still shaky. "But that water felt . . . evil. I saw these, these visions—"

"Visions?" Cole asked, curiosity lacing his tone.

Luna bit her lip, trying to find the words. Cole was still a very new Christian. He had accepted Jesus into his heart, believed he'd died on the cross and been raised from the dead, but he still had questions, things he didn't understand, and as a result, he'd refrained from being baptized. Luna had tried to explain to him there was no prerequisite for baptism, but Cole had claimed he wasn't ready yet.

Which is why, in a moment like this, she had no idea what to say. How did she tell a person who's new to the faith that she, a seasoned believer, was under spiritual attack? That she'd just nearly been drowned by a demonic presence while thinking she was safe—sound asleep even? That scenario didn't exactly bode well for those with an underdeveloped faith. Luna may have been struggling with her own anger toward God, but she wasn't about to say something that would deter Cole from his newfound beliefs. His salvation wasn't her responsibility, but as he stared at her, eyes questioning, she couldn't help feeling like the weight of his entire soul rested on her.

"I don't know what I saw," she said, squeezing her eyes shut and looking away. "It could've been a hallucination, or maybe still part of my dream, but it felt real." She took a deep breath, grateful for the air in her lungs. "I don't know how I ended up in that lake, but we've got to do something about this before the party."

"To hell with the party." Cole stroked her arm, trying to erase the chill on her skin. "We'll cancel it. Let's just leave. Be done with it all."

But Luna shook her head. "No, we can't just leave and expect this to go away." It didn't work like that. "We have to stop it. Put an end to it."

Cole disagreed. "No, Lu. I'm serious. I didn't want to do this party anyway. Let's just pack up in the morning and head out."

"We can't, Cole!" Her voice was shriller than she'd meant it to be, but he needed to understand. "I can't just walk away from something like this. The spirits, demons, whatever you want to call them, they'll follow me." Her eyes widened, a more sobering thought catching up with her. "They'll follow all of us, including Jaxson."

Silence clung to them for a moment as Cole processed her words. "So, what?" he asked a moment later. "Do we perform, like, an exorcism or something?"

She laid her head back against Cole's chest. "Not exactly. That's more of a Catholic thing."

"Then what do we do?"

Luna wished she knew. As the exhaustion and brain fog took over, she fought to recall all she could about demonic spirits, about the darker side of Christianity that was often overlooked by the church—or at least by hers. Luna had been attending a nondenominational church since she was eighteen, where she gave her life to Christ. They'd never preached against possessions or deliverances, but they'd also never spent an entire sermon on anything of the like. Luna only knew of the topic because she'd studied it after Zanella's movie theater art performance during The Gala Games, as Cole called them. He'd recited a verse from the book of Matthew about Jesus casting out a demon and then dropped wild boars from a helicopter, creating a Carrie White–esque bloodbath.

If only she weren't so tired, she could remember what she'd read during her studies—she was sure of it.

"I don't know yet," she said, rubbing her hands over her face. "I need to read scripture."

Thankfully, Cole accepted her answer, then gently lifted her body off his.

"Come on," he said, slowly standing and offering a hand to pull her up, too. "Let's get you cleaned up and back in bed."

Luna wanted to object, to insist they solve everything right then and there, but her body was so drained.

"Lu," he said softly, prodding her.

She let out a deep breath, then nodded and followed him back through the forest to Sol's cabin. Together, they tiptoed inside and up the creaky stairs. At the top of the second-floor landing, Luna tried to walk to her room, but Cole gently tugged her hand and shook his head.

"You are not going to bed like that. Here," he said, leading her to the bathroom. "I'll run a hot shower for you so you can get warm. I'll bring some fresh clothes and a towel, too. Hold on."

Luna didn't object, and Cole was out the door and back in less than a minute. He set a fluffy blue bath towel on the sink, along with a black hoodie and basketball shorts that were definitely not hers.

"There."

He started to walk away to give her privacy, but the thought of being alone in water again terrified her.

Without thinking, she grabbed his wrist. "Will you stay with me?"

She watched as his eyebrows shot up to his forehead, and she stammered, trying to explain. "I-I'm scared . . . of the w-water."

And then understanding flashed in his eyes.

"Of course, Lu. Anything you need."

She nodded, thankful for him and his willingness to overlook the oddity of her request.

He scratched at his jaw stubble for a moment and then pointed awkwardly at the door. "Here. I'll just prop this open and hang out on the other side. Totally here the whole time but with, you know, a little privacy."

"Okay." Luna's voice was scratchy when she spoke. What time was it? Two? Three? She had no clue.

She waited until Cole was on the other side of the door, keeping it partially open like he promised, and then before she could overthink it any further, she stripped off her wet, nasty clothes and stepped into the shower.

The water was immobilizing at first. Icy and hot and paralyzing all at the same time. Images of the bloody flowers entered her mind again, seeping into her vision. For a moment, Luna wasn't sure if she could breathe, and she started to panic.

But then she heard his voice.

"Lu? You okay? I'm right here."

She took a slow, steadying breath and stuck a hand under the stream of water, letting the sting ground her. After a beat of silence, she replied, "Yes," and she meant it. As the hot water boiled on her skin, she let the fear and dirt and grime melt away and swirl down the drain. She took several slow, deep breaths and let herself cry, not caring that Cole could hear her. They were far past casualties at this point.

He'd been there for her through everything, the same way she had been there for him throughout the years. Some people were never fortunate enough to have a best friend, but Luna was.

And she was in love with hers.

She continued to cry until the tears fell away and the water started to run lukewarm. Then, she carefully slipped out of the stall, toweled off, and pulled on Cole's baggy clothes.

"Okay," she said, her voice barely above a whisper. "You can come in. I'm dressed."

Cole pushed the rest of the door open and looked at Luna, a soft smile greeting her. "You look good in my clothes."

She felt something stir in her chest, but in a good way. Before she even realized what she was saying, she slipped a piece of hair behind her ear and asked, "Will you sleep with me tonight? I just really don't want to be alone."

Embarrassment tugged at her, and she hugged her body self-consciously, worried about what he might think the invitation implied. She was exhausted and scared and overwhelmed, and more than anything, just wanted to be held.

By Cole.

He reached a hand out to hers. "Of course I will."

TUESDAY

COLE

He wasn't going to lie—sleeping next to Luna all night, with her tiny body wrapped around his muscular frame, was Cole's idea of perfection.

He had loved slipping his arms around her and comforting her after the events that had transpired. Because he'd come very close to losing her last night. That was not lost on him, and if there was anything this life had taught him, it was that you can't take a moment for granted.

And even though he wanted nothing more than to profess his undying love for her and show her all the ways he worshiped her body, he'd been more than content to simply hold her all night.

Because that's what she needed.

When the morning sun finally rose, creeping through the curtain's shadows, and the crisp fall air seeped in through the windows, Cole gently kissed her forehead and then slipped out of her room before Jaxson or the others woke.

He padded to his room, grateful for the carpeted flooring that masked his footsteps. Then, after a quick shower and change of clothes, he slipped downstairs to the kitchen to brew a pot of coffee. He had no idea what the day might bring, but if there was one thing he was certain of, it was that he needed caffeine—lots of it.

Lemon yawned from her spot on the couch, and Cole smiled at her. "Sounds like you need some coffee, too, huh, girl?"

The pup wagged her tail in response, and for a moment, Cole forgot about the evil presence that potentially hovered over them all.

The world always felt just a smidge brighter with a dog present.

The coffee maker beeped, drawing him back to reality. He poured a fresh cup of black liquid and headed to the backside of the large wraparound porch. He took a sip and let the warm beverage settle in his stomach before chancing a glance at his phone. His agent, Dani, had been blowing him up about the launch party, which was tomorrow. But with everything going on, how could he even fathom something as trivial as a book release? It seemed meaningless in the grand scheme of things.

Dani: Guest list is set at 25. You good with that?

Dani: The caterer is asking for your favorite cake flavor.

Dani: I told him chocolate. Hope that's ok. All good on your end?

Dani: I'm assuming your service is shoddy, but I thought you should know Rose, David, and Clara are confirmed to attend. Thank you again for agreeing to this. I think it'll be great press.

Cole groaned and clicked the lock button on his phone. He'd been waiting for this day for years, the chance to finally meet his niece, and now the opportunity was being presented to him, but at what risk? Luna had insisted they stay, fight this thing off, and keep the party as planned, but was it really safe? He couldn't bear the thought of putting another child in harm's way. He had half a mind to call the whole thing off. Besides, the book would still be published; people would still buy it. He didn't even really want to celebrate with anyone outside of the few people who were already here. What exactly was the point of having a party anyway?

After tapping his thumb against the bottom of his phone several times, he clicked it back on and started typing a response to Dani, making up an excuse about not being ready for a crowd yet. Before he could hit send, though, a rap at the back door caught his attention. He paused, looking up and smiling when he saw Luna. She was still draped in his oversized clothes, a black coffee mug in hand and swollen eyes resting just above her easy smile.

"Hey, Cole."

"Hey, Lu."

They stared at each other in silence for a minute before Luna decided to venture onto the covered porch and take a seat next to Cole.

"How are you feeling?" Cole asked as he scanned her face. She didn't look like a woman who'd nearly drowned hours ago, but she also didn't look like herself.

Luna rolled her neck from side to side before answering, a blank expression on her face. "I don't know. Weird I guess."

Weird.

Cole could agree with that.

He took another sip of his coffee and looked out at the fallen leaves and nearly naked tree branches that surrounded them. The picturesque view would be beautiful under different circumstances. "Have you thought about what we're going to do?"

Luna shook her head. "No. I mean, yes, I've thought about it, but I haven't touched my Bible yet."

Cole bit at the skin inside his lip. "We can still cancel for tomorrow." He assumed she wouldn't go for it, but he had to try one last time. "I was just thinking of texting Dani to say so."

"No," Lu said, confirming his thoughts. "I told you, that won't work. It's better to just figure this all out today. Put a stop to it once and for all. Plus, you deserve to celebrate. You've worked so hard on this book and just spent half a decade locked up." She smiled at him, the corners of her eyes softening. "We could use some joy around here."

Cole still felt uneasy about it, but he conceded. "Fine. What are you going to tell Jax?"

"I don't know. Nothing?" She picked at her nails. "His spiritual beliefs are . . . complicated. I don't really know how to explain this to him."

Cole sat back, twisting his lips as another idea occurred to him. "What if we got him out of here today, for the day?"

"What do you mean?"

"I mean," Cole started, throwing his right leg over the other as he sank deeper in his chair, "what if I called Dani and had her come get him and distract him today while the rest of us do whatever it is we need to. That way he doesn't have to know."

He watched as Luna contemplated his words. Yesterday, he'd been on board with telling Jaxson everything, but that was before he realized what they were dealing with. And if Luna was worried about her son's spiritual well-being, well, he wasn't going to get in the way again.

"What would Dani do with him? Does she even know ASL?"

"No," Cole replied, "but Jax loves to draw and paint, right? What if she took him to the local art studio and let him create something for the launch party?"

That would also get Dani off my back, Cole thought to himself.

Luna ran her hands through her hair, flipping the blonde strands back and forth, the way she always did when she was nervous. "I suppose that could work." She bit her bottom lip and then added, "How soon could she be here?"

Cole smiled. "Let me make a call."

An hour later, Cole gave Jaxson a fist bump and told him to paint something "cool" for the event.

To which Jaxson replied, *"You wouldn't know cool if it hit you over the head."*

Cole stuck his tongue out at him and grinned before Luna cut them off to triple-confirm their plans.

"Now, Grey, you'll take Jax to the art studio on Main Street, and Dani will meet you guys there with all the supplies. You'll help translate, and then you'll both be home by dinnertime once Jax has finished painting?"

Greyson nodded. "Yes, Momma Lu. Don't worry. We'll be fine."

Cole watched as her hands twitched, but Luna refrained from objecting further. When he'd called Dani, she said she wouldn't have time to run all the way out there twice in one day but that she'd be happy to meet Jaxson at the studio so he could paint. They weren't sure Greyson was the best person to take him, especially considering his sign language skills were novice at best, but both Cole and Luna agreed Sol should stay with them since he was the one who'd been living here—and the person who brought up the old myth to begin with.

Not that Cole was placing blame.

"I still don't understand why I can't paint here," Jax said. *"It'd be easier. And the vibe is better."* He bobbed his head, and Luna let out a small laugh.

"I know, I'm sorry. I wish you could, too, but Dani doesn't have time to come out here today. But don't worry, I'm sure you can still vibe"—head bob—*"in the studio with Grey."*

Jax grimaced before giving his mom a hug. *"See you later, Ma."*

"See you later, J. I love you."

Cole rubbed reassuring circles on the small of her back as Greyson and Jaxson waved their goodbyes and headed down the gravel road.

"They'll be okay," Cole whispered next to her.

"I know," she said, nodding as she swiped a quick finger below her eye before clearing her throat. "Okay, where's Solstice? We have research to do."

LUNA

"So you're telling me, all we gotta do is say a little prayer, and all our problems will magically go away?"

Luna felt like scratching her eyeballs out. "I thought you were a believer, Sol."

He drummed his fingers on his exposed knee, his outfit reminiscent of every eighties rock star ever. "I do, but hell's bells. A prayer isn't very rock and roll."

They were sitting around the coffee table in the living room. Luna had spent the last hour buried in scripture and researching online, trying to find a solution to their problems. Her search results had largely yielded one answer: a hedge of protection.

"Prayer is not meant to be rock and roll, Solstice." She grabbed a chip from the smorgasbord of snacks they'd emptied on the table. "Cole, help me out here, please."

Cole and Lemon were snuggled in the large leather lounge chair opposite her and Sol. For a man who was shouldering the weight of some of her burdens, he looked like the picture-perfect version of ease.

"Can you explain it to me again? I'm still trying to wrap my head around it."

Luna flipped her Bible back open, thumbing through the pages as her mind wandered. "So there's this prayer I heard about once that talks about placing a hedge of protection around you. According to the internet, that word comes from the book of Job." She landed on the tab she'd been looking for and skimmed through the passage, refamiliarizing herself with the verses. Her pastor had preached a sermon on Job once, but it was several years ago, and Luna had never studied the book herself. "So Satan and God are talking about this man named Job, and Satan basically says, 'Have you not placed a hedge of protection around this man?' And then God removes it and allows Satan to test Job."

"That doesn't sound very nice," Sol said sourly.

"It was meant to be a testament of faith. God wanted to show Satan that no matter what he did to this man, Job would still love and trust God," Luna said, continuing as the presence of the Holy Spirit grounded her. "Here"—she flipped to the next place her internet search had sent her: Psalm 91—"this is an entire psalm dedicated to showing us all the ways the Lord will protect us, reminding us that we can trust him." She chewed the inner corner of her lip. "The prayer I once heard goes along with this psalm and the hedge of protection from Job. I think we just need to say it, and then, in theory, things should go back to normal."

"In theory?" Cole questioned.

Luna stared at him, unsure why her words felt doubtful. Like she didn't know if she could trust this, whether she could trust God after all they'd been through in recent years.

Her cross necklace felt cool against her skin, resting above her heart and gnawing at her soul.

"Yes," she said suddenly. "Definitely yes. This will work."

I think.

"Well, forgive me," Sol started, "but I think we oughta do something a bit more than that."

Luna sighed, catching Cole's eye. His face had hardened a bit, likely in concentration. She wished she knew what he was thinking.

"What are you talking about, Sol?" she asked.

He slapped his knee before throwing his hand out and gesturing at the door. "I love the good Lord and all, but I don't think we should just rely on words and let ourselves be sitting ducks. I mean, something possessed you to nearly drown last night, Lu."

"I wasn't possessed!" Luna spit out immediately. "I was just . . ."

She couldn't find the words to describe what she'd been, what had caused her to wake up underwater.

"Yeah," Sol said, as if she'd proven his point. "I'm thinking we need a good old-fashioned exorcist."

Luna shook her head. "No. Absolutely not. I told you, that's a Catholic thing."

"Then what was that shit we saw at the movie theater five years ago?"

"I mean, yes, you can cast out a demon like Jesus did, but it's different."

"How?" Sol argued. "Seems like the same concept to me."

But Luna still wasn't budging. "No, Sol. I don't feel confident enough to deal with that. I don't have the proper knowledge or wisdom it requires." In all honesty, she'd probably make it worse. "My parents taught me to stay away from that stuff."

Sol huffed, grabbed a bag of chips, then dramatically threw himself back on the couch. "I never get to do nothing fun around here."

"What if," Cole started, cutting off his tantrum, "we buried the bones?"

Luna scrunched her brows. "Why?"

He shrugged, and Lemon pawed at him, demanding his full attention. "To help lay the spirits to rest. You know, cleanse the place of bad juju."

Oof. Luna's soul shuddered. "Christians don't really believe in that kind of thing."

"The hell we don't." Sol cracked his neck to the side. "That's that purgatory thing my gran is always talking about."

"Again, that's Catholicism, Solstice."

Sol's face lit up. "You know what? Maybe that's what I am."

Cole chuckled, punctuating the absurdity of it all. "What? Catholic?"

"Yeah," Sol answered. "Why not? Makes sense, dunnit? Why I believe in exorcisms and purgatory and whatnot. I think, perhaps, I am a regular ole Catholic." He paused, his face suddenly turning stoic. "Maybe that's why my pop said to avoid alone time with the man in robes all those years ago."

Luna was one thousand percent done with this conversation. "Could you please take this seriously, Solstice?"

"I bloody am!" he bellowed. "I'll agree to your prayer as long as you'll agree to help us put these poor souls to rest. We bury the bones, and that awful bobcat while we're at it. Honor my beliefs, sweetheart, and I'll honor yours."

Annoyance crept up Luna's vertebrae, one by one.

"I think it's a fair request, Lu," Cole said, meeting her gaze. She felt like swearing at the way his warm, honey eyes made her melt, even under duress. "Sol and I can dig the graves, then you can recite the prayer. What harm could it do?"

Luna internally groaned. "I guess . . . *nothing*, technically, but I still don't like it."

"Well, I don't like loads of things you do, love, but I don't rain on your fucking parade."

She shot daggers at Sol. If time weren't of the essence, she would have argued with him for hours. But, instead, she held her tongue and took a deep breath. "Fine. Let's just get it over with then, before Jax comes home."

The men nodded in succession just as a crack of thunder roared overhead.

"Blimey." Sol rubbed his calf, then stood. "I thought I felt a storm brewing. Would've been nice if the big man upstairs could've held off long enough for us to do His work, eh?"

Luna palmed her forehead and blew an exaggerated breath. This was going to be a *very* tiresome afternoon.

COLE

Images of River flooded Cole's mind as he carried the dead animal over his shoulder.

It was a grim comparison, the odor terrible, but the weight of the creature lay heavily on his muscles, making him reminiscent of all the times he'd carried River in his arms while they'd played together. She must have been three or four when they started roughhousing, if you could really call it that. Cole was always gentle with her, but he'd throw her onto her bed or the couch like a sack of potatoes and then laugh as she serenaded him with her little giggles. They were some of his favorite memories.

Now, he plowed through the rain-drenched forest as quickly as he could with the extra thirty or forty pounds biting into his trap muscles. When he'd suggested burying the bones earlier, he had no idea Sol would also suggest burying the cat and then profess Catholicism as his newfound faith. With the way the rain was pelting down around him, he should've made Sol roll this thing up in a tarp and carry it down the hillside himself, but honestly, Cole didn't feel like hearing his complaints. He'd had enough of the singer's frivolous remarks for one day, and it wasn't even dinnertime yet. Slugging this foul-smelling carcass through the storm was a small price to pay for his sanity.

Cole wished he could say the same for Luna. The poor thing had looked like she'd wanted to strangle Sol, if she believed in doing that sort of thing.

140

You do, Cole's inner monologue reminded him.

He couldn't help but smirk, knowing full well he'd happily strangle someone for Luna.

His smile faltered, and he wondered if that made him a bad person.

He didn't know.

Pushing away the thought, he rounded the bend at the bottom of the hill and reached the end of the hiking path, which dumped him out where Sol and Luna were lying in wait.

"Took you long enough!" Sol yelled over the windswept rain, his wild ringlets plastered to the top of his head in a sloppy man bun.

Cole ignored his comment and slung the bobcat onto the ground, water dripping into his eyes.

"Do you think that's deep enough?" Luna asked, stepping up beside him as he stretched out his neck and shoulders.

Cole surveyed Sol's work. "Should be fine." He took another deep breath, then rolled the animal into the earth's hollow pit. Debris sloshed up on him from the freshly made mud.

"Poor thing," Luna said, her voice almost nonexistent as another clap of thunder boomed overhead. "We should name him."

Cole left her to her devices, quickly helping Sol throw the remaining dirt back into the ground before it all turned to clay. When they were finished, he asked, "Are the bones already done?"

"You could stick a fork in 'em, mate!" Sol grinned at him through the downpour, his smile a cross between the Mad Hatter's and Cheshire Cat's.

"All right." Cole nodded. "Lu, this next part is all you."

She bobbed her head but wrung her hands. Cole knew she was nervous to pray out loud. Luna had once confided in Cole that she hated the idea of it. She could pray all day on her own, she'd told him, but introducing someone else into the mix? Luna said it was one of her worst nightmares. Cole wasn't sure he understood, nor shared the same sentiment, causing his next move.

He closed the space between them and ducked his head to her ear. "Do you want me to pray?"

A bolt of lightning streaked across the sky, illuminating her features and highlighting her shocked expression.

"You can tell me what to say," he offered, seeing the confusion on her face.

The corners of her mouth raised, and she smiled, placing a palm on his forearm. "Thank you, but it's okay. I got this."

Cole stared into her blue eyes, squinting and searching for remnants of the truth. In the end, he could tell she wasn't lying. She was strong. She could handle this.

"Give me your hands," she instructed, moving to stand between the two men.

Cole immediately obeyed, a little too eager to take direction from her, but Sol hesitated.

"You're not gonna, like, do a bird dance and transport us into the third dimension like in that bloody TV show—"

"Solstice!" she yelled. "Just give me your dang hand and shut up!"

Cole rolled in his lips to keep from smiling.

Luna cleared her throat and took a deep breath. "I'm going to say a prayer now, and I need you to both pray with me. Not out loud," she corrected herself quickly, "but just close your eyes and bow your heads with me, and it's really important you believe in what we're doing, okay?"

They both nodded, and Cole squeezed her hand for reassurance.

Thunder and lightning struck at the same time, and Luna squealed.

"Um, okay," she started, her voice wobbly at first. "Dear Heavenly Father, Lord, we come to you today, humbly asking for a hedge of protection."

A warm current hummed through Cole's body, and he thought he recognized it as the Holy Spirit. He'd encountered it a handful of times over the years; it was what finally gave him the gentle nudge to believe, to accept Christ as his savior. He sometimes wondered if it would ever return, though, to answer his questions and prepare his heart for baptism.

Maybe that's why it's raining now.

Or maybe it's just a natural part of the water cycle, the earth due for its next bout of precipitation.

"We know that those who believe in, love, and trust you will be saved, safe, and protected," Luna continued, stamping out Cole's thoughts. "We pray that you cloak us with your Holy Spirit, hiding us from any and all evil and familiar spirits and the enemy so that they may not even find us in the spiritual realm."

Her voice faltered; Cole squeezed her hand.

"Please extend this hedge of protection to my son and our friends and loved ones who will be joining us tomorrow night. And Father—" Her voice broke before taking on a more curious tone. "Father God, if there are any souls lingering here, we pray that you would help them move on, and again, please protect us from any evil or wrongdoings."

That's it, Lu. Almost there.

Clearing her throat one last time, Luna concluded with, "We praise you, we thank you, and we love you, Lord. In Jesus's name we pray—"

"Amen!"

Cole opened his eyes and peeked at the others. Luna let out a gust of air, and then, she smiled at him. He bit his bottom lip, proud of her for overcoming her fears and being an example of Christ to him. He was so very thankful for her.

Sol was staring at the sky with his hands on his hips and a giant grin plastered to his face. "Well, would you look at that?" His voice rang out, breaking Cole and Luna's trance and reminding them there was a third person present. A very *vocal* third person. "Seems like the heavens have done opened up."

Cole finally peeled his gaze away from Luna and then furrowed his brows when he realized what Sol was referring to.

The rain had stopped.

The skies were clear.

And a beam of sunlight was shining through the suspended water droplets that made up the clouds.

He looked back at Luna, who was still trying to collect herself. She was completely drenched from the storm and her pants were covered in mud, but she was still smiling.

"Do you think it worked then?" she asked.

Her question caught him off guard. Of course he did.

"I mean, like, all the way," she clarified, apparently reading the confusion on his face. "Do you think all the . . . chaos is over?"

Cole cocked his head, considering her question.

"I sure as shit hope so," Sol answered for him. "Didn't you just fucking tell us we had to believe, otherwise Tinker Bell wouldn't get her fairy wings and we'd be haunted until the end of time?"

Cole couldn't help but smirk as Luna rolled her eyes.

"Okay, okay," she said. "Fine, you're right." She picked up a wet piece of hair, letting it flop back onto her shoulder a moment later. "I can't believe we just did that." Then, she added, "I could really use a flippin' drink right now." She looked at Cole with a new gleam in her eye. "Something that bites."

He felt the heat rush simultaneously to his cheeks and pants as the memory of the first time she'd said that danced in his mind. They'd been standing in his office at *The Chronicles*, discussing Z's gala invite, when Luna had asked him if he wanted to grab a drink. He had felt wildly inappropriate at the suggestion, considering he was still legally married and only separated from Rose at the time, but even then, he couldn't say no to her.

"All right, then, Miss Monroe." He couldn't resist offering a teasing grin. "What would you like?"

"You two disgust me," Sol interjected, rinsing his boots off in a nearby puddle.

To Cole's surprise, Luna laughed and played into Sol's antics. "You only wish I'd bite you, Solstice," she said, snapping her teeth and mimicking a vampiress.

Cole's eyes widened. She was making this incredibly difficult to be a gentleman.

LUNA

AFTER A PIPING HOT shower and a fresh set of comfy, casual clothes, Luna sauntered into the kitchen, graciously accepting a drink from Cole's waiting hand.

"A hot toddy?" she said after taking a sip. "I like it."

Cole offered one of his signature half grins, this time paired with a shrug. "I thought you could use something hot."

Luna felt her cheeks flush, unashamed of their fuchsia color. She'd just warded off a spiritual attack, for goodness sake. If there was ever a time to live and let love in, it was now, right? She and Cole had been through so much together. First The Gala and Cole's trauma with River, then Rose and David. Then came the shocking revelation of Jaxson's existence, Luna being in the throes of motherhood, Cole being imprisoned. This week was supposed to be fun, a celebration as they finally enjoyed life together again, but even that had been tampered with by something evil, something demonic. It was like everything was out to get them, and yet, no matter what, they made it through, better and stronger because of it. They'd always been there for each other and always would be.

They were so much more than friends, and Luna was finally ready to admit it to herself.

Perhaps tonight, she would admit it to him, too.

Something in her felt different at the revelation. Lighter. Like her body and soul were humming in sync with the remnants of the adrenaline she'd just experienced, mixed with a dash of flowery confidence.

Luna smiled, wondering if this was perhaps her old self reemerging.

She sat down and took another sip of her beverage, savoring the warm burn as it melted down her throat. "Thank you."

Cole took a swig directly from the Blue Label bottle Sol had pulled out from the cellar. Then he locked eyes with her. "My pleasure."

Something inside her tingled at those words, and she was pretty sure it wasn't the liquor.

"What time is it?" she asked, that tiny bloom of confidence bordering on the brink of life again.

"Four," Cole replied, his gaze lifting to meet hers.

Luna nodded. "And where's Sol?"

Cole's eyes darkened. "Passed out in his room."

"Oh," was all Luna said, nodding and taking another sip to distract herself from the way the oxygen in her lungs resuscitated at the mere thought of Cole's touch.

Be brave, she told herself.

Be bold.

She straightened from where she was sitting in the barstool and set down her cup. Then, she swiveled in her chair and locked eyes with the man she'd secretly loved, longed for, all these years. She waited on bated breath as the veins in Cole's forearms flexed, indicating how tightly he must've been grasping the counter.

She involuntarily sucked in a breath at the sight of her prison man staring her down, and then, with a small voice, said, "Cole?"

But that was all she got to say, because in less than a second, his body lunged at hers, his lips trapping hers with a kiss.

Luna squealed in surprise but didn't pull away.

Because this was what she'd wanted.

He was what she'd wanted.

The kiss was euphoric. At first, his lips felt like honey, warm and gentle and gooey in all the ways she'd imagined. But then the kiss turned into something else as their lips moved in sync with more urgency, more passion.

Luna felt his firm grip around her waist while his other hand cupped the back of her head. She let out a soft moan, and in response, Cole deepened the kiss. Luna felt him push his body against hers, showing her just how much he wanted her, too, and it all felt so good.

Too good. She didn't want to stop.

She let herself fool her body into thinking she could have it all—have his all—just this once.

But just as Cole's hands dipped down further and hoisted her onto the counter, she broke the kiss, dizzying herself in the process.

Cole didn't understand at first, mistaking her break as an opportunity to kiss her neck, her chin, her chest.

Luna involuntarily moaned again, but this time, she felt a familiar voice of reason slipping into the recesses of her mind. She jerked back, placing a hand out to put physical distance between them.

For a moment, they both sat in silence, breathing heavily and staring at each other, an electric charge in the air.

"Lu—" Cole started.

"I'm a virgin!" Luna blurted. "And I'm saving myself until marriage."

COLE

Cole blinked.

"What?" His voice was low, still out of breath.

He watched as Luna chewed her bottom lip again, only this time, it looked like fear rather than seduction.

"I, I mean, well, I'm not *technically*, technically a virgin," she stammered as her eyes darted away and then back to him. "I'm a born-again virgin. So, like, I-I've had sex, but, you know, then I-I became a Christian, and so, I decided to wait until marriage. To, you know, do the deed again."

Her words came out in a blur, and Cole had to fight to keep up.

"Okay," he said carefully. "So, you're not a virgin?"

"Not technically, no. But like, *spiritually*, yes."

Cole nodded as he let the words sink in. He knew Luna was a believer, so really, this shouldn't have come as a shock. He just assumed . . . actually, he didn't know what he'd assumed. They had never talked about their sex life or previous partners. He realized he knew absolutely nothing about Luna's former dating life.

"But you have had sex?" he asked, trying to wrap his brain around it.

She looked infinitely younger in her embarrassment, reminding Cole of their age gap. "Yes, I lost my virginity before I came to Christ, but I've been abstinent since I was eighteen, when I was saved and baptized.

Cole quickly did the math. "So you haven't been with anyone in—"

"Fifteen years," she finished for him, her voice becoming high-pitched. "Is that going to be a problem, for us?"

Emotions swelled in his chest. He'd be lying if he said he wasn't disappointed. He'd been five seconds away from ripping her clothes off and devouring her, so this definitely came as a shock.

But he loved her. And he knew his reaction in this moment meant a lot. So, instead of begging for her to change her mind like he wanted, he sighed, tilted his head, and grabbed Luna's chin with the tips of his fingers.

"No," he said simply.

Her blue eyes bounced between his dark brown ones. "Are you sure?" she asked, her voice barely above a whisper.

"Of course," he repeated, nodding his head. "That's fine. I can respect that."

He watched as she relaxed her shoulders, the relief visibly falling off.

"Okay," she said through a smile.

Cole licked his lips and looked away, wondering how he was going to navigate this next part. He was curious if *everything* was off-limits, but he didn't think it best to ask.

Instead he said, "I mean, we could, like . . . go to the courthouse."

Luna's jaw dropped, and she hit him, making Cole laugh. "Cole Sloane!"

"I'm kidding, I'm kidding," he teased, even though he wasn't. Not really.

Because Luna was it for him.

He'd marry her today if she let him.

But this wasn't the way he'd planned to propose, so instead, he peppered delicate kisses on her hand, then up her arm, jaw, and finally to her ear. "I've waited five years for you, Lu. I'll wait the rest of my life if I have to."

Something between a moan and a squeal escaped her lips, and Cole grabbed the sides of her face. "Please tell me kissing is okay, though," he begged.

"Yes." Her voice was barely audible over the sound of their heavy breathing.

Cole didn't even wait half a second before pulling her mouth back to his and slowly devouring her lips. She felt so soft and sweet and comfortable. Yet exhilarating and enthralling and enchanting all at the same time. Luna felt like the type of woman worth waiting for. His adventure and his home, all wrapped up in one. He loved her so fucking much.

He should tell her.

Cole began pulling his lips away from her sweet-yet-spicy mouth to do just that, but the sound of tires crunching over gravel interrupted them.

"Oh my gosh!" Luna hopped off the counter and covered her mouth. "Is that Jax?" She didn't wait for Cole to respond before spewing out another series of scattered sentences. "He wasn't supposed to be back this soon. What on earth are we going to tell him? Oh my gosh, I didn't think he'd be back this soon!"

Sensing her nervousness, Cole grabbed Luna's hand, catching it just as Greyson's carefully styled hair came into view through the window.

"Hey," he said, turning her around. "It's okay. We don't have to tell him anything yet if you don't want to."

Luna faced him. Her once-carefree face was now etched with worry lines, and concern swirled in her eyes, bursting in full, electric shades of blue.

"You're okay with that?" she asked after a pregnant pause.

Cole nodded and offered a soft smile. "Of course. I totally understand. We can take things slow—do it at your own pace."

He knew why Luna was doing this. She blamed herself for what happened to Jaxson and didn't feel like she deserved to be happy when he'd had so many unpleasant experiences in life.

He knew because that's exactly how he felt when River died.

"I told you, Lu," he said, clearing his throat and stroking a lock of her honey-colored hair behind her ear. "I would wait a lifetime for you."

A smile spread across her face. "Thank you, Cole," she whispered. Then, she gave him a quick peck on the cheek and turned back to the door.

THE REST OF THE evening passed by in a blur as everyone enjoyed the calm before the storm. The launch party wasn't until tomorrow night, but according to Dani, the vendors would arrive in the morning at eight o'clock sharp.

Cole didn't mind all the fuss as long as it stayed focused on the house and not on him. The idea of being with a large group of inmates—*people*, he corrected himself—again made his skin crawl. He hadn't had much time to think about it, between his insane desire for Lu and the theatrics that had played out at the cabin over the last few days. Now, though, the anticipation of what was to come made his stomach roil.

His story would finally be out in the world. Not Zanella's story, but his. Cole had reported on that lunatic for so long; even after The Gala, his final piece he wrote for *The Chronicles* was all about Zanella's MO.

No one really knew why Cole killed him.

They speculated, but he'd never gone on record talking about the awful confession Z made that night at the library. The one that made something inside Cole snap, changing the very essence of his DNA.

No one knew the role Zanella played in River's death.

And now it was finally his time to tell their story, her story, in his own words.

Cole's body shuddered at the very thought as he sat outside by the campfire.

He tried to take a few deep breaths to calm his nerves, but then he thought of Rose.

And David.

And Clara.

He cocked his jaw, a mess of emotions swelling inside him.

You've been over this before. Been there, done that. Grieved it, forgot it. He wasn't angry at Rose or David anymore. He'd forgiven them a long time ago and moved on with his life—moved on from the ghosts of his past that used to haunt him.

But now everything felt different, like the ground beneath him was shifting and a new ghost was awakening, emerging from beyond the grave, trying to pry itself back into Cole's life.

Because tomorrow, he would meet Clara.

His niece.

River's half sister.

The thought both excited and tormented him.

He polished off the rest of his beer and grabbed another from the cooler. The rest of the gang had retreated for the night, and it was now after midnight. Cole knew he should probably go to bed, too, but for the life of him, he couldn't sleep well here. You'd think after half a decade of sleeping on a lumpy mattress in a prison cell that he'd be sleeping like a king in Sol's guest room, but something about the place felt . . . off.

He looked down at the bottle in his hand, the glass glowing in the light of the dying embers as he reflected on the day's events. He still didn't fully understand what had happened earlier. How his sweet, precious Luna had protected them all and put an end to the crazed events by simply saying a prayer. Cole didn't quite understand any of it, really, but he thought it was pretty badass.

Of that, he was sure.

WEDNESDAY

LUNA

HOLY GUACAMOLE.

Did the past forty-eight hours really happen?

Did Luna really almost drown, snuggle with Cole Sloane all night, bury a bunch of bones and a dead animal, pray *out loud* for a hedge of protection, *kiss* Cole Sloane, and then tell him she was a born-again virgin?!

She needed to lie down.

You already are.

Oh, yeah.

It was barely light outside, but after tossing and turning for hours on end, she realized her body wasn't going to let her sleep. Her mind was too wired, despite the exhaustion she felt.

Is that a thing? she wondered. Can someone feel both completely on edge and alive and anxious but also dreadfully tired past the point of exhaustion?

Yes, she decided.

As a mother, she could confidently say it was a thing.

But that didn't make it any easier.

She pulled one of the too-fluffy pillows over her face and groaned.

What was she going to do with herself?

After deciding that was a problem for another day, one Future Luna would no doubt thank her for, she rolled out of bed and practically floated down the stairs. When she reached the bottom, she'd barely stepped off the landing before a hand grabbed her, making her jump.

"Hey," Cole said, the familiar voice instantly calming her unhinged bodily reactions. "It's just me."

Luna slumped her shoulders before playfully hitting Cole in the chest. "You scared me."

He bent down until his lips hovered just above her ear. "How's this for an apology?"

And then Luna died and went to Heaven.

Okay, not literally.

Ugh, forgive me, Lord!

But if euphoria had a name, it would be Cole Sloane's lips.

OMG, you have to stop yourself before—

"Cole, someone's going to see us," she scolded in a hushed whisper.

"Nobody's awake yet," he grumbled into her neck, his early morning ex-prison voice proving to be just as sexy as she'd feared.

She moused out another squeak-moan and was about to give in, but the sound of a shower turning on upstairs gave her pause.

"Tonight," she said, straightening her back and putting a measurable distance between them. "Tonight, after the party, once everyone's in bed. Then, you can kiss me again." She stuck out her tongue and pranced off to the kitchen, laughing when she looked back and saw Cole's expression.

Tease, he mouthed just as someone came bounding down the stairs.

Luna stifled her giggle and swung around on the balls of her feet, placing her hands on her hips as she waited for the coffee to brew.

"You two are up early," Greyson said, a hint of curiosity laced in his tone.

Cole's response was immediate, as if he weren't affected at all by the previous five minutes. "I'm always up early. You're the one who's early today."

Luna peeked over her shoulder and saw Grey give him a skeptical look as he passed by.

"I know this may come as a shock to you, Cole, but some of us want to actually look good for this party tonight."

Luna handed Greyson a mug. "Wait, so you're up this early so you can start getting ready? The party's not till six."

"I swear," Greyson said with an exaggerated breath, "it's like you two don't even know me."

Luna raised her brows, trying not to laugh as she locked eyes with Cole. "Somebody woke up on the wrong side of the bread today." Her inner child giggled at the *Rugrats* joke.

"Is it so bad that I want to look good for the year's most exclusive, highly anticipated book launch party?" His voice rose on an incline as he spoke.

Cole poured himself a cup of coffee. "I think you're making this a bigger deal than it is, Grey."

"Colestice," Greyson said, using the nickname he and Luna had come up with one night when laughing about the similarities between his and Sol's names. "Have you not seen the latest cover of *Time* magazine?"

That got everyone's attention.

"Wait, what?" Luna asked as she added a dash of creamer to her coffee.

Grey paused and pulled out his phone. After a minute of scrolling, he laid it on the kitchen island. "Here."

Luna's jaw immediately dropped as Cole's mug shot stared back at her.

Released: The highly anticipated story of Cole Sloane will finally be revealed at an exclusive launch party now that America's favorite ex-con is out of prison.

"Favorite ex-con?" Cole repeated the words as they all hovered over Greyson's phone.

"Yeah, it seems doing time has served you well, Grandpa." Greyson clicked the phone back off and slid it into his pocket.

"How did they even get that photo?" Luna asked, a quizzical expression on her face.

"Oh, please," Grey said. "It's all over the internet."

Luna took a second to sip her coffee. "Yeah, but they'd need permission for the high-res image. I'm just surprised the prison let them have it. Actually, I'm surprised they used it at all. There's a huge ethics debate going on now about whether it's appropriate to publish mug shots." She chewed her bottom lip, then looked back at Cole, who had an unreadable expression on his face. "You okay?"

He looked up at her, slowly blinking. "Yeah," he said with a drawn out breath. "Just processing."

Luna nodded. She could understand how this would be a lot for Cole. And he was the type of man who needed time to think, to process, like he said.

So methodical, that one.

"That's exciting, though," she tried, setting her cup down and glancing out the window as a stream of autumn light shone in. "Hopefully this means lots of people will read your book. That was the goal, right?"

Cole nodded slowly, still mentally calculating.

"Yeah," he said after a minute. "That's the goal. Just weird, seeing my face on a publication. I'm so used to just a byline. And all those people . . ."

Luna placed a gentle hand on his shoulder as his voice trailed off. "They're going to love your book, hun. And River's story will finally be revealed—your name cleared."

She knew that must've been what Cole needed to hear because in that moment, she watched all the tension leave his face, her newer *Zen Cole* returning.

"You're right," he said after a beat. "This is for her. All of it is for her."

Smiling, Luna dropped her hand, letting her fingertips linger as she brushed past his biceps.

"Ahem," Grey said, clearing his throat.

Luna and Cole turned to look at him, a sudden reminder they weren't the only ones in the room. Luna felt a rush of heat spread onto her cheeks, but before she could say anything, Greyson said, "Your son is walking down the stairs. Better go hop in a cold-ass shower before he sees what y'all are so clearly terrible at hiding."

If Luna's eyes could've physically popped out of her head, they would have.

"Hey, Mom," Jax said, trotting down the stairs with Lemon at his side.

"Hey, sweetie," Luna replied. *"How'd you sleep?"*

She took Grey's advice and went to the sink to rinse out her now-empty cup, letting the cold water run over her hands and help ground her back to reality.

"Not bad." Jax tugged at the strawberry-blond curls atop his head and walked toward the fridge. *"What time will Dani be here? I want to show you my painting."*

"Eight," Cole answered, walking over to pet Lem.

Luna checked the time on the microwave while Jax continued chatting with Cole. It was a little after seven, which meant people would be here soon. She wouldn't need to start getting ready until late afternoon, and she wondered what she'd do with her free time.

She chose photography.

When in doubt, Luna's camera always won. There was something about seeing the world through a lens that made her think differently, even took her breath away at times. Some thought she did it for the money, and of course she partly did, but in truth, photography was an art, a way of life for Luna, the same way words were a way of life for Cole and painting was for her son.

She had worried that photographing that poor girl's dead body at The Gala would lead her away from the camera, defy her the joy she once found in the art form, but if anything, it drew her closer. When she wasn't worrying about

Jax's school-bullying problems or if he was getting a proper education or if his hearing aids would fit or if she could afford to buy him all the fancy things she never had growing up or all the other overwhelming aspects of motherhood, she was thinking about her art.

Her passion.

And so now, as she sat on the edge of the lake, her camera in hand and pointed at the old dock she'd fallen from just days ago, she felt that familiar calming sense wash over her as she snapped the perfect shot.

It looked broken and weathered, but that's what Luna admired. There was something beautiful about brokenness, or rather, the state of brokenness. Because in her gut, she knew this dock could be restored again, brought back to its former glory and then some if only someone was willing to take a chance on it, yet at the same time, she knew it was just as beautiful now as it likely was the first time a beam of sunlight glinted off the lake, casting a glow on the freshly stained wood.

This dock held a story. Not only had it weathered many storms, but it had also stood its ground and survived the unexplainable supernatural forces of something demonic, something evil, lurking beneath its waters. It still stood tall, having survived the beating of a lifetime.

Just like she had.

It was a beautiful dock.

She snapped another photo and then stood, giving her legs a break from the crouch she'd been in. Her burning thighs thanked her as the sensation soothed itself, and she swung her camera strap around her neck, looking for the next piece of Mother Nature to reveal its hidden secrets to her.

Something in the forest snapped, to the right of her, and Luna turned, curiosity piqued.

She knew it probably wasn't the smartest idea, walking deeper in the woods, all alone after something had just haunted them, but Luna didn't feel scared.

She felt safe. Out here, she was safe from her demons—literally—and the troubles of the real world. Here, at Solstice's cabin, she could finally breathe.

She smashed her boots against the marshlike land and waded through the muddled weeds. The noise sounded again, and this time, it was much closer. Her first thought was that it was a wild animal. A fox or perhaps a coyote. Again, something that should have scared her but didn't as an old longing for adventure desperately tried to claw its way out of her.

As she inched closer to the neighboring trees, the noise got louder. What she'd first thought was a growl now sounded more and more like a groan, and Luna gripped her camera strap a little tighter, suddenly questioning her renewed sense of bravery.

Quietly, she raised the camera to her eye and crouched down again, taking another cautious step toward the noise.

Then another.

And another.

And—

"Ohmygosh!"

Luna gasped, dropping the camera and letting it hang from her neck as she covered her face.

My eyes!

"I know you like to take pictures, love, but this feels a bit too kinky for your speed," Sol said as he covered his naked groin with a nearby leaf.

Ohmygosh, Luna thought. *This is SO not happening.*

With her eyes still covered, Luna shouted, "Put your clothes on, Sol! Cheese and rice."

"Oi, I don't know. I feel pretty free out here like this. Liberated, as you Americans say. Maybe I'll join a nudist colony—"

"Sol!" Luna hiccuped, bouncing on the balls of her feet.

The rock star grumbled but obliged, and when Luna finally uncovered her eyes, she was shocked to see Dani staring back at her.

"Dani? Really?"

Cole's agent fluffed her messy black hair. "What? My job is really stressful, okay. Please don't tell Cole."

Luna scoffed. "Oh, I am *so* telling Cole."

Dani groaned, and Luna shuddered, realizing it was her voice she'd heard through the trees.

"Just keep it on the downlow, please. I'm technically on the clock."

Luna made a face as Dani walked past her. Sure, Luna used to have an itty bitty celebrity crush on Sol when she'd first met him, but after knowing him now, she couldn't imagine doing *that* with *him*. Luna didn't have a brother, but she imagined it was a similar feeling, and she shuddered again, embarrassment and surprise moving through her.

She turned back to Solstice now that he was fully dressed. "You better hope there's no poison ivy out here."

She watched his eyes widen, and she laughed, swiveling on her heel and heading back to the cabin.

"Come on, Romeo. We have a party to get ready for."

COLE

Cole swallowed as he looked at his watch. The party would officially begin in five minutes, and already, several people had arrived. He was upstairs in his room, avoiding the impending crowd while he nursed a beer.

"Knock, knock."

He peeled himself away from his spot at the window and turned to see Luna walking in.

"Wow," he said under his breath. "Lu, you look incredible."

And she did. She was wearing a strapless silvery-blue dress that clung to her body in all the right places, leaving Cole speechless. Her hair was twisted into a side bun, with a few loose curls dangling around her face, and her lips were painted peach.

"Thank you." She smoothed her hands over her dress before looking at Cole with a sheepish grin. "You're not so bad yourself."

Cole sat his beer down and took a slow step toward her. His eyes flicked to the door, which was half shut, trapping the heat of their breath in the room.

Or at least, that's what it felt like to Cole.

"Where's Jaxson?" He took a couple more stealthy, measured steps toward her.

"Um," Lu whispered. "H-He's downstairs helping the caterer."

Cole watched her clasp her left elbow with her right hand, trying her hardest not to fidget. He liked the way he made her body react, even when they weren't touching.

"So, if I did this . . ." He closed the rest of the space between them and put a hand on the door, pushing it completely shut and leaning Luna back against it. He bent his head down and brushed his mouth against her ear, whispering, "No one would know—"

And before he could finish the sentence, Luna's hands were on him, guiding his lips to hers and crushing them against her. Cole felt a jolt of shock, caught off guard by her movements. He recovered quickly, though, and cupped a hand around the back of her neck as his lips moved in tandem with hers. He had only meant it to be a soft, gentle kiss, but it quickly turned into something else.

Something heated. Passionate. Needy.

He moved his lips against hers in a fervent motion, wanting to soak in all of her and make up for all the time they'd missed. Her lips felt like sunshine and chaotic bliss on a hot summer's day, like a shot of whiskey and goose bumps on a cold winter's night. She felt like everything he'd ever needed in a woman and more, and he wondered how he'd gone so long without her in his life.

He deepened the kiss, yet again, and she moaned, sending Cole straight into oblivion. He acted without thinking and slid his roaming hands down to her bottom, stilling when she gasped and broke the moment.

Instantly, he realized his mistake and glided his hands back up her smooth satin dress. "I'm sorry, Lu," he said with a rasp. "You're just so hot, so beautiful. I've wanted you for so long."

She leaned her forehead against his while they fought to catch their breaths. "Me too," she whispered. "But, I'm sorry, I just can't yet . . ."

Disappointment laced its way through Cole, but he nodded against her skin, understanding the words left unsaid. "It's okay. You don't have to apologize." He brushed his thumb against the back of her hand. "I told you, I'll wait forever if I have to. I love you, Luna."

The words rolled off his tongue before he realized what he was saying, but once they were out, Cole felt relieved. Elated, even. Because finally, after all these years, and all these days that felt like years since they got to the cabin, he was kissing his girl and confessing his love to her.

Cole felt whole.

Complete.

Luna pulled her head back and looked at him, her gentle, sexy gaze penetrating him. She opened her mouth, then closed it, then opened it again, all the while sending a wave of mixed emotions through Cole.

"I love you, too, Cole Sloane."

A large grin broke out on Cole's face, and he cupped her face, kissing her again. It was softer, sweeter this time, and he pulled himself away before it could turn into anything else.

He brushed a curl from her forehead. "It feels so fucking good to say that."

Luna pulled in her bottom lip, a lazy smile consuming her cheeks, too. "So fracking good."

This made Cole laugh, and he pulled her in for a hug, brushing his lips against her hairline. "You're so damn cute."

"Holy shit."

Cole had been so distracted as he descended the stairs that he almost missed the magnetism of the room once the party came into view.

Almost.

He stepped off the landing and did a double take as he absorbed the transformed space. Sol's cabin had always been grand and luxurious, but this was a whole new level. What had once been a clean slate with a few modern touches was now an extravagant space full of over-the-top decor that was both haunting and alluring. Cole hadn't seen anything so fantastical and whimsical since . . . well, since five Halloweens ago.

His body shuddered at the thought.

Clearing his throat, Cole took another step into the room, his brain cataloging the details. Above him, white silk draped from the ceiling in a sea of half-moons, and bar tables with candelabras and gold confetti were scattered throughout the open-concept living room, flowing seamlessly onto the back deck. To his left, he noted a large maroon-and-black balloon display, complete with cobwebs and bats—probably for pictures, Cole assumed.

"Drink, sir?" someone asked from behind.

Cole kinked his head to the side and graciously accepted a glass of champagne from one of the servers, downing it in one gulp. He sat the empty glass back down on the man's tray and grabbed a second, nodding a silent thanks as he spotted a stack of his books on what must be the signing table, along with a large retractable banner that sat behind it.

This was everything he'd worked for, and he couldn't help but feel a small ounce of pride swell in his chest.

"This is so exciting," Luna said, coming up behind him with a plate of food already in hand.

Cole smiled, his features relaxing at the sight of her as she unabashedly stuffed her face.

"What'd you get?"

"Oh my gosh." Luna swallowed and wiped her mouth with a tiny square napkin. "What didn't I get?"

Cole started to listen to her ramble on about the fancy grazing table Jax had helped the caterers set up in the dining room, but just then, a flash of red hair caught his eye, sending a surge of adrenaline through him.

Rose.

LUNA

"Do you want to try a bite?"

Luna peeked at Cole, her heart fluttering at the sight. His normal five-o'clock shadow had been swapped for a clean shave, and his wavy brown hair was carefully gelled back. Not to mention he was also in a suit.

If she wasn't careful, she might drool.

"Hm?" His voice sounded disoriented.

Luna repeated herself. "Do you want a bite?" Her cheeks colored when she realized how that sounded. "Of my app. Do you want to try one?"

When Cole still didn't answer, Luna followed his gaze, looking for whatever was distracting him.

And that's when she saw her.

Bright red waves of hair shone in the fading evening light as Rose Sloane walked in the room.

"Oh, frack." Luna laid down her croissant and wiped her face with a napkin. She wasn't the jealous type, but it would *maybe* be good to not be totally stuffing her face when her secret boyfriend's ex-wife walked in the room.

Boyfriend? Someone's rather confident in themselves.

Luna scowled.

Shut up, self! So not the time.

She watched as Rose walked in, her curvaceous figure highlighted by the black velvet dress that hugged her body. Luna swallowed, smoothing a hand over her own gown, suddenly feeling insecure in her twelve-year-old-boy frame.

Don't think about that right now.

Luna smiled, appreciating the kind thought her inner monologue threw her way. She shook off the insecurity and reached for Cole's hand, giving it a light squeeze. "You okay?"

That seemed to pull him from whatever inner turmoil was going on inside his head.

"Yes. Fine." He squeezed her hand back, then curved his lips into a soft smile. "Thanks, Lu."

She felt the butterflies take flight in her lower belly, their wings fluttering all the way up to her heart.

And then all 542 of those wings broke, disintegrating into the crevices of her heart.

"Clara's here," she said simply, her gaze transfixed just beyond Cole's shoulder where she saw the back of a small child's head inside the doorway.

She felt Cole's movement as he dropped her hand and turned around. Luna took a step forward, squinting her eyes for a better look and gasping when the girl turned her way.

She looked exactly like River.

"Cole!" Dani walked over, her heels clicking against the polished hardwood floors. "Clara has just arrived, and we'd love to get some photos."

He cleared his throat to respond but not before Luna cut in.

"How 'bout a little sensitivity, Dani? The girl just walked in, and Cole has never even met her." She made a shooing motion with her hand. "Give us a few."

Cole shook his head. "No, it's okay—"

"No, it's not!" Luna argued. She threw Dani a pointed look. "You wouldn't want your personal life on blast, would you?"

The threat in Luna's voice was loose, strained. She would never publicly share the details of Dani and Solstice's sexcapade she'd accidentally walked in on earlier, but she would absolutely tell everyone here if this woman didn't back off.

Dani seemed to understand. "Yes, of course. Sorry, you're right. Go, mingle. We'll come back later." She rubbed the tip of her maroon stiletto nail before running her fingers through her black curls. "But we do have to get started with the reading soon, so don't take too long."

Luna stuck her tongue out at Dani's back as she walked away. "Rude."

A half-hearted smile deigned Cole's lips but then quickly diminished when the final member of the trio walked in.

David.

Luna chewed the inside of her lip as her eyes bounced from Rose, to Clara, and then to David before finally landing back on Cole. She wished more than anything she could be inside his head right now so she knew what to say, how to help. She wanted to give him the time and space to process all this, but she also wanted to hold his hand, rub his back, and kiss his cheek, to tell him it would all be okay.

She sighed. Life would be much easier if she were a mind reader.

Jax waved at her, distracting Luna. *"Hey, Mom. Could you help in the kitchen for a second?"*

Luna put up a finger to her son, then glanced at Cole again, hesitant. "Do you want me to come with you? To meet her?"

Cole's hard stare was unreadable for a moment, but then she saw him notice Jax. "No." He shook his head. "It's okay. Go on. I'll be fine."

Luna felt like he very much would not be fine.

"Are you sure? Because I can—"

"Lu," Cole interrupted her. "It's okay. Go. Help Jax. I'll catch up with you later."

Stuck between feeling a tad stung and completely understanding, Luna nodded and gave his arm one more gentle pat before graciously making her exit.

COLE

It had been four years since he last saw her.

Rose had come to visit Cole in prison once the divorce was finalized, shortly after giving birth to Clara. It was hard seeing her, but not detrimental like Cole had expected. By that point, all his pain had morphed into anger, which over time, eventually fizzled out, first by way of his therapist, then his pastor. And once he found his heart was fully healed, or as healed as it could ever be, he knew without a shadow of a doubt he was in love with someone else.

The comparison between Rose and Luna was intangible.

But seeing her here, now, with her fiery red hair and the familiar attributes of River lingering over her skin, his chest squeezed, if only just a little.

And then Clara walked in.

Followed by David.

And his world shattered.

Cole gave himself a moment after Luna walked off with Jax, trying to ready himself for this conversation, this interaction. The moment he'd been both dreading and looking forward to for years.

This is for you, Riv.

Cole took a deep breath and marched forward.

He weaved through the small web of people that had conglomerated in the open living space, heart beating wildly in his chest as the child came fully into view. She was four years old now, and except for the red hair, she looked identical to River at that age. The mere sight of her was haunting, and Cole felt an old flame of anger glowing inside him, an ember that had been dormant for many years. Not toward the child, of course, but at his brother and ex, because of all the people in the world she could've slept with, Rose had to choose Cole's brother, David, and together, they'd created a child that shared the same DNA as Rose and Cole's daughter. She even had the same last name, for fuck's sake.

It was like looking in an alternate universe, a parallel world mirroring and mocking and taunting what could've been his, what *was* his.

A hint of nausea lined his throat.

"Cole." Rose's voice.

He hadn't realized he'd been staring, his eyes glued to Clara's face.

A throat cleared. "Cole, thank you for inviting us." This time it was David, and the gruffness in his tone finally broke Cole out of his trance.

Cole looked at his brother and nodded. "Of course." He turned to Rose, his movements curt and awkward. "Thank you for coming."

Then, without another word, his eyes fell back to Clara. She was smiling at him, twirling a little red curl around her finger.

"My mommy says you're my uncle and you just got unlocked out of the big house and that's why I've never seen you before but you're not really a bad guy, just a daddy who defended my sissy."

Cole's eyes widened, shocked by her response.

"Clara," Rose chastised. "That is not polite."

The little girl scowled. "What does polite mean?"

Cole still felt so many things, but despite it all, he smiled. He smiled and stifled a laugh before clearing his throat. The long-lost stinging sensation of tears burned his eyes, and he blinked them away quickly.

"Hi, Clara." He held out a hand for her to shake. "It's nice to meet you."

"Did you wash your hands after leaving the bathroom?" she asked, nervously holding her palm midair. "I don't like germs, and sometimes, people don't wash their hands after they go potty, and it's yucky."

Cole's timid smile morphed into a full-blown grin, accompanied by a soft chuckle. "Yes, yes, I did wash my hands."

Rose and David both mumbled apologies as Clara proceeded to shake Cole's hand.

"It's okay," Cole reassured them, his eyes never leaving Clara. "It's very important to wash your hands."

"She's a bit of a neat freak," Rose said, ruffling her daughter's hair.

"That's not a nice word, Mommy."

Clara had a bit of an attitude. Cole liked it.

"It's good to see you, bub." David wrapped an arm around Cole, slapping him on the back. Cole returned the gesture, then pulled away.

"You too." And surprisingly, he meant it. Despite what he'd done, David was still his brother. Cole loved him, even through the pain and betrayal. Because that's what families do.

His eyes flicked to Rose. She was still a harder pill to swallow. In a way, she had been family, too, forever connected by River's blood.

But River was gone now.

And Rose wasn't his blood.

Although he'd forgiven her, he felt no sudden urge to pull her into a hug. She was a boundary he needed to keep at arm's length. And that was okay.

"So are you my uncle?" Clara's sweet voice chimed again.

"Yes," Cole said, returning his gaze to her. "I certainly am."

She tilted her head to the side. "Do I have to call you Uncle Cole?"

Cole laughed again, and he felt his heart warming—squeezing and moving and adjusting to make room for all the newfound love he had for this child. "Not if you don't want to."

Clara pulled her lips to the side, the gesture strikingly similar to River. "I don't think I like that word. I think I'll just call you Cole."

He nodded, pursing his lips and placing a hand on his chin, as if deep in thought. "Okay. I think that sounds good to me, kid."

"Sorry, I don't mean to intrude, but we'd love to snap a couple photos if that's okay?" Dani had reappeared with the publishing house's photographer standing at her side.

Cole straightened, looking to Rose and David for approval first.

"Yes." Rose ran a hand through her hair and fluffed her bottom curls. "Yes, that's fine."

"Okay, great." Dani feigned an overly exaggerated smile, then led the four of them over to the balloon arch.

Cole obliged with all of her requests, posing for multiple photos, first with everyone, then one of just him and Clara, then one with his brother and him shaking hands. He went through all of the motions, feeling slightly disconnected from time and space, as though his brain couldn't quite comprehend what was happening, all of his previously unsettled emotions wrestled into a state of comfort.

Or at least, comfort adjacent.

"All right!" Dani clasped her hands. "Thank you so much, guys. I think we got a lot of good stuff." The photographer mimicked her sentiment, and Dani glanced at her phone. "Cole, feel free to mingle for a few more minutes, then we'll get started."

He nodded just as Luna's blue dress swayed into view. Luna caught his eye from across the room, and without thinking, he winked.

"So, your coworker, huh?"

Rose's voice startled Cole.

"I'm sorry, what?"

"Your coworker," she repeated. "Luna. She was the one who went through The Gala with you."

"Oh," Cole said nonchalantly. "Yes."

When he failed to offer more, Rose pressed on. "Are you two together now?" Clearly, she had seen the wink.

Cole contemplated his answer for a few moments before responding, stuffing his hands in his pockets to bide time. "You could say that."

Lu caught his eye again and smiled, the dimple in her left cheek showing. Fuck if he didn't want to ditch this conversation and bite it.

"I'm really happy for you, Cole," Rose said, drawing him away from his fever dream. "You deserve to be happy."

Cole scoffed but refrained from making a sarcastic remark. Instead, he decided to wave Luna over. "Is it okay if I introduce her to Clara?"

He looked at Rose and almost laughed at the shocked expression on her face before she schooled her features. "Um, of course." She cleared her throat. "Yes, that would be nice."

AFTER A QUICK INTRODUCTION, it took all of five seconds for Luna and Clara to become best friends. Lu was a natural with children. Cole had seen it in the way she interacted with Jax, but seeing her here, holding silly conversations, mimicking Disney character voices, and making Clara laugh—it was as if she were born to do this.

It made him wonder if she wanted more kids. He ruminated on the thought for a moment, then decided it best to distract himself by mingling with the other attendees.

Cole made his way to the bar on the patio and ordered a glass of whiskey. Leaning against the bar top, he thanked the server and took a sip as he surveyed the crowd. It wasn't large by any means, but it was still a decently sized group. Everyone was scattered about, standing at the small circular tables the stagers had placed methodically throughout, careful to avoid the large outdoor heat lamps. Cole recognized most of the faces: His editor, the publishing house's photographer, and an editorial assistant he'd met earlier were nearest to him, surrounded by a mix of former colleagues and a handful of other authors his agency had invited. Between them, Rose, Clara, and David, and his crew with Luna, Jax, Sol, Greyson, and Dani, he estimated about twenty people were in attendance, not including the staff.

"I suppose it's go time," he mumbled.

Cole threw back the rest of his drink and made his way around the room, shaking hands and making touch points with everyone. He was a bit stiff and awkward at first, but once he'd finished making the rounds, he felt like quite the social butterfly.

Luna and her damn phrases were apparently rubbing off on him.

"There you are!" Dani waved at him from across the room. "Are you ready?"

He nodded, flexing his jaw muscles as she walked over. "Are you sure Sol or somebody else can't do this? Crowds love him." It was a weak last-ditch effort that he knew wouldn't work.

"Not a chance," Dani deadpanned.

He sighed, accepting his fate as he followed her back to the balloon arch, where someone had added two chairs and a microphone. Dani grabbed the mic, pulling it off the stand and tapping it a few times to draw everyone's attention.

"Hello, hello," she bellowed as the music faded into the background. She waited for everyone outside to wander in before continuing. "Hello, and wel-come! Thank you all so much for coming to celebrate the launch of *The Great Chase* by our very own Cole Sloane!"

The audience cheered, with Sol ringing out a few louder-than-necessary yelps. Cole waved at the crowd, blushing and smiling at the same time.

Dani turned to him, putting on a theatrical show. "As you know, Cole here was also just released from prison."

"Hell yeah, mate!"

Everyone laughed at Sol.

Dani walked a few paces to the left, grabbing a hard copy from his signing table. "And we are just so honored to have him with us tonight to read the opening of his much-anticipated tell-all about Graham Zanella."

Anxiety bubbled under Cole's rib cage. Reading his own words in front of people felt like a special form of hell.

"So without further ado, I'm going to officially pass the microphone off and introduce you to Cole Sloane, author."

He took the mic, his ears humming loudly and nearly drowning out everyone's cheers.

Don't screw it up.

He grimaced, blocking out the negative thought, and moved to take a seat in front of the backdrop. "Uh, hello, everyone." His voice was rough, strained even to his own ears. "I tried to get out of this, but Dani wouldn't let me."

That elicited a small chorus of laughs from the audience.

"Not because I don't appreciate you all being here," he continued, easing his way into the performance. "I just don't do well with public speaking. Probably why I was a reporter at a paper, before being incarcerated."

He smiled, insinuating it was a joke, but the only person who laughed that time was Luna.

Correction: snorted.

"Okay, then," he said, shifting uncomfortably in his seat as sweat started to gather between his brows. "Let's get started."

Perhaps the most befuddling element to all of this was
Graham Zanella's true identity. The man behind the
mask.

—Cole Sloane, *The Great Chase*

LUNA

Luna sat from a distance and smiled as Cole read the opening pages of his book. She'd read it a dozen times already, but hearing him read it with the proper inflection of how he'd intended every word, every sentence, it inspired her.

Apparently it inspired her so much that she dropped her food, splattering a mess of fancy cheese and leftover grapes on the floor.

"Doodle pop!"

A few heads turned toward her.

"Sorry, sorry!" she hissed under her breath.

Her internal monologue started popping off, chastising her for her clumsiness.

Why are you the way that you are?

She groaned, not wanting to pay her mind any attention and instead wanting to crawl inside a hole.

A server handed her a napkin, and she thanked them before quickly cleaning up the mess. She excused herself from those around her and retreated to the kitchen to throw her plate away. But before she could, the grazing table caught her eye.

One other small snack wouldn't hurt, if she didn't drop it.

She beelined for the table and nearly smacked head-on into a server, causing her to yelp. "Ohmygosh! I'm so sorry!" The person backed away from her, and that's when Luna noticed the mask.

The half-faced raven masquerade mask.

"It's okay," the man said before mumbling something else.

Only everything he said at that point was incoherent to Luna.

Instead of listening, her thoughts returned to a recurrent nightmare. One with a bludgeoned man, dead teenagers, and *her son's head on fire.*

It all came rushing back at an alarmingly fast rate as she stared at the man. It's not that his physical appearance was similar, but his mask. It was almost an exact replica of the one Zanella wore the night of The Gala.

Is this a coincidence?

It had to be. There was no way—

Stop. You're fine. Jax is fine.

Except, now that she thought about it, had this man previously been wearing a mask? She'd been here when the crew first arrived, and none of the waitstaff was in costume. Actually, she believed she specifically told Dani *no masks* when they were planning this. She was worried it would be too triggering for Cole.

She never once stopped to think about how triggering it would be for her.

"Miss?" the man asked.

"Hm?" She blinked at him several times, trying to piece together the puzzle, and as she stared at him, she noticed something else.

He had blue eyes.

Just like Zanella.

In an instant, Luna grabbed the man's hands, turning them over repeatedly, checking for tattoos. Although she hadn't noticed them at the time, Cole had filled her in on Z's true identity and the nautical tattoos Cole's old roommate Harley had had on his hands.

"What are you doing?" The man pulled his arms back, confusion lacing his tone.

"I-I'm sorry." Luna let go, staring at the floor in shock. "I'm so sorry, you just . . . you reminded me of someone is all."

He scurried off, leaving Luna alone with her thoughts.

And then the lights went off.

Oh no.

She abandoned her empty plate at the food table and ran back into the main room where Cole and the guests were. She, along with everyone else, waited on bated breath, hoping the lights would flicker back on.

But they didn't.

After a few moments, Dani walked back to the front, the sound of her heels clicking louder than bullets. "Well, this is something we did not account for." She laughed at her own joke, her lame attempt at humor winning over a few pity laughs.

Luna looked at Cole, locking eyes with him through the low light of the candelabras. Thankfully, it wasn't pitch-black, but it was still dark enough to give her pause.

Something was wrong.

She didn't know how to explain it, but something deep within the pit of her stomach told her this wasn't supposed to happen. This wasn't a situation where, *Oh, the breaker just went out* or *the storm cut the power.*

No, this was something dark.

Something sinister.

The prayer hadn't worked.

Immediately, her eyes danced around the room looking for Jax.

"Spooky," he signed when her eyes snagged on his.

Her panic subsided for a millisecond. *"Very spooky."*

Cole stood now, placing the microphone and his book down. He made eye contact with Luna again, then waved her over.

Dread pooled in her stomach; he must have sensed it, too.

"Lu—" he started, but his words were cut off by a flashing red light.

In a moment of pure terror, Luna dropped her hand to his, immediately grabbing it.

"Dani," Cole said, his voice low and urgent. "What the hell is going on?"

His agent turned to face him, and the look on her face confirmed Luna's worst fear.

Something *was* wrong. This wasn't part of the program.

Before Luna had time to question it further, though, the entirety of the waitstaff marched inside from the patio, all in a line, and all wearing masks.

Raven masquerade masks.

"What the bloody hell is this shit?" Sol's voice boomed over the crowd. "I know it's Halloween, but for fuck's sake, let's not relive the most tragic night of our lives, Dani."

"I didn't do this!" she argued, her pitch hitting a high note as the red strobe lights continued to flash. "Katniss, what's going on? I said no to all the theatrical ideas."

Luna followed Dani's gaze to the woman she'd been introduced to earlier as Cole's editor.

"I didn't sign off on this," Katniss said, taking a few steps toward them. Then, she turned her head to her assistant. "Paige, did you have something to do with this?'

The woman quickly shook her head, looking like a deer caught in headlights. "No. Cole was just supposed to do the reading, followed by the signing with a few press photos. That's all."

Shoot, shoot, shoot.

Luna's heart rate spiked as she and Cole locked eyes again.

"You don't think—" she started.

"Impossible," Cole interrupted her.

The servers finished lacing their way through the room, the line of masked men and women passing Cole and Luna before circling the signing table.

"What're you blokes doing?" Sol tried approaching them, but they ignored him. "Come on, take those fucking masks off."

He reached for one then and tried to pull it off the man, but the person elbowed Sol and he yelped.

"Hey!" Cole stalked over and slapped his hand on the man's shoulder, and just as Luna thought he was about to throw a punch, a siren blared.

The same siren that sounded at The Gala five years ago.

No.

"Cole, what is happening?" Luna was moving from paranoid panic to downright terror.

As the siren and strobe lights continued to go off and the crowd began to mumble and scatter, the servers circled the signing table. Each one picked up a book and held it in the air.

And then they started chanting.

"The lake! The lake! Is it real or fake? The lake! The lake! Is it real or fake?"

They marched in their circle, moving their arms up and down, over and over, shoving the books into the air.

"The lake! The lake! You make us break. The lake! The lake! We make you ache!

A mix of unease and dread rose through Luna's stomach, then her esophagus, and threatened her throat lining.

"The lake! The lake! Not yours to take! The lake! The lake! Not yours to take!"

"I *so* did not sign up for this!" Greyson yelled from behind Luna.

The waitstaff continued their chant through the wail of the sirens, and then suddenly, it all stopped.

The chant, the sound, the lights, the movement. For approximately twenty seconds, all was still.

And then the masked crew began to whisper a renewed chant.

"The lake, the lake, their bones you take. The lake, the lake, their skeletons awake."

Luna had no idea what was happening—no idea what their words meant. Her face was etched in a permanent scowl as she tried to make sense of it all.

And that's when the bones fell.

Luna screamed as dozens of skeletal remains dropped from the ceiling, hovering only mere inches above everyone's heads. She ducked at first, not realizing they were attached to strings, but before she had time to process anything, each masked server struck a match, lowered Cole's book to the flame, and set them all on fire.

"What the fuck!" Cole screamed, shoving his way through the crowd, acting immediately.

Luna knew she should move, should do something other than just stand there and stare, but it was all she could do. Stand there and stare and watch as the embers licked at the spines of the books. Some of the waitstaff were still holding their books while others had tossed them in the air, and Luna watched as they fell carelessly around the room, flames flying everywhere. Around her, she could hear screams and sense movement, but mentally, she was caught in a trance. Her mind was elsewhere as she was transported back to the night of The Gala when she watched the library go up in flames as she held her baby boy and waited for the ambulance.

"Lu, watch out!" Cole yelled as he rushed by her, a large trash can of water scraping her elbow.

She leapt out of his way, her body slowly reawakening, and watched as he poured the water onto the fire, extinguishing some of the flames. Luna snapped into action then, running to the hall closet and snatching an armful of blankets.

"Grey!" she called, tossing him one. "Here!"

Greyson followed Luna quickly, and together, the two draped blankets over the remaining books scattered on the floor. She looked for Cole, started to ask if that was it, if they needed more water or blankets, but then the siren began bellowing again, and the hairs on her arm rose.

Jax, she thought. *Where's Jax?*

She swiveled around, searching for her son. "Jax!" she yelled before realizing her mistake. *No, no, no.* She ran toward one of the candelabras and snatched it, then started waving her arms furiously. "Has anyone seen Jax?"

People scurried all around her. She tried scanning their faces, but it was all such a blur. Too many moving bodies in a dark sea of chaos.

And then a dome light turned on above the stairwell, highlighting the wall and a very clear message written in blood.

Are you ready to play, Luna?

Here's the part you've all heard before:

Boy gets invitation.

Boy plays game.

Boy kills opponent and goes to prison.

Not exactly your classic love story, but it's essential
to *this* story that I reiterate all the details.

—Cole Sloane, *The Great Chase*

COLE

Cole stared at the words in horror.

Are you ready to play?

The words from his own invitation flashed through his head.

Are you ready to play, Cole?

Followed by thoughts of Luna, the woman he'd fallen desperately in love with.

Are you ready to play, Luna?

Finally settling on Jax, the child whom he loved like his own.

Are you ready to play?

"Dammit!" he screamed before hurtling his fist into the wall. This was not happening. There was no fucking way this was happening.

"Cole." Luna's voice was low yet urgent.

He looked at her, then spun around, searching for Jax. Without thinking, he ran toward the front door, running his hands against the wall, searching for light switches. His fingers found them, but after several tries and no lighting, he ran to the other rooms, repeating the same motions and ending with the same results.

Dammit!

He hit the kitchen wall and pushed himself off of it.

Think, think, think.

"We need to find Jax!" Luna yelled, running out onto the back patio. "He's Deaf! And it's dark out!"

Cole could hear the terror in her voice. He internally cursed again, his innate need to protect the ones he loved kicking in.

"Sol!" he yelled over the hysterics of the crowd. "Do you have any flashlights?" He paused, searching for the singer. "Or better yet, do you still have fireworks?"

Solstice emerged from a dark corner in the living room, throwing his hair into a messy bun. "Yeah, but I'm not sure how that's going to help us."

"We need the light," Cole spat immediately. "If Jax is outside, it'll alert him, and he'll come back."

Sol nodded, understanding then. "Right. I'm on it, mate."

Cole sucked in his bottom lip as he took in the aftermath of whatever the hell had just happened. The fucking bones were still hanging from the ceiling, various skulls and clavicles and femurs dancing above him, taunting them all. His eyes flicked back to the masked servers, who were floating throughout the room, and he thought of the weird chant they'd shouted before burning his books.

The lake! The lake!

His mind raced as he tried to understand their words, tried to make sense of it all, before he reminded himself there was no time for that now.

They had to find Jax.

And he had to keep Luna safe.

"Lu!" He started to run back outside, but then he noticed a small figure huddled under the kitchen table.

Clara.

The sight annihilated him, completely stopping him dead in his tracks.

"Clara!" He ran to her, crouching down to the floor where Rose and David were trying to coax her out. "Clara," he repeated. "It's going to be okay, sweetie."

The little girl looked at him, the terror in her eyes almost too much for him to bear. "What's happening, Daddy? I'm scared."

He knew she was talking to David, but the question struck him right to his core.

"I don't know, sweetheart," David said, interrupting Cole's despair. "But we're getting out of here. Just grab my hand, and Mommy and Daddy will take you home. You're safe."

Cole desperately needed to believe that was true.

But he never got the chance to ruminate on it because an eerily familiar sound made the skin on his neck crawl.

"Dear Miss Monroe." The computer-generated female voice echoed through the house, and Cole's heart stilled. "We are pleased to inform you that you have been cordially invited to participate in our next event: a launch party slated for Wednesday, October 31, 2029. I understand you've been searching for your son tonight, and we're pleased to know we have your attention."

No.

Fucking *no*.

Cole stood and ran to Luna, who stared at him with wide eyes, tears already cascading down her porcelain skin.

"Before you can find him, though, you must complete a series of three tasks. My team will deliver the information for each one, and you must complete them to advance to the next level. Then, if you succeed, I will reveal Jaxson's location, where we'll have the opportunity to meet."

"Fuck this," Sol said from behind. "Cole, I thought you killed this mother-fucker."

Cole's tone was harsh. "I did."

The electronic voice continued. "I understand this is outside my usual antics, but I do hope you'll accept my invitation."

Cole pulled the strands of his hair. This was not fucking happening.

"Are you ready to play, Luna?"

LUNA

"No," SHE WHISPERED.

This isn't happening.

That was the only thing Luna could think at that moment. She was living her worst nightmare, stuck in a state of grief-stricken misery. Tears rained down her face, thoughts of River and the other beautiful children from The Gala who committed suicide flashing through her mind before the haunting images of Jaxson on fire returned, ever present in her inner torment.

"Hey, Lu, look at me." Cole's domineering voice tried to cut through her misery, but she couldn't shake it. Couldn't pull herself from the downward spiral her mind was thrusting her in. "Luna!"

That time it worked. Her eyes snapped to his, searching for solace. "He can't hear, Cole. What if—"

He grabbed her shoulders and planted his feet firmly in front of her. "We will find him. Do you hear me?"

She nodded, wiping the tears from her face. "Okay."

It was the only thing she could say.

Chatter broke out among the others in the room. Some ushered themselves outside, others mumbled fearful sentiments, but it was Greyson's question that caught her attention.

"Who the hell is this person?" he asked. "Are you sure Z was dead, Cole? Like dead, dead?"

Cole shot him an annoyed glance. "Of course, I'm sure." He flexed his jaw. "I squeezed the life out of that man and then watched them extract his body."

"It's fucking Roger, I bet," Sol said, interjecting. "Just look at this bone garland he bloody well sent us."

"This isn't a ghost," Luna whispered.

Sol scoffed. "Fine, not a ghost. A *demon*."

Luna looked at him, contemplating the very words she'd uttered to him a few nights ago.

"There are no fucking demons, Sol." Cole tipped his head to the side, then said quieter, "We already took care of that."

"Unless we didn't," Luna mumbled without thinking, a different type of fear paralyzing her. "If my faith wasn't strong enough—"

"No," Cole said, cutting her off. "Stop that line of thinking."

But she shook her head and continued anyway. "Cole, if any one of us didn't fully believe, then it may not have worked. The Bible says spirits can come back sevenfold if there's any doubt . . ."

Had she done this? Caused this mess?

Had she failed her son in the worst way possible, yet again?

"Lu." Cole jerked her chin, albeit gently. "Look around. There are people wearing masks who marched in and set my books on fire." He paused, letting the words soak in. "These are not demons or campfire ghosts"—he turned his head toward Sol—"or Zanella's ghost, for that matter. These are real people."

"But who would do this?" she asked, nearly shaken to her core.

"We're glad you asked." A sinister voice that Luna didn't recognize slithered into her eardrums.

She turned and looked, but not in time to see which person it came from. Instead, she watched in horror as the servers began forming a military-style line, along to the steady beat of a slow clap that quickly turned futile. They began to hum, the a cappella performance sending an uncomfortable chill down Luna's spine. Then all at once, the noise stopped.

Luna sucked in a breath, and all was silent.

And then they yelled in a unified voice, "We are Zanella's Army!"

Luna blinked.

Zanella's Army?

"What the hell is that?" Cole asked.

"Like Dumbledore's Army?" Sol scoffed. "Hate to break it to you lads, but JK Rowling kind of has the market on that."

"We are the ones who question society now," they all yelled. "We will carry out Z's mission from beyond the grave."

Luna gasped, nearly suffocating herself from the sharp intake.

"We are," they continued, "Z's Army!"

Z's Army.

"A fucking copycat killer, great!" Sol threw up his hands. "Goes nicely with your copycat name. Yeah, might as well call you the ZA and go fetch my magic wand."

"Shut up, Sol!" Luna snapped. The servers were humming again before slowly breaking out into a fiendish laughter, making her skin crawl. She was trying to think, trying to process, but she couldn't in the midst of this unholy chaos.

She rubbed her temples, then faced Cole. "They're impersonating him, like they're . . . recreating his work."

"Replicating it," Cole confirmed, his gaze hard as he studied the *army* of people.

The servers began to dance and clap and chant again, and it was all so unnerving, Luna couldn't help but cry. How could she have been so stupid? So foolish as to think this was all some demonic attack, instigated by a freaking ghost story! She knew someone was watching them but had let herself be talked out of her fears and talked *into* something else entirely. What a *stupid*, stupid fool she'd been.

And to think it was *these* people! People she didn't even know but who were so obsessed with the likes of Graham Zanella that they waited until Cole Sloane was out of prison so they could hijack his launch party, steal her son, and freaking torture them all. Z's art had always been chaotic and dangerous, but he'd never crossed a line until the night of The Gala.

That's what scared Luna the most. Because Z's final performance had apparently been the opening act for whoever these people were. There was no telling what they would do.

"How do we stop them?" she asked Cole, her voice timid and meek.

Cole swallowed.

And then Luna realized she already knew the answer.

They'd already told them what they had to do tonight.

She just didn't want to say it.

Apparently, neither did Cole.

"We have to play their game," Luna confessed.

Cole held her gaze, a beat of silence passing between them. "We have to play their game."

Great, Luna thought. *Just great.*

She knew she wasn't supposed to question the Lord, knew sin and evil were never part of his original plan, but right now, she felt incredibly hopeless.

Please, God. Please, find him. Protect my baby, and don't let him be hurt.

Cole squeezed her shoulder. "We need to get everyone out."

"Good luck doing that, mate," Sol said from beside the window. "The bloke has ruined everyone's cars."

Luna's eyes widened. "What?" She rushed over to Sol, nearly shoving him out of the way.

She squinted but she was unable to fully see what Sol was referring to, so she ran outside, her candelabra still in hand.

And then her heart skipped a beat.

"What the heck?" She stood gawking, soaking in the scene.

Someone had destroyed every single vehicle. Even from a distance, she could see tires slashed, windshields busted, doors thrown open, and—

Her eyes widened.

Were those *fingers*?

Her heart thumped in her chest as, upon further inspection, she realized she was staring at dozens of human phalanges, sprinkled across the cars like demented confetti.

"We tried calling the police." A new voice sounded from behind her, and she turned, spotting Rose, who was clutching a very scared Clara. "Nobody has service."

Luna groaned. Of course they didn't.

Knowing it was true but refusing to believe it, she ran back inside and grabbed her own phone from her purse.

No service.

"Dang it!"

More tears were streaming down her face, when suddenly, she couldn't breathe. Her chest constricted, tightening more with each passing moment, and her eyes dilated. What was happening? She'd never experienced this sensation before. Couldn't explain it, or contain it.

In a desperate attempt, she finally gasped, falling to the staircase.

"Cole!" She hated relying on him so heavily, but it was all she could think to do.

He must have heard her because he immediately rushed over. She looked up and met his eyes, his dimly lit face not enough to calm her.

"You're okay," he said.

She didn't believe him. "What's happening?"

He crouched in front of her, removing his suit jacket and placing it around her shoulders. "You're having a panic attack."

What? Luna didn't understand. She didn't get panic attacks. That was Cole's thing. She'd felt anxiety before, of course, but she'd always felt the presence of peace, the sense of Jesus settling over her, whenever the nerves took over. But this was different. This felt like her lungs were drowning in that lake again, her breath too shallow to call for help.

Where are you, God? Why is this happening?

"Here." Cole grabbed her palm and held it up. "Name five things that are true right now."

"What?"

"Name five things that are true." When she still didn't understand, he grabbed the tip of her pinky and pushed it down. "Your name is Luna Monroe."

She blinked, still unable to catch her breath.

"You have a son named Jax." Cole tried pushing down her ring finger, but his words had sent her into hyperventilation mode. He let go and tried again. "We are in a cabin in the woods."

"With psychopaths who kidnapped my son!" Luna shouted.

Cole moved on to the middle finger. "My name is Cole Sloane."

Luna looked back at him, holding his gaze as he tugged at her pointer finger, then thumb.

"You are wearing a blue dress. You are sitting on the stairs."

She slowly felt her chest start to ease, but not quickly enough.

"Again," she said.

Cole obeyed, pressing her fingertips back into the air, then slowly bending each one down at the knuckle as he spouted out five more facts. When he was finished, Luna sat up straighter, taking several more steadying breaths.

"Better?" Cole asked.

She nodded, too overwhelmed to verbally answer. Because while yes, the air had returned to her lungs, her son was still missing, and they were still trapped with no way out and no way to call the police. They were stuck alone in the woods with a group of murderers who was forcing them to replay the most traumatic events of her life, and if Luna's intuition was correct, it was going to be much worse than the first time.

Much worse.

Blinking away more tears, she retracted her hand from Cole's and clutched her chest. "We have to find him," she whispered.

"I know," Cole said. "We will. I promise."

At that, Luna felt like she could stand again, and she rose from the stairs, testing her strength. When she didn't completely collapse, she pressed a hand to the railing and removed her shoes. If they were going to do this, she wasn't going to be slowed down by heels she was likely to twist her ankle in.

"Did you see Clara—"

Loud shots erupted through the room, terrifying her into oblivion and cutting her off. She screamed, then fell off the stairs and onto the ground with Cole's body draped over her.

"Get down!" he yelled.

More shots echoed in the hollow space between the rooms, and Luna's ears rang in the deafening disturbance. She began to weep again, Jaxson's whereabouts her only thought.

Then the familiar, dreaded siren sounded again, and the shooting stopped. Neither Luna nor Cole dared to look up, and after a startling minute, the alarm was quickly replaced by the electronic female voice.

"Many years ago, before a construction company overhauled this property, it was a Native American burial ground. More specifically, it was a burial mound that was uprooted and replaced with the Rhododendron Lake."

Oh no, Luna thought, the chant from before now ringing in her mind.

The lake! The lake!

The mock Siri voice continued. "Since man deemed it appropriate to dig up the remains of such a precious cultural practice, we have decided it only seems fitting for you to replace them as your first task."

Replace them?

"So, tonight, our team members have taken out the unnecessary participants for this event, deeming them willing sacrifices for this first challenge."

Luna was still lying underneath Cole, but at this point, she felt him lift up on his arms and saw him glancing around the room as he held his body weight with his elbows.

"The fucking caterers," he spat.

"What?"

"The servers in the masks—they're back and holding guns. It looks like they just . . . *shot* everyone."

Luna's breath hitched. She started to ask him more, wanting to know who was dead or alive, but the voice continued.

"It is said the spirits of these folks remain here, haunting the woods and looking for victims they can prey on to take vengeance. If you are so unlucky, their voices will invade your thoughts, curling up inside your brain and taking root until they can bloom into a fully formed possession, a manipulation of the mind, if you will. So, in an act to appease them and finally put their souls to rest, we are challenging you to extract the bones of your dead teammates now and bury them beneath the lake."

"What the fuck, mate?" Sol cried from the porch. "No one said anything about Indians in me ghost story! And how do you bury shit under a lake? Mental, all of ya."

"Our associates will provide you with the necessary tools to complete this task. Only after you are finished, and only then, will we reveal the next act. We hope you will accept this challenge as Jaxson's life depends on it. Thank you, and welcome to act one of The Launch, where you are now officially part of the art."

COLE

Impossible.

Fucking impossible.

"Who the hell are these sick fucks?" he whispered.

Luna's body was shaking again beneath him, and he pulled her into his arms, unable to do anything else in the moment as they both tried to process what they'd just heard.

"This is vile," Luna spat. "And cruel! What do they mean extract the bones? How can they expect us to do this?" She wiped a glob of snot off her nose. "We don't—even—know who they've killed!"

Her words snapped Cole out of his matrix of thoughts, and he turned his head, straining the muscles in his neck as he tried to see which of his friends had just potentially been slaughtered. It was difficult to see at first, or rather, difficult to make out in the dark lighting. A few of the candelabras had blown out, and the red strobe lights were off, dimming the room to near darkness.

"Mommy!" A child's voice cried from the back deck, and Cole wanted to throw up when he realized who it was.

Clara.

He'd completely forgotten she was there.

"Where are Rose and David?" Luna asked, still a puddle of tears in his arms.

Cole shook his head, a hardened expression on his face. "I don't know." His voice was low, but then he heard Clara scream for Rose again, and fear consumed him as he wondered whether they'd been shot. He stood, carefully untangling Luna's arms from around him, then ran toward the direction of Clara's voice. The gunmen stood around laughing, mocking him, but they allowed him to move freely. Cole tried his best to ignore them, but—

"Fuck!"

He tripped over something and fell, hitting his head on the corner of Sol's coffee table. His face warmed as a small trickle of blood slipped its way down his face. Cole winced, but not because of the pain.

He sat, paralyzed by fear, because he'd realized what he'd tripped on, *who* he'd tripped on.

A dead body.

No, a *pile* of dead bodies.

Cole was lying on someone's arm.

Move, he thought. *There's no time.*

He fumbled into motion, panic and adrenaline fueling him.

"Cole!" Clara ran toward him the moment he stepped foot outside.

He wrapped his arms around her, holding on to her for dear life. "Are you okay?"

The child instantly burst into tears and squeezed him. "I don't know where my mommy or daddy are," she sobbed. "I ran outside to hide and then the loud noises started. I'm scared, Uncle Cole!"

His heart throbbed as he held her tiny body next to his. He had to get her out of there. *But how?* The servers were still standing guard inside, masks and guns in place. He assumed none of them were going to shoot him. At least not now. The rules of the horrific challenge were made clear, and he assumed no one else was at risk so long as he and Luna obeyed orders.

But that didn't mean Clara was safe.

Not knowing what else to do, Cole scooped her up and ran down the side of the back deck, refusing to take Clara back inside. He rounded the side of the house, then came out near the edge of the semi-wraparound porch.

"Where did you last see your parents?" he asked, trying to survey his surroundings while also shielding her from the trauma as best he could.

"I don't know!" Clara cried.

From afar, Cole spotted Sol, who was waving a hand at him. A small wave of relief washed over Cole, thankful his friend was alive, but the feeling was fleeting as he moved closer and saw what Sol was waving to.

Fuck, fuck, fuck!

He flinched as his gaze snagged on the familiar face of his brother, who was lying face-up with a bright red stain seeping through his white button-up shirt.

His eyes were unmoving.

Instinctually, Cole wanted to run, wanted to hug his brother's body and mourn, but his mind stopped him before his body betrayed him.

Clara couldn't see her father dead.

"Clara!" Rose's voice pulled him away from the sight, not allowing his heart even a moment's notice to grieve for his brother.

"Mommy!" The child writhed in his arms, and Cole let her go. "Mommy! I'm scared!"

"It's okay, sweetheart." Rose limped toward them from behind a large SUV, her arms outstretched. "Come here, baby."

Clara ran to her, meeting Rose in the middle and nearly knocking her off her feet. Cole moved to help steady her before whispering in her ear, "Don't let her see over there."

He pulled back and looked at Rose's terrified expression, her face turning grim when Cole mouthed, *David*.

"No," she whispered.

They locked eyes, and for a very brief moment, Cole felt an ounce of sorrow for her.

And then his adrenaline kicked back in when the red strobe lights turned on again inside.

"Just get her out of here," Cole warned, clearing his throat in a lame attempt to keep his own tears at bay. "You can't leave, but you can hide." He whipped his head around, catching Sol motioning him inside. "Go. Take her and run. Find somewhere safe to hide"—his eyes snapped down to her bleeding leg—"and here." He unbuttoned his top and shrugged it off. "Use this to wrap around your leg and try to stop the bleeding once you've gotten a safe distance away."

Rose hesitated for a moment, then grabbed the shirt from Cole's hand and threw it over Clara's head. Cole turned to leave them but paused when he heard, "Cole?"

He turned back to look at her, the tension pulled taut between them like an invisible string.

"Thank you," she breathed.

Cole nodded once, then exhaled and ran back inside the cabin, silently praying his efforts were enough to keep Clara safe.

"Attention! Luna Monroe, Cole Sloane, Solstice Blackwood, and Greyson Miller, please report for duty!" one of the masked staff members bellowed through a megaphone, his voice that of a demented sergeant. "Act one of The Launch begins now! As you may have heard, your job is to extract the bones of the deceased audience members here tonight and then bury them *beneath* the lake."

Had they *drained the lake* for this?

Cole watched in agonizing horror as the other five waiters emptied the bullets from their gun chambers, set their rifles down, then pulled out axes and knives from their backpacks. Their actions occurred simultaneously, all in one synchronized moment of terror.

"We have provided you with the necessary tools to do so. In honor of the old Legend of the Rhododendron Recluse, you will only need to remove their arms and legs. We have kindly decided to bypass the kindling part of the legend, for time's sake, but you will need to chop off the femur, tibia, fibula, ulna, humorous, and radius of every deceased individual here."

The acidic taste of vomit crept up Cole's throat, and he swallowed the disgusting liquid before it could spew out of his mouth. Luna stood beside him, surprisingly quiet. He chanced a peek at her and noted the swollen, red bags under her eyes and the puffiness of her cheeks. A harshness had washed over her, and she no longer looked like a damsel in distress but a mother willing to do whatever it took to save her son.

LUNA

A COLD, HARD FEELING gripped at Luna's insides.

She couldn't allow herself to feel, think, or focus on anything other than what was being asked of her. It was a task that she didn't want to comprehend. It was vile and disgusting. Something no human should ever have to do.

But as she stood there, staring at the masked strangers as they held their axes and knives in a merciless act of horror, she knew there was no other option.

If she wanted her son back, she was going to have to do whatever these psychopaths demanded.

Not allowing herself to waste another minute, she stepped forward and held out her arms.

"This is ridiculous, mate," Sol said, throwing out his own arm in an attempt to stop her. "We're not fucking doing that. You're off your rockers if you think this is in the name of 'art' or 'social justice,' lads."

Luna agreed with Sol, even thought about voicing how they were getting this all wrong, taking it too far. But she locked eyes with the man who'd been holding the megaphone, and even through the thin slats of the raven mask, she knew there was no getting out of this.

"Move, Sol." She pushed his arm away, then closed the rest of the distance between her and the nearest waiter. She pulled the tools from their hands, their weight and shape foreign in her dainty hands.

Luna, her internal consciousness whispered. But she ignored it. Ignored every attempt to stop her from this atrocity, because even though she didn't want to break God's commandments, there's nothing she wouldn't do, no length she wouldn't go, to protect her child.

She would not fail him again.

With both items secured in the palms of her hands, she turned back around, facing Cole and Sol. "You don't have to do this with me, but I can't stand by. I can't say no. I have to do this." Her mouth trembled as the tears that lined her lashes threatened to disobey her, but she held her gaze steady all the same.

Cole immediately nodded, then walked around her to a woman with red hair and grabbed the morbid instruments. Luna swallowed, a minor token of relief invading her.

"You two can't be serious." Sol looked from right to left, then left to right. Luna waited for his response. "This is—" He scoffed, throwing his hands on his hips. "I mean, we did some fucked up shit back at The Gala, I'll give you that, and saw some even more fucked up shit in the pen, but this?" He stopped, hanging his head. "I don't know, mate. I don't know if I can—"

"It's okay," Luna cut him off. "I understand, Sol. You don't have to do this."

"Actually, he does," the man bellowed through his megaphone, making them all jump. Luna assumed him to be the leader of the pack. "The rules of the event are clear. Everyone who attended The Gala that is here and alive tonight must complete each challenge, or you lose."

Luna's heart dropped. "You can't be serious." Her voice was barely above a whisper.

The man lowered the device and spoke in a normal tone. "Those are the rules. Either Sol and Greyson join you, or Jaxson's location will forever remain a secret."

Luna's chest constricted again, the tightness screaming at her as it longed to break free. But she couldn't let it. She couldn't succumb to her own shortcomings right now if she was going to save her son.

"Sol—"

"Oi, piss on ya." He spit on the masked man's shoe. "Give me the fucking ax."

Thank goodness.

Luna let out a giant breath, but something else the man said snagged in her thoughts. "You said Greyson." She hadn't heard or seen Grey since the bullets erupted. Her eyes widened in shock. "Where is he?" She spun around, scanning the dead bodies at her feet. "Greyson!"

"He wasn't at The Gala." Cole's harsh words filled the silence as Luna began weaving through the fallen troops. "Never came inside."

"Doesn't matter," the man said. "He was there; he participated in a parallel proximity. His presence is required."

Luna held in a scream as she accidentally stepped on a woman's hand. She jumped away, then gasped when she saw the woman's face.

Katniss.

Katniss was dead.

Until now, Luna had refrained from identifying any of the injured parties. From the moment the bullets hit the air, something inside her snapped. Shifted into full momma bear protection mode as she realized these people were not here to play games or make a statement.

They were here to steal, kill, and destroy.

Just like the devil.

But now, seeing Katniss's sweet face slack-jawed and lifeless, her eyes cold and unmoving, Luna had no choice but to acknowledge it. Because these people weren't just strangers to her. They were people she knew and cared about. People she loved. Katniss may have been far removed on that chain, but she was a person in Cole's life, which automatically placed her in Luna's, too.

Small tears swelled in her vision, and she started to cry again.

"Grey's probably smarter than the rest of us," Sol said, snapping her back to reality. "Probably ran off with the dog."

Lemon. Luna's jaw dropped. *Ohmygosh, Lemon!*

"I put her in the crate upstairs before the party," she said, looking at Cole as more tears glistened in her eyes. "She must be so scared."

"Ticktock, ticktock," the man said, his voice lilting with a singsong edge to it. "You don't want to run out of time."

Luna scrunched her nose, not knowing what that meant; it sent her heart ricocheting. What were they doing to her sweet boy?!

"We'll check on her later," Cole said. "Right now, we need to find Greyson so we can get this over with." He strode past Luna and began checking the bodies on the floor, his own body moving in a rhythmic motion that Luna wasn't accustomed to. "He's not here," he said after a few minutes. "I'll check outside."

Luna nodded quickly, then began checking all the rooms on the main floor. If he'd hidden somewhere, she wouldn't have blamed him, but she didn't have time to think about what she was asking her friend to do, only what was necessary for Jaxson.

"Grey!" She flung open the bathroom door, then marched to the laundry room when she didn't see anything. "Greyson!" He wasn't there either. Just when she was starting to panic and think the worst, Luna jerked open the coat closet and found Greyson cowering in the corner.

"Grey," she breathed.

He was shaking, and something Cole had said earlier returned to her. Greyson had never been inside The Gala. He'd only seen the aftermath as they broke out of the front windows, barely escaping before the entire building went up in flames. Other than the cave scene, which involved dead fetuses on display, he'd never had a firsthand encounter with Zanella.

The poor man looked petrified.

"I don't wanna die, Luna," he whispered.

She nodded, swallowing and closing her eyes. "I know. Neither do I." She crouched down now, placing a hand on his shoulder and meeting him at eye level. "But they have Jaxson."

Tears rolled down Greyson's face, and he didn't even bother wiping them off. "Do you really have to cut those bodies?"

Luna bit the inside of her cheek, willing the stinging sensation of their reality to wash away and hoping more than anything that something distant and far removed would replace it.

"Yes." She listened to him wheeze, and then she took another deep breath and delivered the news. "And so do you."

Grey's eyes widened. "Uh uh," he tried. "No way. In fact"—he tried grabbing the door handle and closing himself back in the closet, but Luna blocked him—"I don't want them to find me. Either move or get in!" he hissed under his breath.

"Greyson!" she whisper-screamed. "You don't understand. They will not tell us where Jaxson is unless we all do it. You, me, Sol, and Cole." She huffed, ignoring the awful look on his face. "I'm sorry. I hate to ask this of you, but he's my son, Greyson. You have to do this." Her voice cracked. "We *all* have to do this. We have no choice."

Grey looked at her now, really looked at her, and Luna felt the impending dread creep into her stomach as she awaited his answer.

"Please, Greyson," she begged. "I would do the same for you."

His eyes bolted back and forth between hers before he finally tore his gaze away and let his head fall into his hands.

"He's not outside!" Cole yelled as he ran back in through the front door.

Greyson looked up then, first in the direction of Cole's voice, then back at Luna. She held his gaze steady for a moment longer, then felt her stomach do a somersault when he offered her a simple nod.

"I found him!" she called. "He's alive. We're coming!"

I would hate to imagine what Z would've done next had
he escaped me that night.

                        —Cole Sloane, *The Great Chase*

COLE

Cole wished he could pretend like the next series of events didn't happen.

That he didn't take the knife.

Didn't pick up the ax.

Didn't chop apart people he loved like Jeffrey fucking Dahmer.

But he couldn't, because he did.

Seeing Greyson walk out of that closet with Luna had nearly shattered him. Grey was the last barricade standing in their way, so when he conceded, it made everything real. Up until that point, Cole had done his best to distance himself from this alternate, horror-filled reality where deranged killers were attempting to recreate Graham Zanella's *artwork*.

Except, it was nothing like Z's artwork. What they were making them do was something far darker, far more unhinged. Far more sinister.

"So what?" Sol crouched beside the dead carcass that Cole recognized as his editor. *Katniss.* "We just start hacking?"

He met Cole's gaze, and for a moment, Cole stuttered.

"I, uh . . ." He cleared his throat and tried again. "Yes." He walked around the living room, pulling the bodies apart into a neat row. "They said arms and legs. Sol, help me move them."

It took a minute for the rock star to oblige Cole's request, and when Luna noticed his hesitation, she stepped in.

"For goodness sake, I'll do it."

Cole paused, nearly dropping the dead person's arms. "Lu?" His throat was scratchy.

"Not now, Cole. Please," she said, using all her might to try and move his editor. "Let's just do it."

He scooted the oversized journalist he'd been adjusting over, then moved to help her. "Here, let me."

"I can do it."

"Lu—"

"I said I can do it!"

Cole stopped dead in his tracks and looked at her. Tears rolled down her face, and her cheeks were nearly raw from them. Cole had experienced significant lows in his life, and he realized that he was watching Luna claw her way out of hers right now.

This was her rock bottom.

"Ticktock, ticktock!" The masked server danced around the room, megaphone waving in the air as the others swayed around the room, mumbling their lake chant under their breaths.

"Okay," Luna said, wiping her nose. "Five bodies here." Cole turned back and looked at her. "That means one for each of us, and then—"

"I'll do two." Cole grabbed his ax and knife from where he'd laid them on the floor.

Luna nodded, wrapping her hands around her own weapons. "I guess we'll do these, and then move outside."

Silence greeted her as Cole, Greyson, and Sol all stared at the deceased victims on the ground. Cole had intentionally rolled them onto their stomachs so he wouldn't have to see their faces, but Luna hadn't been strong enough to turn hers. The glassy, unmoving eyes of his editor stared up at him—the sky, the heavens—and Cole wondered if Katniss believed in God.

And then before he realized it, Luna had thrown down her knife, gripped the ax with both hands, and rained it down on Katniss's arm, splintering her skin as it cracked open and spewed blood everywhere.

What have we done?

He watched as Luna picked up the ax again, his own body too stunned to move. His once-sweet, fragile-yet-feisty Luna had been replaced by someone darker, harder. Still wearing her blue satin cocktail gown, she towered over Katniss's body, ax raised, with blood splattered on her face as small blonde ringlets fell from her carefully curated bun, and he knew in that moment she'd never be the same.

She screamed as she brought the weapon down again, and something inside Cole snapped.

He couldn't watch this anymore.

Eager to get this over with so they could move on to the next task, he stepped up to the reporter's body and sent up a silent prayer.

Please forgive me, Lord.

And then he followed Luna's lead.

He held the ax over his head, took a deep breath, and plunged the weapon into the man's leg. Cole shuddered as he felt the metal dig into the corpse's fatty flesh, then nearly choked on his own vomit when he yanked it out and tried again, repeating the action until he hit bone.

Noticing Greyson and Solstice just staring at them, Cole snapped his fingers in front of their faces. "Let's go, boys."

He didn't dare chance another glance at Lu, afraid of what he might see.

Afraid that his heart might never recover from seeing her this way.

Instead, he trained his eyes on the bloody mess in front of him. The man's thigh was now cut wide, and muscles and tendons were splayed against his pale skin. Cole inhaled a deep breath, instantly regretting it when the stench of blood and guts infiltrated his nostrils.

"Fuck." He breathed into the hem of his shirt, desperately seeking a reprieve.

This was so much worse than he thought.

Next to him, Luna had dropped to her knees and had picked up the knife. Cole squeezed his eyes shut and willed himself to continue as he heard Greyson crying and Sol cursing in the background.

It's for Jax, he reminded himself. *Do it for Jax.*

After another laborious breath, he swung back the ax and continued hacking until he loosened the man's legs from his torso. He threw the ax down and yanked the lifeless limbs as hard as he could. The bones resisted at first, but after another hard pull, he successfully separated the patella from the femur.

Falling backward, he quickly dusted off his hands, then made quick work of the knife. He plunged it into the man's dismembered flesh, cutting away loose muscles and tendons until he had a solid visual on the bone. Hesitating for half a millisecond, he shuttered, then plunged his entire hand into the mess he'd created and pulled out the bone. Loose fatty cells clung to it, dangling in the glow of the dim candle flames scattered throughout the room.

Cole stared at it for a moment longer, trying to process what he'd done, and then he retched onto the floor, unable to control his bodily functions anymore.

THE NEXT SEVERAL MINUTES passed by in a montage of blurs, cries, and bones. With each additional arm and leg he chopped, Cole found it increasingly easier to keep his bile at bay. When he'd finished removing the extremities from the two men inside, he immediately marched outside, not wanting to give the adrenaline a chance to wear off.

"Ticktock, ticktock. You've almost reached the end of the clock," Cole heard the deranged masked man sing into his megaphone.

"Come on!" Cole yelled, leading the others outside. Lord only knew what else these people had planned for them tonight.

Or what they had planned for Jaxson.

Cole shuddered, determined to protect this child and get them out of this mess.

"All right . . ." His eyes quickly scanned over the remaining bodies lying in the yard. "There's only three left. Grey, Sol, let's hurry and finish it."

"I can do it." Luna walked out of the house, and an even deeper sadness settled over Cole as he took in her presence. She was drenched in blood, her hair somehow frizzy and slicked with sweat, and a terrifying look blanketed her face.

"Luna." He willed her to look at him. "It's okay. We've got this. Rest."

Silent tears streamed down her face, and she nodded fervently. "Thank you."

Cole nodded, then picked up his ax, the knife already secured in his belt loop. He walked to the bodies, his own limbs moving without thinking, but just as he was about to swing the ax at the nearest target, he froze.

David.

His brother's body had already started to change, a purple hue coloring his lifeless skin. Cole barely recognized him.

"I can do this one, mate." Sol stepped in front of him, but Cole placed a hand on his friend's shoulder.

"No," he said, his voice hoarse. "It's okay."

Sol tried to interject. "Cole, come on—"

"No," Cole said, louder this time, as moisture licked the back of his retinas. "It's okay. I can do it."

He waited for Sol to move, then took another step closer to David. He could feel the others' eyes on him, but he didn't care. All he could think about was his brother. The man—boy—he'd grown up with. David was three years younger than him and had made their childhood both a living nightmare and the biggest adventure Cole had ever been on. David was a loose cannon, a dreamer. Some-one Cole had always aspired to be, although he would never admit that.

David had been a wonderful brother.

Until he wasn't.

Thoughts of him with Cole's wife, the betrayal the two of them had inflicted—it all came rushing back in an instant.

He hurt you, a tiny inner voice whispered. *He deserves this.*

Cole's rib cage felt like it was cracking open. Despite what the enemy was trying to tell him, his brother didn't deserve this. No one did. Despite what David and Rose had put him through, this was not something he'd wish on his worst enemy.

This was cruel. A horrible punishment that Cole would forever bear the responsibility and guilt for. Because that's why everyone was here tonight—to celebrate him. To celebrate his stupid fucking book.

A humorless laugh escaped him as he thought back on the meaningless frivolities of the party they'd created. The risk they'd posed to all the attendees.

Cole hated it.

Every ounce of it.

"Come on," Sol tried again. "You've done enough. Go take what's-her-face over there."

But Cole couldn't. Couldn't take his eyes off his brother and risk letting someone else put him through one more minute of misery.

"It should be me," he said, his voice firm. "I brought him here. I deserve this." He tightened his grip around the ax handle as he thought about how Clara would have to grow up without a father.

This is your fault, the voice whispered.

He grimaced, his gaze never leaving his brother. "It should be me."

Sol hesitated but eventually walked away, leaving Cole alone with his demons.

His eyes traced over David's head, then over his shoulders, down his arms and to his legs, landing at his feet.

Then, without overthinking it anymore, he raised the weapon high above his head and whispered, "I'm sorry, bub. I wish it had been Rose."

LUNA

Luna hated herself.

She hated herself, and in this moment, she may have even hated God.

Because there was clearly no more good in the world.

And He clearly wasn't coming to save her.

She swung that damned ax for what felt like hours as she hacked off a human's arms and legs before plunging the knife into their wounds, skinning them like an animal. She felt the man's flesh buried under her fingernails, and her arms were coated in blood. She looked like Carrie White after the prom.

Except no one was obeying her or the cries in her mind to stop.

God wasn't getting her or her son out of this one.

She had to do it herself.

And it nearly destroyed her.

It had been horrific slamming the sharp edge of the ax into the stranger's body, but nothing compared to the grotesque feeling of plunging her hand inside his corpse, then gripping his skeletal figure and pulling, relying on the knife to help her tear the remaining ligaments away from the cartilage.

Before she knew it, Cole and the others had finished and retreated outside, but when Luna offered to help, they told her to stand back. She'd nearly felt a ripple of relief until she realized who Cole had to dismember.

Watching the man she loved physically destroy his brother's corpse would be seared into her brain for the rest of eternity.

Because she did that.

She caused this.

Luna shuddered as a breeze rolled by, and she thought again about how she hated herself.

"Okay," Cole said after some time. "I'm done."

She watched him throw his ax onto the ground, then take slow, unhinged steps back toward the cabin. His previously slicked back waves were now falling out of place, framing his face. Blood glistened on his forehead, but it was no comparison to the red liquid that coated his forearms, matted and tangled in his body hair.

I'm so sorry, Cole.

"Fuck this bullshit," Greyson screamed, his appearance equally as unruly as Cole's. "Fuck. This. Shit!"

His voice rose an octave with each word, making Luna shudder. She started to open her mouth, but he yelled again before throwing his ax at a nearby tree. It plunked against the wood, then fell to the ground, making a dull thud.

"Shit's demented, mate." Sol removed his jacket and tried to wipe off some of the blood and guts from himself. "No use crying about it now, though. Loads more to do."

Grey griped something back at him, but Luna tuned them out, standing and walking back inside to the masked torturers.

"We're done."

She watched as six heads snapped her way.

Slowly, the man she recognized as the ringleader walked forward. His figure was tall and slender, the only intimidating thing about him the raven mask on his face.

"I don't see any dirt on you." His voice was low and disgustingly sultry.

"What, the blood and guts not enough for you?" Luna fired back.

He smirked, sending an unwelcome shiver down Luna's spine. "You have to bury the bones. Or did you forget that part?"

Damnit.

Luna winced, her entire world shattering.

She had, in fact, forgotten.

Images of her, Sol, and Cole burying bones only yesterday went through her mind. It felt like a fortnight ago.

"That's going to take forever!" she argued.

Cole walked in behind her, his footfalls heavy.

"We'll do it later. Let us move on to the next task." He stood beside Luna now, his bloodstained physique glowing in the firelight. "Jaxson is Deaf, in case you've forgotten. He's probably terrified."

But the man wasn't relenting. "Ah, ah, ah," he said in his stupid singsong voice. "You know the rules. Complete each task to move on to the next. If you don't, then no Jax. Simple as that."

A fresh surge of adrenaline rushed through Luna's body as she tried to understand why this was happening. What had she done in her past life to deserve this? *Ugh*, Luna didn't even believe in past lives! What was she thinking? This night was making her crazy, sending her into a pit of doom and despair she feared she'd never escape.

"Where are the fucking shovels, bloke?"

Sol's voice grounded her, if only for a moment.

As if on cue, the other five masked servers—Luna thought she should call them henchmen at this point—each whipped out a shovel from behind their back.

"Here you are," the leader said as the others all extended an arm.

Luna, Cole, Solstice, and Greyson inched forward, each reluctantly taking a shovel, but a fifth server remained standing with a shovel still in hand.

Cole was quick to ask what they were all thinking. "Who's that for?"

"Ah!" The stupid, evil ringleader clapped his hands together. "I'm so glad you asked. You see, we caught somebody here playing possum while you were busy chopping up your friends." He stepped around Luna and the crew and walked out onto the back deck, returning later with a wide-eyed woman whose hands were bound with rope and her mouth covered in duct tape.

"Dani!" Luna cried out before she could stop herself.

"I found her hiding under the deck out back." Mr. Terrorist, a.k.a. the ringleader guy, grabbed Dani by the back of her neck and ripped the duct tape off with his other hand. She screamed, but he kept going. "Thought you'd escape tonight's adventures, did ya?"

"Please," Dani cried, tears streaming down her face and leaving a trail of mascara. "Please just let me go. I won't say anything."

He laughed, cutting the rope off her hands in the process. "Yeah, right." He finished removing the tie, then shoved her into Cole and Solstice. "You may have cheated death tonight by surviving the initial shooting, but now, that makes you a part of it. A part of *this*."

He paused for dramatic effect, and Luna's hatred grew. How many more people had to suffer, had to die tonight?

"Haley!" the man yelled as he snapped his fingers. "Dani's shovel, please."

The woman, Haley, walked forward, offering Dani the shovel. Luna waited on bated breath to see what she would do. She hated that another person was being dragged into this, but Jaxson's life depended on it.

Dani looked at Haley, her gaze quickly dropping to the tool. "Do they really have him?" she whispered.

Luna nodded slowly, biting the inside of her cheek to stop the onslaught of tears.

"What happens if I—"

Luna cut her off with an urgency in her voice. "They'll kill him." They hadn't explicitly said this, but Luna knew it was true the moment she said it.

Dani's eyes widened more than they already were, and slowly, she nodded.

Then, she picked up the shovel.

COLE

Dirt.

Mud.

Sweat.

Blood.

Tears.

It all blurred together in Cole's mind as he trudged through the swampy grass, making his way to the lake. Cole never imagined he'd have to dig another grave in these woods. So much for Sol's "Catholic" approach. A lot of good that did them.

"Do you really think they drained the lake?" Luna's tiny voice traveled up to Cole's ears.

He glanced down at her, wanting more than anything to comfort her and wipe that sad look off her face. "Probably. I guess we'll see in a minute."

He continued his trek through the muddy forest, the rest of the crew not far behind him. They each carried a trash bag full of human remains. Cole had offered to carry Luna's, but she'd resisted. Under normal circumstances, he would've fought her, but he needed to reserve his energy for God only knew what else was to come. He'd already chopped off people's limbs, hacked his own flesh and blood from his brother's deceased carcass, and now they were forcing him to bury the remains. His stomach curdled as he wondered what could possibly be worse than this.

Nobody else spoke as he led the pack, brushing a low-hanging tree branch out of the clearing when they reached their destination.

"Well, damn. They bloody well did it, didn't they?" Sol pushed past Cole. "Drained the whole fucking thing."

Cole scrunched his eyes together, trying to process what he was seeing. It would normally take months, years even, to drain an entire lake of this size. How had they possibly done this in one day's time?

It didn't make sense.

Or perhaps, in a way, it did.

These people were like a wannabe vigilante group, like the copycats in the *Joker* movie. The loud, delirious gang of vandals who painted their faces with clown makeup, yet were never able to perfect it, no matter how hard they tried.

That's what these people were.

Vandals trying to wear Z's skin, the mask of a dead man.

They were bound to get it wrong from the start.

Cole carefully stepped over a large tree trunk and approached the now-empty pit that, just days ago, he'd pulled Luna and Lemon out of after two near-drowning incidents.

Lemon.

Cole shuddered, praying the dog was safe.

"How is any of this possible?" Dani broke her silent streak as she observed the waterless lake.

Cole's response was rapid. "Dunno. Somehow these people always find a way."

"They've probably been watching us," Luna said, crossing her arms as she stopped to take in the sight. "Tracking us, planning this whole thing for years. Makes me sick."

Cole snapped his gaze to her, wanting to somehow fix this, but Luna pulled herself out of her own trance and threw the bag of bones onto the ground.

"Come on," she said. "Let's get it over with."

Cole, Solstice, and Grey followed suit, but Dani stood still, her feet firmly planted on the ground.

"You guys can't be serious," she said.

Cole and Luna paused, each already marching into the mud with their shovels.

"We don't have a choice," Luna said quickly, then set back to walking.

But Dani still wasn't moving. "We can't just . . . bury these . . . these *people*!" She wrapped her arms around her midsection. "We'll go to jail!"

Cole involuntarily flinched. "Well, we don't exactly have a choice now, do we?" he snapped.

Dani looked appalled by the tone of his voice, but Cole didn't care. His only mission was to bury these fucking skeletal remains and be done with it so they could move on to the next task.

But that thought process was quickly interrupted by Greyson throwing his shovel on the ground and wincing. "Jail? I never thought about *jail*! I'm a gay man. Do you know what they'll do to me in *jail*?" His voice rose higher each time he said the word, causing Cole's jaw to clench.

"We'll figure it out later, mate." Sol wiped a fleck of mud from his left eye. "These fuckers are going to kill us if we don't play their demented game tonight."

Dani gnawed on her thumbnail. "There's just got to be another way."

Cole shook his head, following Luna into the muddy pit. "The only way out is through."

LUNA

Sweat dripped from Luna's pores, mixing with the blood and mud that coated her skin.

It swirled in a marbled pattern, resembling paint colors spattered on an art palette.

A fitting image for the mess they were in.

She'd been digging for several minutes already, and her arms burned from the weight of the friction, her muscles flexing and tensing as her heart beat loudly in her chest. Luna knew very little of Indian burial grounds—had never even known this site had been one. Shame incinerated her as she thought about the disrespectful act she was committing.

Without warning, a white-hot bolt of lightning struck the sky, followed by a roll of thunder. Luna paused, allowing herself a moment to catch her breath as she looked up.

Then a single raindrop fell on her lashes.

"Oi, fucking hell, mate!" Sol grumbled in the background. "This is all a bit too familiar, innit!"

Luna felt her entire world collapsing around her. Or maybe it was her lungs. At this point, she couldn't tell the difference. She only knew that she desperately had to get her son back. Had to save him. Had to protect him the way she never could the first time.

Her chest cavity suddenly felt like it was trapped under two hundred pounds, like Emmett was lying on her, the way he used to before he passed.

Only there was no Emmett.

There was no Lemon.

There was no Jax.

She felt like melting into a puddle, blending right there into the mud to be buried with the bones of her former acquaintances and the curse of a resting place disturbed.

She wanted to give up. Wanted to give in and let the universe take her.

But she couldn't.

Jaxson still needed her.

Her faith had failed her tonight, but in a desperate attempt to hold on to hope, she whispered, "Jesus, *please*."

She threw down her shovel and hopped into her small hole. Pellets of rain fell around her now, and she prayed the droplets would wash her soul, cleanse it from the anger and disgust she felt toward her creator right now.

"Deep enough!" Without even glancing at the others, she flung her leg out of the grave, then the other, and ran for the bags.

One by one, she lobbed them at the others. Cole, Solstice, Greyson, Dani. Each responded in their own way, Cole being the only one who didn't groan—a small respite in the moment.

Finally, she retrieved her own bag and ripped it open, laying the remains in the makeshift grave.

I'm so sorry, she thought as she set the bones into the hole, trying her best not to dwell on this man's family who was probably waiting at home, wondering where he was.

Once the last bag was empty, Luna threw it aside and quickly retrieved her shovel yet again. With fury akin to a live wire pulsating through her veins, she tossed a pile of dirt back into the ground, then again and again and again, until the messy carnage started to disappear. She continued until the entire plot was filled, patting it down with the head of her shovel upon completion.

"Done!" she screamed, throwing the tool down.

Fresh mud streaked down her cheeks, accentuating the hair plastered to her face. The rainfall was atrocious now, and she prayed that whatever happened next was indoors. That her *son* was indoors, staying warm and dry and untouched.

She waited for the others to quickly finish, then took off sprinting, full speed ahead.

"We're done," Luna spat. "What do you want next?"

The man grinned at her, a toothy, shit-eating grin that made her skin crawl. "I was starting to think you'd given up."

Luna's heart stuttered. "Of course we didn't. My son's life is on the line." She observed his rigid posture, how he appeared to carry himself with confidence, yet something about him seemed inauthentic. "Who are you anyway?" She exhaled a heavy breath, watching as he squared up to her. "What's your name?"

The man's full-fledged grin dropped to a half smirk. "You, my dear"—he touched the tip of his thumb and forefinger to her chin, making her flinch—"can call me Herod."

The air left Luna's lungs.

"Hey!" Cole was beside her now, grabbing the man by the neck and shoving him away. "Get your hands off her."

The man—whom she refused to call Herod—laughed. "Always coming to her aid, like a lost puppy." Cole tightened his grip around his neck, and another woman came forward, a gun in hand. "You better call off your dog, Lu."

She shivered. No one other than Cole had ever called her that.

Who *was* this man?

Who was *Z's Army*, and why were they targeting her?

"Cole," she said gently. "They've got a gun."

Cole responded immediately. "I know. Doesn't make a difference to me—not if this asshole is going to put his hands on you."

She heard the gruff tone of his voice, a small part of her heart swelling. "Cole," she repeated calmly. "We just have to get Jaxson."

Cole continued holding the man at arm's length, his hand gripped around the stranger's throat as the woman held a gun to him. Solstice, Greyson, and Dani had all arrived by now, feet apparently glued to the entryway.

"Just think about Jax," Luna whispered.

That time her pleas worked. Cole dropped the vermin—but not without shoving his body back a few feet. Cole himself staggered backward, chest heaving as he looked at Luna. Under different circumstances, she might have noted how hot he looked.

But these weren't different circumstances.

They were fighting for her child's life, and this sinister man had just named himself after perhaps the most evil Biblical ruler:

Herod. King of the Jews.

The ruler of the Massacre of the Innocents.

She suddenly felt dizzy.

Still smirking, the man pulled out a small device from his pocket and hit a large red button. "I hope you're ready for this next part, Lu. I have a feeling it's going to pack an extra special punch for you."

Her heart felt like it had iced over in her chest. All sense of feeling gone as the shock from the first task sat frozen in her core. Nothing would break her after what they'd just done.

Nothing except losing her baby.

"Bring it on."

The red strobe lights from earlier began flashing again as the familiar siren blared in the background. Luna continued to hold the man's stare in a deadlock, daring him to break contact first, as Siri's voice penetrated her ears.

"Congratulations on completing the first task. Not many would've been able to accomplish what you have, so we commend you for your hard efforts. It is the least we can do to make it up to our Native American brethren."

"Oi, please," Sol said. "Stop pretending like you demented fucks actually give a shit about any of this. Z would've never done it this way."

Luna kept her stare trained on *Herod*, not disagreeing with Sol.

"For your next task," the female-generated voice continued, "we will allow your bodies a brief reprieve. We understand the physical toll act one took, so you will be pleased to know you may remain seated throughout the duration of the next act . . . if you can handle it."

Anticipation leaked into every hollow crevice of Luna's body.

"You will also be pleased to know that for act two, you will be documenting a live-performance act, just like you did at The Gala."

Dani gasped.

"Our team will now escort you to the back patio, where we have created a makeshift theater for your viewing pleasure. They will provide you with all the necessary tools to execute the task."

Finally, the man broke Luna's gaze, only to bark an order. "Let's go!"

Luna flinched but recovered quickly.

Then felt the cold barrel of a gun shoved against her throat.

She wanted to spit on this man.

Without thinking, she moved quickly, wading through the disgusting mess of blood and guts from the cadavers they'd chopped before.

They really couldn't have taken the time to clean up this mess? she wanted to say as she stepped onto the back patio, annoyed with the lack of care these people poured into this stupid event. Zanella would've never been so reckless.

But, instead, as she lowered her shirt from her nose and took a staggering breath of fresh air, Luna looked up and lost all sense of functionality.

COLE

No.

Cole blinked once, twice, then in rapid succession as he tried to make sense of the view before him. Somehow, in the hour or two since this insane night had started, these people had managed to set up a glass-encased scene in the middle of Sol's backyard. It looked like something pulled straight from Joe Goldberg's basement, complete with a bed and two humans inside.

One adult male.

And one teenage girl, gagged and bound on the bed.

"No." He shook his head, not wanting to believe what he was seeing. "No fucking way."

"You all did good work in drawing attention to the human trafficking crisis in our country during act one of The Gala. Documenting the execution of that senator made headlines for weeks, which led to further investigation of his campaigns and the rescue of hundreds of innocent children," Siri's mock companion said, making Cole's gut twist. "But what you failed to do was draw awareness to the sexual abuse crimes that happen in our everyday lives, unrelated to trafficking crimes."

Cole shook his head vehemently as one by one, the masked servers delivered red theater chairs, staging them in a tight row in front of the glass cage.

"Popcorn!" a new voice yelled as a small bald man in a tuxedo rolled a vintage popcorn cart by. "Get your popcorn here!"

"They can't be serious," Dani said, shock ringing in her voice.

Cole didn't turn to acknowledge her. He couldn't tear his eyes away from the poor girl who was tied up and on display, likely about to be horribly violated in this sick, twisted mind game.

"I hate this." Greyson threw his hands up, marching away and staring into the opposite direction. "I hate this night, and I hate this game, and I hate this fucking event. Worst launch party ever!"

Cole ignored him, trying beyond reason to process what was about to take place.

"You will now witness an unsettling scene demonstrating these crimes," the electronic voice said, confirming everyone's shared fear. "You must complete the task if you wish to advance to the next level. And remember, Jax is counting on you. Good luck, and happy documenting."

Sol snorted. "Happy documenting. Bravo, you sick fucks!" He clapped his hands, then motioned toward the glass cage. "Excellent lighting and acoustics you've got here. Really, a job well done. I can't wait to see how all of our precious art turns out and how well it really cuts down on fucking rape!"

The rock star's unhinged voice finally caused Cole to look away from the atrocity in front of him. Sol had stomached everything up until this point. All three acts prior to The Gala, The Gala itself, and the weird events that took place here earlier in the week. Hell, even the body chopping tonight. For as theatrical as he was, he'd done it all without much gripe. Cole had never put much thought into it, but he always assumed the singer had seen worse in his life. Or at least, worse things than the rest of them had.

The fact that this act was setting him off unnerved Cole to no end.

"Brav-fucking-o!" Sol screamed and clapped again, punctuating Cole's thoughts. "At least you kept the heat lamps on, though. That was thoughtful of you—"

The woman Herod had called Haley strode forward and smacked Sol in the face with the butt of her rifle. He fell to the ground, cupping his wound and groaning.

"That ought to shut him up for a minute at least," Haley said as she towered over him.

Herod returned now with an armful of supplies. Notebooks, pencils, pens, recording devices, and around his neck, a camera.

Lu.

Cole turned to her. "Lu?" He took a step toward her. "Lu, you okay? You got this?"

But she didn't answer. Wasn't even listening it seemed. Instead, she just stood there, staring blankly at the glass cage, her eyes tracking the man's movements as he stalked from side to side.

"Luna?" he tried again, this time using her full name.

"What's the matter, *Lu*?" Herod mocked, coming to stand in front of her, blocking her view. "Feeling a little triggered, are we?"

Triggered?

Cole looked from Herod to Luna, then back to Herod. "Luna, what's he talking about? Are you okay?"

"Oh!" Herod screamed. "This is rich. You mean he doesn't know?" He pointed at Cole, then removed the camera strap from around his neck and hung it on Luna's, causing her to wince. "Your little Lu here was molested when she was fourteen. About the same age as our sweet Clementine there in the box."

Molested.

Cole's lungs seized.

Was that true?

"Luna," he said gently.

But Herod answered for her. "Tell them, Lu! About how it was your high school math teacher. That's why she donated her eggs, really."

Cole's world was spinning, as if everything he knew was tilting on an axis.

"I thought . . ." he said, trying to piece it together. "I thought that was because of your sister."

At least, that's what Luna had said at The Gala when Zanella revealed that Luna had donated her eggs, resulting in Jaxson's unique conception.

"It was," Luna finally said, clearing her throat, as if that would make saying it easier. "Partially." She swallowed, then tried again. "I was scared of having a sick child, but I also—*dammit!*"

The word came out like a hushed yell as Luna covered her face, but Cole heard it just the same. Luna had only ever cursed in front of him once, and it was at The Gala when the sex trafficking survivors were about to kill their offender.

Oh.

His face fell as realization dawned on him. It was all starting to make sense now.

"It's okay," he said, clarity setting in. "You don't have to explain." He started to pull the camera off her neck. "And you don't have to do this."

Her hand shot up to his. "Yes," she said, pulling his palm back down. "Yes, I do. For Jax." Her voice was barely above a whisper.

For Jax.

Of course she had to. They all had to, or Jaxson would die.

There was no way out of this.

Only through.

So, even though it was the last thing he wanted to do, Cole dropped her hand and looked back at the man who resembled evil reincarnated.

"Fine. Let's get this over with."

LUNA

Luna took her seat, front and center, ready for the show.

She felt disconnected from time and space, yet somehow still in tune with her body. Everything felt tense, every muscle and nerve ending pulled taut. Her skin prickled like pins and needles were tattooing every inch of her flesh, all while she tried to remember to breathe.

It had been nearly two decades since that slimy man had touched her, defiled her, took her youth and her innocence with it. She was fourteen, struggling to keep up in her Algebra I lessons, when her teacher, Mr. Carr, offered to tutor her after class.

In truth, she'd found him attractive and harbored a secret crush, so her cheeks had flushed a deep fuchsia when he offered. Luna had agreed immediately and dressed up the next day, knowing she'd be alone with him. When the time came and the final bell ended, she'd rushed off to his classroom, eager to learn and spend one-on-one time with him.

"Hi, Mr. Carr," she'd said with a bit too much enthusiasm in her voice. "Thank you so much for agreeing to tutor me. I'm having the hardest time with this stuff."

A hint of embarrassment had crept up her spine, but she'd shaken it off, reminding herself he was there to help and not make fun of her like the kids in class had.

"Of course, Luna." He'd beamed, standing from behind his desk. "You're a bright girl. I know with a little help, you can get these concepts. Integers and all."

She remembered blushing again as he flashed a bright white smile at her, a sensation that continued to blossom throughout the lesson.

Until it didn't.

Halfway through the first assignment, he'd stopped her during a moment of incessant babbling by placing a hand on hers. "Luna." His voice was low and steady. "I didn't really invite you here to practice algebra equations."

Her heart rate had sped up tenfold, so loud she was sure he could hear. She swallowed and took a deep breath.

"Then, why did you invite me here?" She involuntarily bit her bottom lip, not entirely sure why she'd done so.

"Because," she remembered him saying, a dark gleam in his eye, "I think you're beautiful."

He'd placed a lock of hair behind her ear then, and Luna shuddered in her seat now, the ghost of his touch still haunting her today.

"And I've been dying to do this."

Immediately, he'd drawn her face to his and entrapped her in a kiss. Luna was only fourteen and had only kissed one boy before: Matthew Johnson, her first boyfriend, and it had only been once—a quick peck on the lips.

It was nothing like Mr. Carr's kiss. His lips moved quickly and angrily, like a force to be reckoned with, as he darted his tongue into her mouth.

For a moment, Luna had enjoyed it, indulged in it even, the thrill of it all. But then reality set in, and she pushed him away.

"Mr. Carr, I'm sorry, but aren't you married?"

"Shhhhhh," he'd said, shushing her by crushing his lips back to hers. "Let's not talk about that."

Alarm bells went off in Luna's head. She'd found the man attractive, yes, and she had enjoyed this at first, yes, but this had just been a silly fantasy that formerly existed in her head. She wasn't actually out to destroy a marriage. She wouldn't be able to live with herself.

Luna tried pushing him away again. "I'm sorry, but I think I should go."

She'd stumbled as she tried to get up from her chair and gather her things, but he'd grabbed her arm and yanked her back down. "You're not going anywhere."

Luna shuddered, the memory of it all still alive and dancing, itching beneath her skin. She'd tried so hard, so desperately, to get away.

It hadn't worked.

He threw her body onto the floor, forced her clothes off, and stole her innocence against her will.

She got a C on her final report card that year.

"Luna." Cole's voice pulled her out of her trance, and she blinked several times. "Are you okay?"

No.

Were any of them really okay?

She nodded once, then looked back at the glass enclosure, locking eyes with the young girl named Clementine. She was just a child. The same age Luna had been when it happened. The same age Jaxson was now.

Her skin pulled tauter, threatening to crack at the seams, exposing her heart.

You're gonna be okay, Luna mouthed to the little girl.

Clementine saw it and held her gaze, the fear and terror apparent in her eyes.

"I shouldn't have to do this," Dani said as one of the servers held her at gunpoint. "I'm not an artist! Or a documenter, or whatever the hell you call these people. I'm a book agent! What am I supposed to do?"

"Sell the rights. Take notes for your tagline," Haley said, shoving Dani forward as she jabbed the AR15 into her back. "Let's go."

Dani started to object again, and Luna winced.

"Dani, please just shut up and do what they say!" she yelled. "Please." Her voice cracked as she stared at Dani's washed-out face. "I just want my son back."

A beat of silence passed as Dani looked back and forth between the gun-woman and the people in the cage. A harsh wind swept by, leaving a chill in the air.

"Fine." Dani took her seat begrudgingly. "But I'm not eating any damn popcorn."

Luna let out a relieved sigh just as Sol laughed.

"Hah!" He slapped his knee and stood. "I'll have some, mate! Why the hell not? Can't watch a rape scene without a good snack. Wouldn't be much of a horror movie without it, eh?"

He continued to laugh maniacally, the unhinged sound sending a new wave of goose bumps across Luna's flesh.

Apparently, it had affected Greyson, too. "Sol, please, can you just shut the fuck up so we can be done with this." He spoke with no absolution in his tone.

Luna opened her mouth to echo Greyson's sentiment, but the same red lights from inside the cabin started flashing in the glass cage while the siren sounded again.

"Showtime!" Herod shouted, grabbing his own bag of popcorn.

Luna's gaze fell back to Clementine, who was still staring at her, wide-eyed and fearful.

It's okay, Luna mouthed again. *It's okay.*

The girl nodded, then squeezed her eyes shut as she braced for impact. Luna pressed her own eyes closed, reminding herself to breathe.

"Eyes open, Lu!" a female voice called. "Don't forget to take pictures!"

Luna grimaced but obeyed, opening her eyes and seeing Haley, who she now deemed second-in-command, staring right at her.

"Snap, snap." She mimed clicking a camera, waiting for Luna to follow with the real motion.

Fuck this woman.

Luna took a deep breath, then looked back at the cage. The man had already undressed himself, the only thing remaining his boxers. A rigid chill rushed down Luna's spine as she watched him yank the young girl's leggings down to her ankles, then reach inside his waistband.

Breathe.

She pulled the camera up.

Breathe.

Clicked the shutter once.

Breathe.

Then pressed the button again.

Muffled sobs escaped Clementine as her exposed skin hit the air.

"Hello, gorgeous," the man cooed, and his disgusting voice could be heard for miles. Luna squinted, trying to figure out how it was possible, but then she noticed the small headset around his ear, similar to the one her pastor wore on Sundays.

The predator raised a hand, ready to touch this poor girl, all while Luna and the others sat, unable to rescue her from the trauma Luna had caused.

Breathe.

Breathe.

Breathe.

Luna raised the camera and pressed the shutter button, exhaling slowly.

"I wanna—"

The man's voice was drowned out by Luna's own predator, the disgusting leer and lilt of his voice creeping into her ear canals like a spider, even two decades later.

That's it, Luna. Good girl.

She shuddered at the live memory, the smell of his coffee breath still rigid in her nostrils. Like it happened yesterday.

The man in the box stalked around Clementine to the front side of the glass and ripped the duct tape from her mouth. She screamed, and Luna felt Cole squeeze her hand. It was meant to comfort her, but all it did was further cement the unwanted feeling of a man touching her body.

She retracted her arm and tried not to let the guilt consume her.

"That's right, scream—"

Don't scream, Luna, Mr. Carr's voice whispered in the back of her mind as she watched the vile man grab Clementine's hair by the back of the neck. *You don't want to get caught and fail my class, do you?*

"Please!" Clementine pleaded.

Breathe.

Breathe.

Click.

"That's right, sweetie." The man stood, then removed the last of his clothes. "Beg—"

"No! No!" Clementine screamed, but it was no use.

In one swift motion, the man turned, pressing his bare backside against the glass and positioning himself in front of the girl. Luna turned away, unable to watch, but that didn't stop her from hearing a muffled gag escape through the pedophile's headset.

Breathe—

Luna choked on a sob as tears slid down her face. Her entire body felt numb. No, scratch that. It felt hot, like white-hot shame plastered against her skin, itching with the intensity of a thousand sunburns. She felt disgusting, vile. She wanted to scratch her skin until she'd destroyed every last cell and could burn herself from the inside out.

The man screamed more orders at the child, and Luna gasped, losing control of herself.

"Ah, ah, Luna darling!" Herod's voice twisted her insides. "Jax is counting on you. You only get to the next task if you document the whole thing."

Breathe.

Breathe.

Breathe.

Luna nodded violently, then held her camera back up and clicked several photos in rapid succession as a muffled cry escaped her.

"That's it," Herod said. "Don't be afraid to really get in there. We need all the best angles, truly."

The pins-and-needles feeling was back, aggravating her flesh as her pulse ricocheted in her chest. Somewhere, deep in the recesses of her mind, Luna felt something telling her to stop, to sit down and not listen to this man, but she couldn't do it. Couldn't listen to the tiny voice of reason that hadn't saved them from this situation in the first place.

"Lu!"

Cole's voice was louder than the one inside her head, but she still didn't listen. There was only her and Clementine, and this man and the echo of her abuser. She had to do this, had to get it over with and put an end to it.

For Jax.

Slowly, and in a trancelike state, Luna stood and drifted closer to the glass cell as the monster moved behind the girl.

Shh, Mr. Carr's phantom whispered, the memory of his hand clamping over her mouth making her shudder. *I'm almost done.*

Luna stopped at the cube, close enough to make out the freckles on Clementine's cheeks. She trailed the tiny constellation all the way up to the girl's eyes, where she held her gaze. Luna took a deep breath, trying to be brave for the child.

With a small thud, Clementine threw up her hand, letting her palm catch on the glass. Luna wrinkled her brow for a moment, but then understanding dawned on her. She offered the girl a meek smile, then planted her own palm against the window, attempting to align it with Clementine's—this small yet monumental gesture the only lifeline between the two victims.

"It's okay," Luna said loudly. Then, in a softer, quieter voice, she repeated, "It's okay."

Clementine cried but nodded, scrunching her fingers against the glass, as if trying to break through, desperate for someone to save her.

And then her hand dropped.

Click.

Click.

Click—

COLE

COLE'S WEAK STOMACH MADE it approximately five minutes into the act before he vomited, covering his feet in acid.

He'd endured so much trauma in his life, and so much more even moments ago when he had to rip out his brother's bones. Somehow this seemed worse than all of it.

Almost.

After he'd emptied the contents of his stomach and written down enough notes to pretend like he gave a fuck, like he would actually write about this later, Cole threw his notebook down in protest once the man in the cage started screaming about his orgasm.

"That's enough." He marched down to Luna and, remembering how she'd flinched earlier, stopped abruptly when he reached her. "We're done, Lu. It's over."

She finished capturing one last photo, then dropped her camera and turned to him, her face completely ashen. Even in the midst of the worst night of their life, with blood and guts and sweat and fear laced into her features, she was still beautiful as ever.

It broke Cole's heart.

"We're done, Luna. The task is over."

As if on cue, the red lights began flashing, a siren sounding over the loud-speakers. She nodded curtly at him before walking away from the glass prison. Cole watched as she removed the camera from her neck and promptly dropped it into Herod's awaiting hands.

"Here." Her voice sounded foreign to Cole. "All done. What's next?"

She seemed to move in a daze, like a spirit caught between life and death, not quite knowing where her tormented soul was supposed to go. Perhaps Sol's purgatory theory had some truth to it.

"Luna." Cole walked after her, ignoring the peanut gallery as he went. "Lu, are you okay?"

"I'm fine, Cole." She avoided eye contact. "What's next?"

Her question was directed at Herod, he knew, but Cole wanted to stop her. To shake her and make her look him in the eyes and tell him she was okay.

But that wasn't his place. Not in this scenario.

He had no idea the mental toll she had just undergone, and worst of all, he had no idea how to help her through this.

So he closed his eyes and did the only thing he knew.

He prayed.

God, he started, picturing Luna's bloodied, battered, and broken body. *Please, help me help her. Help us all through this. Help us survive tonight.*

Herod, in all his five-seven or five-eight stature, faced Luna and Cole and the rest of the gang with a smug curiosity. "I must say," he began, a wicked grin overcoming his face, "I'm surprised you all completed that. If I were a betting man, I'd have lost. Jax is lucky to still be alive."

"Where is he!" Luna screamed, her shrill tone making Cole jump. "What have you done with my son? Where's my *baby*?"

If Herod was also shocked, he didn't show it. "Now's not the time to throw a tantrum, Luna darling. Only one more task left to go if you want to save your sweet boy's life."

"Just tell me where he is!" Luna's demands melted into sobs. "Just tell me where my baby is."

No longer able to stand on the sidelines and watch, Cole swooped in and wrapped an arm around her. "Come on, Lu. Let's go inside for a minute."

He was anticipating her to put up more of a fight, but to his surprise, Luna turned her head into his chest and allowed him to lead her away. With a heavy heart, he quickly walked them through the sea of bodies inside and took her back to the stairs. There, her limbs turned into a puddle, and she fell into him, sobs wracking her body.

"I just—want my baby, Cole!"

He shushed her and rubbed her back, pulling her fully into his embrace as he sat on the staircase. "Shh, shh. It's okay, Lu. It's okay."

"But it's not okay!" she yelled back, her inflection rising in anger. "They have him, and I don't know what they're going to do to him, and that poor girl was just *raped* while I sat by and watched and took fucking pictures! I took *pictures* of the worst moment of her life, Cole, and there was nothing I could do about it! None of this will ever be okay again!"

"Dammit, Luna, look at me!" He grabbed her chin, forcing her to pause and make eye contact with him. Her eyes were bloodshot, the skin surrounding them swollen. "I know this is hard, okay?"

She snorted as snot fell from her left nostril.

"This sucks ass. This is terrible. I know that. You're scared, and you just experienced a traumatic event from your past. I get it, okay?" He sucked in a breath, then continued. "When I lost River . . . Well, you saw me. I was a wreck. I couldn't sleep, couldn't function. I had PTSD episodes all the time. It was an unimaginable grief."

Another whimper escaped her, and she looked down, squeezing her eyes shut.

"But hey." Cole firmly but gently lifted her chin back up and waited until she looked at him. "Jaxson is still alive, okay? He's still alive, and even though this has been the worst fucking night of your life, your baby boy is still alive. He's still breathing, and we have a chance to save him. That's the good in all of this."

She held his gaze for a moment, then broke away, trying to catch her breath. "But we don't know that! They could have already killed him and are just taunting us, making us do these terrible things. I'm such a terrible mother! How did I let this happen? How did I fail to keep him safe again? I mean, what if . . . what if they—already—killed—him?"

She was struggling to breathe. Cole had experienced it enough times himself to know. His protective instincts took over, and he gripped both sides of her face.

"Luna, we're sitting on the stairs."

"Wha—"

"I'm holding your face."

She looked at him but still couldn't breathe.

"You have blue eyes."

She shook her head furiously.

"Your hair is—oh, fuck it!"

Cole let go of her and ran to the kitchen, nearly tripping on the way. He flung open the nearest cupboard and grabbed a tall glass before shoving it under the sink.

"Come on, come on." He tapped his fingers against the rim of the glass, waiting for the water to fill up. Then, he hurtled back to the woman he loved. "Sorry for this, Lu."

And he threw the cold water over her face.

LUNA

Luna gasped.

Air filled her lungs, and she took several steadying breaths, trying to calm her racing heart.

"Breathe, Luna. Just breathe."

She blinked, a cool drop of water falling from her lashes. Slowly, she clutched a hand to her chest, focusing on the physical sensations coursing through her body.

After another deep breath, she finally looked up at Cole. "Thank you."

He nodded, then hooked his arm around her neck, pulling her to his chest. "Water," he whispered, nuzzling his face into her hair. "Sometimes that's the only way to ground yourself. Although I typically prefer hot water instead of cold, I figured you might get pissed if I flung boiling hot water at your face."

Despite herself, she laughed. The sound was devoid of humor, but it was a relieving sensation all the same.

"What are we going to do, Cole?" She stared blankly into the void; nobody had bothered to shut the front door.

She heard him take a deep breath, and then he pulled away and said something that shocked her. "We're going to pray."

Luna nearly snorted. "I don't think that's going to help us." A lot of good her *attempted* hedge of protection prayer did.

Cole furrowed his brow. "Of course it is. You taught me that."

She shook her head, now laughing for real. "Look around us, Cole." Her eyes landed on the balloon arch that was meant to serve as a backdrop for photos. It was now covered in blood splatters, and Luna swore she saw a piece of flesh tucked in between one cluster, a tendon hanging loosely from a fake bat. "Praying isn't going to save us from . . ." She paused again, struggling to get the words out. "From . . . these monsters."

"Hey," Cole said, his voice full of concern. "Luna Marie Monroe, you know better than I do that's not true. God is always good, always there for us when we need him most, even in hopeless times like this. You taught me that after the car accident, remember?"

Memories of Cole's Jeep ramming into her small car flashed into her mind, followed by a montage of hospital images. She remembered the drugs, the pain, the antiseptic smell of the recovery unit. But most of all, she remembered Cole's confession as he sat in her room and admitted he'd wanted to die. That his reckless drunk driving accident that had placed them both in the hospital was a nearly completed suicide attempt. Luna had held him that day and spoke truth into his life, reminding him that Jesus loved him, even if Cole had stopped loving him.

I love you, Luna.

She gasped.

I will always love you.

The powerful yet gentle conviction from the Lord consumed her every thought.

There is nothing you can do that would separate me from you.

Luna clutched her chest. Then, for an entirely different reason, she began to wail.

I'm so sorry, Jesus.

The pain from her guilt began squeezing her insides, but then the Lord spoke again.

It is well, child.

And the invisible clutch she'd placed on herself released.

Luna continued crying, her mind spinning from the emotions. All night, she'd felt fear, resentment, anger—the fleeting feeling of hope when she'd desperately tried to call upon a God who was supposed to be there for her, yet had allowed these horrendous things to happen to her son and her friends.

She'd felt all these things and more toward her savior, not just tonight, but for a long time. Perhaps from the first moment she discovered she had a son. The bud had begun to grow the night of The Gala, and instead of stopping it, stomping on it with her muddy combat boots, Luna had allowed the bitter arrow to root itself deep within her heart.

She had been slipping further and further from Christ for years, and tonight, when Jaxson disappeared, she felt her anger morph into something else entirely: An absence of faith.

An abandoning of hope, realizing that all was lost, and God was not going to save her from this nightmare. Her doubt and bitterness had fully bloomed, nearly growing over her steadfast love for the Father.

But then God.

Luna smiled through her tears, suddenly overwhelmed and in awe of the Lord. Because just when she was about to submit to the darkness, to give in to the devil's mind games, Jesus revealed himself, proving that he'd been there all along. Pursing his daughter. And he used Cole Sloane to do it, a man who'd only recently been saved. Luna had prayed for his salvation so many times, and now there he sat, begging *her* to believe, to have hope in a savior who cares. The act stunned her, and it was enough to cut the root, killing all the resentment in her heart.

She didn't know why God had allowed these terrible sufferings to happen tonight, but some things were beyond human comprehension. Hadn't she just been reminded of that in the book of Job?

Luna turned to Cole and pulled his massive, muscular frame into a life-changing hug. "I'm so sorry, Cole. You're right. You're so right." And then in a softer voice as she leaned back and rested her forehead against his, she whispered, "I'm so sorry, God. I'm so sorry, Jesus."

I'm so sorry, Jax.

She continued to sob, repenting of her sins while Cole held her, until finally, the presence of the Holy Spirit washed over her.

You are forgiven.

Luna could finally breathe again.

For she was a child of God, redeemed by the blood of Christ.

"Thank you, Cole," Luna said, taking his hands into her own. "Let's pray."

COLE AND LUNA EMERGED from the house, their fingers entwined as they strode hand in hand toward Herod.

"Lucky little Lu, always having Big Bad Cole come to her rescue," Herod said, stroking the beak of his raven mask. "I have to say, I really thought you were a goner."

Luna resisted the urge to roll her eyes.

"Just get on with it." Sol stood from his crouched position near the edge of the deck and turned to face them. "What's the third task? I'm starting to miss my Deaf little mate."

Haley swung the strap on her gun around her back and raised her hands. "*You can't even sign that well.*"

Luna's eyes widened. First in fear, then in shock. If Haley knew how to sign, perhaps she was the key to finding Jaxson. Luna had failed to track her movements before, but now she vowed to stay vigilant.

"I am growing rather bored, actually, so oh well. Why the hell not?" Herod pulled the small device from earlier out of his pocket. "You've made it this far. Let's see how you perform in tonight's third act."

Watching with intense trepidation, Luna followed his hands, her heart beating wildly with anxiety. His thumb hit the large red button, and within seconds, the lights were flashing, followed by the siren blaring.

How the heck had no one discovered them yet? They were in the woods, isolated, yes, but at the rate in which they kept doing these things, surely there had to be a park ranger or camper within a ten-mile radius who could see or hear this. A balloon of hope inflated Luna's chest as she clung to the thought.

Maybe somebody is *coming.*

"If you are listening to this, then congratulations, because you have made it to the third and final task of the night." The robotic female voice stung Luna's eardrums. "Jaxson will be pleased to see his mother soon."

Jaxson.

She gasped as a new thought occurred to her. What if they *made* Jax part of the act? What if they were forcing him to play along as some twisted ode to his part in The Gala?

What if they tried to make him commit suicide or light himself on fire again?

Panic flooded her body; she shook her head furiously.

"For this next part, you will be escorted back into the woods, to the lake where you completed act one."

Blood-smeared bones.

Hacked bodies.

Mud pits.

It all flashed briefly in her mind.

"This time, however, you will be pleased to find the water is now refilling the lake. The only problem is—"

Don't say it.

"—Jax has been chained to the bottom."

"No!" Luna screamed, and her legs gave way underneath her.

This was her living, breathing nightmare.

The only thing worse would be if they added flames to the mix.

Which could still happen.

She squeezed her eyes shut, attempting to stave off the tears.

But it was no use.

The water that poured from the corners of her eyes might as well be akin to the hundreds of gallons they were using to refill the lake.

She felt her lungs constricting again, and then Cole picked her up, holding her steady as she tried to ground herself, both physically and spiritually.

"We will provide you with the key to unlock him, but only if you complete the final challenge."

"What the fuck is it?" Cole cried with a deep, throaty voice.

"Our team will now escort you to the lake, where Luna, and only Luna, will find further instructions. The rest of you are to join her, but you must not intervene. If you do, Jaxson will die."

Much like her heart, Luna's mind wanted to race, but it was caught in slow motion, processing everything like a broken shutter speed.

"After all," the voice continued, the noise muffled in Luna's head, "a good journalist must never interfere."

The lights shut off, and the sting of invisible ice pierced through Luna's skin.

Then she ran.

COLE

"Luna!"

Cole took off after her.

"Wait up!"

He jumped off the deck, then nearly fell as he slipped in mud while trying to round the corner. Herod and the others laughed somewhere in the background, but Cole kept going, not giving them a second thought.

"Come on!" he yelled over his shoulder, bellowing to the others. "Let's go!"

Sol grumbled while Dani and Greyson cried, but they all followed orders, snapping back into their twisted fate.

"Lu!" He saw her blonde hair flying in the wind. "Lu, we're coming with you!"

"He's in the lake, Cole!" she screamed back. "We have to move."

Deciding to save his breath, Cole continued to pound his feet against the muddy earth. All around him, flecks of mud and dirt sprayed outward, creating a dusty storm in their wake. The others trailed not far behind, racing against time, as he tried desperately to catch up to Luna and Jax, all while a million thoughts clouded his vision.

What had they done to the poor boy? And what were they going to make Luna do? This night had been horrendous so far, but at the very least, Cole had been there for Luna. Able to help her in all the ways he could, even if it meant offering a shoulder to cry on. Now he was expected to sit on the sidelines, front and center, and watch her carry out something demonic on her own, all while her son was at risk of drowning while chained to the bottom of a fucking lake?

It was sick.

Everything about this was sick. It made him want to kill someone, perhaps almost as badly as he'd wanted to kill Zanella.

He internally groaned at the thought of the artist, hating the way the man had tormented him and all but forced his daughter's hand at suicide. The only thing that could make tonight worse was if they somehow did the same to—

"Watch out, mate!" Solstice grabbed Cole's arm just in time before something—Cole didn't know what—almost knocked him over.

He fell hard on top of Sol but quickly pushed himself back up.

"What the hell was that?" Greyson yelled while Dani screamed.

Another large round creature shot out from behind a tree, and this time, Cole caught the gleam in its eye, reflected by the moon.

"Pigs," Cole said simply. "Fucking pigs."

The animal huffed, then ran directly at them.

"I think you mean *boars*! These are fucking *boars*, Colestice!" Greyson screamed as he ran by Cole, pushing him down again.

Cole grimaced as he landed in another pit of mud. "Dammit, Greyson!"

Grey's screams were his only response.

"I should've known the bastards would unleash feral swine after us! Why not? Bringing it all full circle, eh!" Sol yelled, then laughed again, his maniacal side returning and sending shivers down Cole's spine.

"Swine?" Dani screamed, hiding in a bush. "Pigs? Is this because of the movie theater? The whole *Exorcist* thing? Oh my gosh, you did not describe them well enough in your book, Cole!"

He rolled his eyes. "Nobody cares about the book anymore, Dani. Let's go!"

He offered her a hand before dashing off again. With a huff, he jumped over a large rock that was jutting out in his path just as another boar shot out of the dark, narrowly missing Cole as it ran by. His instinct was to flinch, to hide, but he filtered through his thoughts before remembering that wild pigs will not necessarily harm humans unless they feel threatened.

In theory, that should have made him feel better, but given the circumstances, it didn't.

Because who knows what they had done to these poor animals. How they got them here, if they'd harmed them, how long they'd been here. They were probably just trying to escape, trying to survive, the same way Cole and the others were.

For a moment, he empathized with them.

Until he heard Luna scream.

"Lu!" He sped up, the muscles in his thighs burning in protest. "Luna, are you okay?"

"Get off me!" was her only response, and Cole's heart plummeted.

They were so close to the lake. He could almost see it, just beyond the trees.

Which meant Jax was close, too.

He refocused on the mission ahead, his eyes locking on Luna. From a distance, it was hard to make out what was happening, but as he closed the gap between them, he saw that a pig was dragging Luna by the hem of her dress. Her leg looked like it might be bleeding, and he was hit with a sense of déjà vu.

Dammit.

"Get off her!"

Without thinking, he lunged for the animal, causing it to squeal and release its grip. Cole didn't have anything to hit it with, so he mustered all his strength and shoved it into the trees, praying it wouldn't retaliate.

"Come on!"

He scooped Luna up and continued running, albeit at a slower pace, trying to put distance between them and the animal. If they were lucky, it would just race off, likely scared, but Cole wasn't waiting around to find out.

"Are you okay?" he yelled, adrenaline pulsing through his veins, even though he was desperately out of breath.

"Fine," she answered immediately, then shrieked, "Look! There!"

Cole snapped his gaze to the scene in front of him and nearly halted. They'd reached the lake, and there, in the middle, was Jaxson.

Luna started waving her arms frantically. "Jax! Mommy's here!"

Cole could feel her slipping down and out of his arms, but he hadn't assessed the damage to her leg yet. "Wait," he said. "You're hurt!"

"I'm fine," she snapped back, shoving her arms off his broad chest once her feet hit the ground.

Cole watched her limp toward the lake, and that's when he finally took it all in. Because not only was Jax chained up—he was housed in a glass cage, similar to the one Clementine had been in. Only this one was much smaller, as if it had been custom-made for him. The object sat in the middle of the lake as a thin layer of water ebbed around it. Cole trailed his gaze, noting the small round holes that lined the edges of the cage. The voice had said they were refilling the lake, but Cole felt a small fraction of relief because at this rate there was no way Jax was in danger of drowning. Whatever they made Luna do, she would crush it way before the lake filled up enough to infiltrate the glass cylinder.

Jax would not drown tonight.

They would save him.

Luna would save him.

You must not intervene.

"Jax, baby!"

Luna continued to scream while waving her arms wildly, but Jax was facing the other way.

"Where's Herod?" Luna asked, whipping back around. "What's next? That stupid recording said the task would be here, but I don't see anything!"

Cole scanned the rest of the area. He could see large pipes thrust into the rocky sludge that lined the lake—probably how they'd managed to drain it so quickly—but other than that and Jax, nothing seemed out of place or staged. He turned around to see if the others had arrived just as he heard another woman's screams.

Dani.

Why had they made her come? Cole swore, wanting to help but knowing he couldn't leave Luna and Jax now that they were here. He sent up a silent prayer that Sol or Grey would protect her.

Another boar shot out of the dark forest, racing along the northernmost side of the lake, punctuated by Greyson's scream.

"What the devil are these things doing here?" Grey stumbled over some old pieces of driftwood as he made his way over to Cole. "I thought we left the animal abuse behind when Zanella died."

Cole gave him a once-over; he didn't have any visible injuries. "You okay?"

Grey huffed, leaning over and placing his hands on his knees. "No, Colestice. I am very much not okay right now."

The mention of his nickname told Cole that Greyson was fine for now. "Where are Sol and Dani?"

Greyson shook his head. "She fell back there again. Sol's trying to help her. I ran when another pig came after me."

In the distance, a red light started blinking. Cole walked toward it, squinting. Even from afar, he could tell the light was similar to the one from the cabin, yet smaller. And it was moving.

"Hey, Lu." He reached for her arm, catching it and spinning her around. "Look. I think they're coming."

"Oh, praise Jesus." She tossed one final glance at Jaxson and started jogging toward the light. "Herod!"

Adrenaline pounded through Cole's veins as negative thoughts infiltrated him. He had a terrible feeling, deep within his gut, that he'd been trying to ignore all night. But now that they were here, he knew he must admit to himself what he'd been dreading most so that he could be prepared. He needed a plan of attack so he could survive, so he could save Luna, Jax, and the other person in his life whom he now loved most.

Clara.

Despite watching her and Rose flee, Cole had been terrified all night that the crew would capture and harm the little girl. He just hadn't wanted to voice it, for fear of bringing it to fruition somehow.

His niece and River's sister—she was the perfect target in this twisted game where Zanella's wannabees seemed to know everything there was to know about them. He cursed himself for agreeing to invite her here tonight. Cursed himself for agreeing to the stupid party in the first place. What was he thinking—dragging everyone to a cabin in the woods on Halloween night? In hindsight, it'd been a terrible, selfish idea Cole had latched onto because he was apprehensive about being in a crowd.

This was all his fault.

As the red glowing light moved closer, Cole vowed to do whatever it took to protect Clara, Luna, and Jaxson.

He just had to figure out how.

LUNA

"Come on, come on," Luna mumbled under her breath as she tapped her foot.

She'd been standing near the entrance of the lake's clearing, not wanting to go too far for fear of losing sight of Jaxson, but feeling more anxious than ever before. Her baby still hadn't turned around to see she was there, and she'd never been so disheartened that he couldn't hear. Being Deaf made Jaxson part of a special group, one that got to experience life in an entirely different way. She'd sat through countless lectures in her college ASL classes about how to respect the Deaf community, and she had been doing her best to honor their culture since the moment Jax came into her life.

She wanted him to love himself and learn to reframe the negative self-thoughts he had, especially in the wake of his bullies. Something that wouldn't be an issue if she'd just sent him to that Deaf school in Columbus, like Jaxson's interpreter suggested. But something inside her had cringed at the thought. She'd already missed out on so much of his life. She couldn't possibly fathom sending him away to a boarding school where she'd only see him on holidays and weekends. The idea had been absurd to her.

But now, as she stood at the edge of the lake's clearing, she couldn't help but feel like she'd chosen wrong, yet again.

"

She vowed, when they got out of here, she would take another look at the program.

A noise sounded nearby, pulling Luna from her thoughts. She glanced right then left before the red light appeared, clearly now, as Herod and his crew rounded the trunk of a large oak tree.

"Finally," she breathed. Then louder, said, "Let's get this over with! What do you want me to do?"

The words came out rushed, nearly drowning out the hint of a familiar sound yet again, one that made her skin crawl.

No, she thought. *No, they couldn't possibly—*

"Luna, dear," Herod said, marching straight toward her and revealing a leash in his hand. "I believe Miss Lemon was looking for you."

Luna's heart dropped to the bottom of her stomach.

"No." She shook her head. "Don't you dare hurt Lem girl."

Herod laughed, relinquishing the leash and letting the dog run to Luna. "Who do you think I am, Luna? Honestly, we would never hurt a dog."

She let out a massive sigh of relief.

"But you are going to."

And her heart immediately stopped, paling her already ashen face.

Luna wrapped her arms around the poor canine, clinging tightly to her furry body. "What do you mean?"

Herod and his crew laughed. "Oh, I think you know exactly what I mean." He stepped around Luna and Lemon, shoving his hands into his pockets as the others spread out, twirling their guns like batons. "If you want to save poor Jaxson from drowning and make it out of this alive, then you'll have to drown little Lemmy Lou in this lake here."

Fresh tears poured down Luna's face.

"It's tragic, really. So terribly sad. Everyone knows it's easier to kill a human than it is a dog."

Herod's voice blended into the background as a million thoughts ran through Luna's head. She stared into Lemon's sweet puppy-dog eyes, and her chest cracked wide open. She couldn't possibly do this. Luna loved animals—especially dogs!—almost more than she loved people. And she'd gotten Lemon as a gift for Cole.

Lemon was going to be their dog.

Their family pet.

There was no way she could do what they were asking.

"That's so cruel," she finally said after clearing her throat. "You can't hurt an innocent animal. She's just a dog. Man's best friend! I mean . . . look at her!" Luna stood, carrying Lemon toward Herod. "You cannot possibly ask me to do this."

He held her gaze for a moment, then flicked his eyes to the dog. "Unfortunately, it has to be this way since"—he pulled his phone out and hit play, speaking in tandem with the female-generated voice—"euthanasia is a highly controversial topic in today's society. For your final task, we're asking you to execute this method of death and instant pain relief by deliberately killing one of your own to see where you stand."

"But she's not even sick! That's just murder! That's not the purpose of euthanasia!" Luna's insides twisted. "This isn't something Zanella would have done." None of it was.

The man pressed pause on the recording. "Unfortunately, Lemon Drop *is* sick. She got into a bit of rat poison earlier this evening, so the way I figure it, she's got about a day left before the internal bleeding takes her."

No.

No, no, no! Not Lemon.

Luna's soul cried out as her physical body began to betray her. She looked down at the dog, who whimpered in her arms before nuzzling her snout into Lu's chest. It was the same whimper she'd heard right before Herod and the others arrived, and now it made so much sense.

Lemon wasn't just scared.

She was poisoned.

Sick and likely dying.

"I hope you burn in hell," Cole said. "All of you."

Herod laughed and pressed play on the recording again, reciting the final phrase of the night right along with Siri. "Who do you choose, Luna? Lemon, or Jax?"

She buried her face into Lem's fur and sobbed. Because of course she chose Jax. She had to. What kind of mother would she be if she let her son drown to save her poisoned dog who would die tomorrow anyway?

It was all just so cruel and unjust, and if there were ever a time to need a savior, it was now.

God, please, she silently begged. *I know this wasn't your plan. I know evil wasn't by your design, but please, please, save us from this. Don't make me do this. Please, save them both. Save all of us.*

With fresh saltwater tears still running down her face, she opened her eyes and took a large breath when something over Cole's shoulder caught her attention.

"Jax!"

She rushed around Cole, waving a hand at her son before cursing and turning back. "Can you sign to him? I don't want to put her down. Tell him it's okay, and we're going to save him."

Cole quickly nodded, relaying the message with his hands. She watched as Jax nodded, and even though it was dark, she could see the fear in his eyes.

"I'm scared."

That was all it took. All it took for the hesitancy in Luna's heart to cease.

Because in an instant, her momma bear instincts took over, and she knew what she must do.

She cleared her throat and spoke again, her voice low. "If I kill the dog, you'll let him go? And this will all be over?" She didn't look at Herod, but her question was directed at him.

"Scout's honor." He made a three-finger salute.

Luna sneered.

That a-hole would've made a terrible Boy Scout.

"Okay," she said, nodding and swallowing. "Okay. Cole, tell Jax it's okay and to turn around. I don't want him to see this."

Cole's hands flew in a furious movement, but Jax shook his head.

"I don't want to. Please. I'm so scared."

Luna placed a hand on Cole's arm, then took a measured step into the water, closer to her son. *"It's okay. Just turn around. You're safe now."* She signed with one hand up in the air, the other still holding on to Lemon tightly.

"Mom!"

She started to motion for him to turn around again when large floodlights turned on, illuminating the small lake. Luna blinked, shielding her face and trying to adjust her eyes to the new lighting. How had they installed these? How had they done any of this, actually? Was there a freaking psychopath vigilante fund she wasn't aware of?!

"The fuck is this shit?" Sol bellowed, announcing his arrival. "Oi, Jax buddy!"

Luna looked up in time to see Sol waving his arms at Jaxson, not understanding what she was about to do.

"You better hurry, Luna. Ticktock, ticktock." Herod was holding the small device yet again in his hand, and upon pressing the button, a large gush of water shot out from each of the embedded pipe drains.

Luna quickly scanned the perimeter, clocking six of them.

"Dang it!" she cried as Lemon squirmed in her arms and Jaxson banged against the glass.

Now or never, Lu.

Out of time and options, Luna lunged forward, wading through the messy waters. They rushed by quicker than she expected, and she almost lost her footing. Jaxson was approximately fifteen or twenty feet from her, and a part of her wanted to rush right up next to him so she could free him the second Lemon was . . . gone.

But then the other, more rational, part of her brain reminded her that she needed to shield her son from this, and she held her ground, digging her heels into the sand.

"How do I know this isn't a trick?" she yelled over her shoulder. "How do I know you'll really let him go?"

"I guess you don't!" Herod yelled, laughing loudly over the rush of water. "But what other choice do you have?"

Luna had never wanted to kill a person before, but right now, she felt an entire universe of rage seething beneath her skin. When this was all over, she would—

Lemon barked, pulling her from her thoughts. Luna looked up and saw the pup was staring right at Jaxson, trying to warn Luna of the water that was now filling the bottom of his glass enclosure.

"Dang it, Lemon. Why do you have to make this so difficult?" Tears cascaded down her dirty, blood-caked face. "Why do you have to be such a good girl?"

Lemon blinked and whimpered in response; Luna knew she was out of time.

"Cole!" she screamed. "Can you please shield Jax from this?"

"On it!" he yelled.

But the woman who'd used sign language during the last act intercepted him, blocking his movement with the barrel of her rifle. "Ah, ah, ah. No interference!"

"I'm not interfering with her! I'm not touching the dog. Please, just let me stand with Jax so he doesn't have to see this," Cole pleaded while Luna fidgeted.

The woman looked at Herod, who nodded after a moment.

"Fine. But you better not touch Luna or the dog, or Jax dies."

A rush of cold air blew out of Luna as Cole dashed by her and through the water. Lemon whimpered again and tried to run after him.

Luna clung to her tighter. "It's okay, girl. It's okay." She kissed the dog's head. "I'm gonna make this fast for us, okay?" More tears rained freely, dampening her pet's white-blonde fur. "I'm gonna make this quick, baby, I promise."

And then Luna took the deepest breath of her life, flexed her fingers, and plunged Lemon into the water beneath her.

COLE

Cole was nearly to Jaxson when he heard Lemon's first squeal.

The sound felt like someone was scratching his brain, sending pain signals to every connected fiber in his being. He writhed in sympathetic pain, wincing as he heard Luna crying in tandem with the dog—their dog. Never in all his worst nightmares could he have imagined this.

"Cole, what's going on?"

His eyes locked on Jax as Cole tried to silence the sounds. For once, he was thankful Jaxson was Deaf. This was a noise he could never unhear and wouldn't wish on his worst enemy.

"Your mom is getting you out right now, buddy. Just hang tight another minute."

With Jax now directly in front of him, Cole did a once-over to evaluate the damage. Jax had a bruise on his upper cheek, with a small cut along his jagged jawline, but other than that, he seemed to be okay physically. Cole finished his initial evaluation, then took a quick glance over his shoulder to ensure Jax couldn't see what was happening.

He wished he hadn't.

Luna was elbow-deep in the water as it continued to flood in around her, while she used all her strength to hold the poor dog underneath. Cole could see Lemon's body flailing beneath Luna's grip, and Luna struggled to keep her under.

Cole shuddered and turned back around. If only there was another way . . .

Jax waved, catching his attention again. *"What's happening?"*

Cole shook his head. He had no idea how to respond.

Slowly, he raised his hands, trying to think of something, anything, when Lemon's muffled gurgles turned into a large, very audible yelp. Cole's eyes grew wide, and he spun around. Happening in both slow motion and within seconds, Cole saw Luna stumble backward and fall underwater while Lemon shot out of her grip and charged at Herod. Judging by the look on his face, he was significantly caught off guard, and by the time he'd reached for his gun, Lemon bit him, sinking her teeth into his flesh.

Yes! Cole huffed out a laugh. "Thatta girl, Lem!"

A shot fired through the air, grounding Cole back to reality. Without thinking, he dove into the water as it continued to pour into the lake, and he swam to Luna. He heard another shot go off, and he came up for breath, searching the scene to see what was happening. They'd said if he intervened, then Jax would die, but this may be their only chance to escape.

He had to act on it.

Moving in a blur, he saw Lemon charging at one of the servers and clamping down on the woman's ankle, causing her to fall.

Cole pumped his fist into the air.

Fucking get 'em, Lem.

His eyes scanned quickly now, and he saw Sol battling with Herod while Dani and Grey were fighting the others. To his left, he heard Luna cry, and he shot off into the black waters yet again in search of her. The water was ice-cold, just as it had been mere nights ago when he rescued Luna from her sleepwalking spell—which he now suspected was something else entirely—but he paid no mind to the goose bumps lacing his arms. Inside, his chest was on fire, and his body raced against the clock as he fought the current to find her and figure out a plan.

With another swish of his arm, Cole hit something hard yet soft. He grasped Luna's small frame with both arms and led them to the surface.

Luna gasped as soon as they broke it, sputtering water from her lungs as Cole hit her on the back. It took her a moment to breathe, to function normally, but when she did, her eyes widened, fear consuming her.

"Jax," she whispered.

Cole's eyes darted back to the glass tank, where Jax remained as more water leaked in. It was to his abdomen now, and Cole knew they didn't have much time before Jax would suffocate—or be shot.

"Listen to me," he said, looking back at Luna. "I need you to run and hide."

Another gush of water burst through the pipes, causing Cole and Luna to shift as they grew unsteady in the moving water.

"What? Cole, no—"

"I'm going to save him," Cole interrupted her. "I'm going to smash the glass, and I'm going to get him out of here. But he still has that ball and chain on his leg, so I'll have to carry him." He paused, grabbing Luna's hands. "I can't protect him and you at the same time."

Luna stared at him, searching his eyes and trying to understand. "Cole, I don't need protection."

"Luna, please. There's going to be glass everywhere in the water. I don't want you to injure yourself more than you already have, and I can't carry both of you. So I need you to please listen to me and swim to the opposite side of the lake, underneath the water to protect you from the bullets, and then I need you to hop out and run while I get Jaxson. Do you think you can do that?"

What he really meant to say was, *Can you trust me?*

Luna bit her bottom lip, a trace of dirty water falling off. "Yes," she said after a moment. "Yes, of course."

"Okay." He squeezed her hand, then let go. "You head over now. I'll wait as long as I can, and then I'll bust open the tank and get him out of here. I promise you, Lu."

"Cole, wait!" He had started to back away, but Luna stopped him, tugging on his hand and pulling him back to her. "I love you," she said once he was facing her again. "I love you so much. Please go save my baby."

And as another bullet popped off in the background and another cry hit the air and thousands of gallons of water rushed into the lake and Jaxson pounded on the glass cage, Cole grabbed both sides of Luna's face, and he kissed her.

For one brief moment, everything felt right in the world. Like no matter what happened, he would always have this kiss to come home to, these lips to hold on to for dear life, as a reminder that all their problems would eventually melt away, the worry vanishing from their skin.

But everything wasn't right, and the weight of their lives stacked on him like a thousand boulders.

So in a moment of absolute and total clarity, he broke the kiss, rubbed her cheek, and dove back under the water, desperate to rescue Jaxson.

Underneath the lake's surface, the dark, murky waters encompassed him again, but he didn't have time to linger on the fact that he could barely see. Time was of the essence, so Cole swam as hard as he could, following the direction he thought would lead him to the glass cage.

The water swayed dramatically as he pushed his arms with full force, fighting against the current. He had no clue how much water they had dumped in by now, but the constant rush made it nearly impossible to move quickly.

Eventually, his hands struck against something that felt like glass, and his heart leapt with joy. He broke free from the surface with a large inhale as he tried to catch his breath. Behind him, Cole could hear shouts, but he drowned them out the second his eyes landed on Jaxson.

The child's eyes were wide, his cheeks tear-stained and his hands tugging at his hair the way they always had when he was nervous.

"Watch out," Cole signed.

Jax furrowed his brows, the fear still evident in his gaze. *"What?"*

"Move! Breaking you out!"

Finally understanding, Jax sank to the back right corner of the cell and nodded, indicating he was ready for whatever Cole was about to do. Cole nodded back, then took a deep breath and glanced around him, trying to pinpoint Luna's location. At first, he saw nothing, and his heart pounded. Then, a millisecond later, he saw her blonde hair pop out from across the lake, almost to the edge.

"There we go, Lu," he mumbled to himself. Then, he turned back to Jax. *"Here goes nothing."*

Cole unfurled his fingers, then clenched them into tight fists, summoning every ounce of grief, anger, pain, and defeat he'd encountered tonight. He harbored all that negative energy and then forced his body against the mud below him, against the current around him, and into the glass enclosure in front of him.

It didn't budge.

Dammit!

His shoulder stung as it made contact, but that didn't stop him. Cole tried again, and then again, failing miserably both times.

What is this shit made of?

Taking a breath, he waded backward in the water, thinking. If he wasn't strong enough to break this, then he needed something else, some other way to get Jaxson out.

A piece of wood flew through the water and hit Cole's arm.

"Ouch!"

He grimaced, offended that the current had betrayed him by sending broken bits of wood his way, but then a spark of hope ignited inside him, and he dove underwater again. His body throbbed as he swam, but he persisted until he was at the bottom. He forced his eyes open, ignoring the sting from the filthy water, and he placed his hands against the earthy bottom, digging until he found the perfect rock. With his hand clamped around it, Cole swiveled his body back around and kicked his feet off the ground.

A shot grazed his left ear as soon as he resurfaced, and he cursed, clutching his ear. He had to be quick now.

Without thinking or looking back, he motioned for Jax to move again and hit the hefty rock at the glass.

"It'll never work!" a voice yelled from land.

Cole drowned it out by hitting the cage again.

And again.

And again.

Until slowly, a crack formed.

It was small at first, and then all at once, a large divide split the paneling, similar to how an earthquake appears in the ground. Cole let out a choked laugh, then reared back and hit the glass again, this time shattering it and freeing Jax.

Just like he promised.

He dropped the rock immediately and helped Jaxson climb out.

"Come on, buddy!" He knew Jax couldn't hear, but he didn't need to. He clung to Cole immediately, pointing at the large weighted ball and chain that was still on his ankle. Cole cursed, knowing there was no time to carry him out now. They were coming for them.

He plunged his hand underwater, and by some miracle, he brushed the surface of the rock he'd been using. He slipped his fingers around it, all while blood poured down the left side of his neck. He held up a finger to Jaxson, signaling for him to wait, and then Cole dove once again into the water, searching with his fingers until he found the ball and chain. Moving as quickly as the current would allow him, Cole flung his arm against the links as many times as he could, silently screaming when it broke.

Thank you, Lord.

He swam to the surface, sputtering from the water he'd inhaled. "*Go!*"

Jax's eyes grew wide, and he started to argue, but then an arm wrapped around Cole's neck.

"*Go!*"

Without another word, he watched Jaxson swim off into the night, then he turned around to see who was attempting to kill him.

"Oh, you've got to be fucking kidding me."

JAX

Cold.

Wet.

Darkness.

The sting of silence.

Those were the sensations that surrounded Jax as he swam through the traverse of moving lake waters that night. He had taken a deep breath as soon as he saw the hands plastered around Cole's neck, then took off, diving underwater and swimming as fast as he could. He'd never been much of a swimmer, but those few lessons his mom had paid for their first summer together were apparently paying off because now he swam with a vengeance.

Pieces of driftwood and trash floated by him as he plunged through the darkened waters. He brushed most of them away, but then a sharp object pierced his thigh, and he winced, pausing to extract it. Whatever it was had broken skin, and he knew he was bleeding. Coming up for air, he held up the item, his stomach curdling when he realized what it was.

Someone's bone.

Jax shuddered, then tossed the skeletal remains aside before continuing his trek, not daring to look back. Cole had said he would protect him, that everything would be okay; Jax feared if he looked over his shoulder, he would soon realize it was not.

And he didn't want to live in that reality yet.

He took another deep breath and plunged beneath the water, having no idea where he was going or what he was going to do next. Only that he had to get out of here and call for help. He saw a woman earlier talking about plugging a cell booster back in—or at least that's what he thought. Jax wasn't great at reading lips, but he was almost positive that's what she'd said. He just needed to find a phone, and then he could try.

A large vibration reverberated through the water, sending an instant chill up Jaxson's spine. He couldn't be sure, but his gut told him it was a gunshot.

He swam faster.

You're gonna be okay.

Cole's words played on repeat in his brain, and he prayed the same was true for his mom. He had to trust Cole would protect her.

Because he didn't know what he'd do without a mom.

Without *his* mom.

Jax had lived so much of his life without parents. Growing up in those awful foster homes, being beaten and abused by more than one pretend parent, only to later learn his true identity and the origin story of how his Intended Parents, surrogate mother, and Luna had all abandoned him. Or at least he thought. That's what that idiot Zanella had told him when he'd plucked Jaxson from the group home he'd been living in.

Jax remembered feeling broken and vindicated all at the same time, finally knowing the truth of his upbringing. He'd been so hurt, so destroyed, and he let Zanella take advantage of that and talk him into participating in The Gala. He'd told Jax that was the only way to move on from this horrible life and stick it to his parents for the way they'd treated him. *Poetic justice*, he'd called it.

And Jax had tried. He'd tipped the lighter over, lit the flame to his head, and was prepared to end it all.

But then Cole saved him.

And Sol helped him escape.

And Luna welcomed him with open arms, pouring love into him every chance she got.

She was a great mother.

The best, really.

And Jax couldn't live without her again.

Reaching the shore, he bobbed his head up, carefully peeking over the water's horizon. He could see Cole held at gunpoint on the opposite shore and his mom tied up, kneeling. Jax's heart raced with panic. He couldn't tell where Sol, Dani, or Greyson were, and he hoped that didn't mean they were dead.

You have to save them.

At this new thought, he stealthily hoisted himself out of the water, never taking his eyes off his mom or the man he'd come to love like a father, Cole. They were both facing his direction, which meant the bad guys were positioned the opposite way. As long as Jax didn't make a sound, he could crawl away.

Something sharp stung his neck, and he clamped a hand over his mouth, trying not to shout.

Way to go, moron.

He chastised himself, then swatted at his neck. Small black goop on his fingers revealed a dead mosquito.

Great. Fucking great. He'd almost killed them all because of a stupid bug.

Wiping his hand off on his wet shirt, Jax rechecked that no one was coming for him, rolled off the bank, and slithered into the grass. For a moment, he lay there, not daring to move a muscle as he got attuned to his surroundings. As a Deaf person, his other senses had become more aware, more heightened and acute. He may not be able to hear someone approaching, but he could sense it.

Feel it.

After scanning the area as far as he could see and getting a feel for the ground, he deemed it safe enough to move and army crawled to the edge of the forest. He thought about how this would all be so much easier with his hearing aids, but one of the masked women had taken them after grabbing him. He snarled at the memory.

What he wouldn't do to wrap his hands—

Movement in the distance caught his eye.

Jaxson froze, his body on high alert. If they caught him now, it would all be over. He had to be absolutely certain no one had—

A boar ran out in front of him and to the lake.

Jax remained still as a statue until he was confident no one—or anything else—was around him.

Finally, he let out a breath and kept moving, his feet treading cautiously over the terrain. It was Halloween night in Ohio, which meant the beauty of fall had already died, giving way to dropping temperatures, rain, and mud. He had to remain diligent, careful, mindful of every step. One wrong move, one broken tree branch, and he could give himself away.

He couldn't let that happen.

Heart pounding, he continued to move, not entirely sure of where he was going but putting distance between himself and the others no less. He would eventually either run into the highway, where he could flag someone down, or end up back at the cabin, where he could search for a phone and dial 911.

Seconds felt like hours as he tiptoed through the forest, survival mode his only method, his only thought. He just had to keep moving—

A leaf bobbed in the corner of his eye. He paused again, trying to remember if there'd been a breeze.

It could be another animal, another wild pig stuck in this mess of a horror game. Or it could be Lemon. Cole had tried to hide what was happening, but he knew his mom was holding her seconds before the chaos erupted. Jax hadn't seen which way she went, but he knew the dog wasn't dumb enough to stick around and find out what else was on the agenda for her tonight.

After a moment, he lifted his left foot, readying himself to take a small, tentative step, when the leaf nudged again. Suddenly, an eerie sensation crept up his vertebrae, stilling his heart.

Because someone was behind him.

And they were breathing very heavily.

LUNA

Luna stared at the ground in front of her.

Hoof marks from the pigs were ingrained in the mud, creating a pattern. One that swirled in circles, causing Luna's eyes to cross as she trailed their inconsistent path.

"Eyes up!" the voice yelled.

She was being held at gunpoint. Had been tied up, thrown onto the ground, and mocked horrifically by the person who stood before her.

"I can't believe you're the one doing this," she said, her voice barely above a whisper. "What is wrong with you? That's Jaxson you were holding hostage. My son! You were going to kill him." Venom and confusion both dripped from her lips. "I can't believe it."

She looked up now, locking eyes with the vicious, unassuming monster.

Dani.

"Ah, you're always so dramatic," Dani said, waving a hand. "Jax was never going to die. That was just part of the game, to get *you* here." She swung her eyes to Cole. "And *you.*"

Anger flooded Luna. "You could've gotten us here without traumatizing my son!"

"Let us go, Dani," Cole demanded. He was being held at gunpoint by Herod, who smirked.

Luna shivered with rage, but there was one silver lining in all this.

Lemon and Jaxson had escaped.

That was all that mattered. Now, she just had to keep the bad guys distracted long enough for them to find help.

"What the devil are you doing this for?" Sol asked from his spot on the ground. They'd tied him up, too. Luna still didn't know where Greyson was. "I thought we had sumthin', Dani. The way you screamed—"

"Enough!" Dani pointed the gun at him. "I only slept with you to throw you off. After you caught me trying to sneak off to check on the water pump situation, I had to . . . improvise."

Luna shook her head, shock and disgust overwhelming her. "It was all you," she said, taking a moment to let the words settle in. "Not just tonight, but everything that happened this week leading up to the party. It was all you . . ." Her mind flashed back to the bones, the campsite, the *near-drowning* experience.

Dani cocked her head, her lips curling into an evil grimace. "Of course it was. Who do you think told Sol about the *Rhododendron Recluse*?"

Luna felt faint. "Sol! I thought you said Wrenner Scott told you that."

Sol grumbled. "Sorry, love. You know my memory's pretty shite."

Dani snickered before biting out a retort, but Luna didn't hear whatever it was. All her mind could think was *why*?

"Why, Dani?" She pinned her with a stare, desperate to know what could have possibly possessed Cole's *book agent* to orchestrate all this. "*Why*, Dani? Why would you do this to us? To everyone?" These people, this *army*, had murdered and assaulted innocent people tonight—nearly killed a dog! She didn't know who she had expected to be behind it all, but it certainly wasn't *Dani*.

Dani pursed her lips before smoothing a black flyaway hair. "Isn't it obvious?"

Luna furrowed her brows. It absolutely was *not* obvious.

"You know, for investigative reporters, you're really all a terrible bunch."

"I'm not a fucking—"

"Shut up, Solstice!" Dani barked, cutting him off.

Luna shook with fear, but she didn't dare look away.

"Is this because of the book?" Cole asked. "Please tell me you didn't do all this for book sales, Dani."

She snorted. "No, Cole. I didn't do all of this for *book sales*, although that will be a nice bonus."

A gust of wind rolled by, causing more goose bumps to rise along Luna's skin. Behind her, water continued to gush into the lake; by now, it had to be close to being full.

With the bones she'd chopped up earlier buried underneath.

"Please," Luna whispered. "Please just let us go. We won't tell anyone it was you."

Dani swung the gun back her way. "I'm afraid I can't do that. See, the plan was never for you to make it out of here tonight, little Lu. Jaxson was never going to die, but you were. You and Cole both."

Fear grappled Luna. "But why? What have I ever done to you?"

"What have you done? What haven't you done?" she screamed. "What haven't you *all* done?"

Luna still didn't understand. "I am truly sorry if I—"

"Oh, it's way too late for apologies now." Dani started circling around them. "I'd say about fifteen years too late."

Fifteen years. What was she talking about?

"That's how long it's been since you donated your eggs, yes?"

Luna's eyes widened. Then she spoke hesitantly. "Yes, but—"

Dani sighed dramatically. "You really are a slow bunch." She pinched the bridge of her nose, rubbing her eyes. "Luna, have you ever wondered who the father of your child is?"

Of course she had. Luna had wondered almost every day for the past five years. It used to haunt her, plague her, that she didn't know. Likely never would.

She'd begged the fertility clinic to tell her, to release the information, but they wouldn't. Said it breached a confidentiality clause of some sort. And because she didn't have the funds to pursue further legal action, her only option was to pray God would send her answers one day.

Apparently that day was today.

"Of course I have," she finally said after a rushed breath.

Dani stopped her tyrant parade long enough to crouch in front of Luna, her sweat-streaked face mere inches from hers. "And do you remember who else donated their sperm to that fertility clinic?"

Her eyes pierced Luna's gaze, and for a moment, Luna stopped breathing.

"No," she whispered, not wanting to accept this answer. "Impossible."

Dani smiled, the twitch of her lips resembling something feral. "Not impossible at all, my dear. It's in fact very, very possible."

"What are you talking about?" Cole cut in.

But neither woman answered him. Instead, they remained in a deadlock gaze as Luna processed this new information. If what she was saying was true, then that meant—

"Graham Zanella is Jaxson's father." Her voice came out as a whisper, but Luna felt the conviction, the truth of her words, the moment they left her lips.

"What?" Sol and Cole asked in unison.

"That's right, babe," Dani said, using her forefinger and thumb to slightly pinch Luna's chin. "Daddy Z, delivering one last surprise from beyond the grave."

Denial started to wash over Luna as her heart retaliated. "No," she said. "This doesn't make sense. If Z knew he was Jax's father, then why didn't he tell us at The Gala?" Then she asked a question even more important to her. "Why did he convince Jaxson to attempt suicide?"

Something just didn't add up. Unless—

"He didn't know," Dani said, finishing the thought for her. "He died never knowing what happened to his sperm. He always said he didn't want to know, no matter how much I begged him." She paused, chuckling in frustration. "I used to say, 'You won't give me a baby, but you'll dish them out to whores at the clinic like candy. The least you could do is find out who they are. Who the kids ended up being, how their lives are.'"

Luna reeled from the shock of this news.

"Did you just say he wouldn't give you a kid?" Solstice asked.

Dani popped her neck, then nodded, slowly. "Mhm." She turned and faced the boys, a stoic expression on her face. "Graham Zanella was the love of my life."

Oh, fudge. Luna groaned. *A jilted lover. Just what we needed around here.*

She felt like crying at the absurdity of it all.

But her mind wouldn't let her. Because she was too busy working the pieces together in her brain like a puzzle: Dani had been in love with Z. That was why she was after them. Because Cole killed Zanella, and Luna . . . what had Luna done? Other than unknowingly create a child with Z.

Ugh! Graham freaking Zanella is Jax's father?!

She shuddered again as more thoughts clicked into place. *This* was why her son loved art. Why he had weird quirks and mannerisms that felt familiar in a way she couldn't identify.

It was probably why he was so troubled. Why the clinic had never released the information, because they were afraid of Zanella, even though the man was dead. Who knows what he had threatened to do to them if they ever released that information.

So how did Dani get it?

"How do we know you're not lying?" Luna asked suddenly.

"Please." Dani scoffed. "You know it's true. Look at the boy. He's the spitting image of Graham. And that artwork?" Dani pursed her lips. "It reeks of his father."

Luna slumped her shoulders, defeated.

She was beyond exasperated at this point.

"So why do you want me dead, then? It's not like I had any say in all this. I didn't even know Jaxson existed until five years ago."

"Because!" Dani shouted this time, sending a new wave of chills through Luna, making her shudder. "Didn't you hear what I said? Zanella was the love of my life, and he refused to give me a baby. Then come to find out, he fathered one with *you* of all people, and that boy comes out looking like the spitting image of my Graham. He should be *mine*. He belongs to me, and I'm going to take him."

Jax was never going to die.

The words from earlier echoed in her mind.

She was never going to kill him because she wanted to *keep* him.

"We're going to carry on his father's legacy *together*."

"Like hell you are!" Luna spat back. She hadn't come this far to let another psychopath kidnap her baby. She would go to the ends of the earth to save him. "He's *my* son."

"Yeah, the son you never—"

A shotgun blared, and Luna jumped.

"Dammit!" Dani screamed, falling backward and clutching her shoulder. "Herod! Get him!"

Luna's eyes widened in terror, assuming the worst.

No, no, no. Jax, you were supposed to escape.

But a different voice interrupted them.

"Let them go, you Raisin Bran assholes!"

Greyson!

"Nobody even likes you!"

More open fire hit the air, and Luna fell as Cole jumped to cover her. "Stay down!"

Luna screamed, her ears stinging in the aftermath of the bullets. Then, for a moment, all was quiet.

"Did he—"

"Shh." Cole shoved his body off Luna's. Then—

"No!"

COLE

WHERE MOMENTS AGO GREYSON had been their knight in shining armor, he now lay on the ground, face-up with blood pooling in the pit of his chest.

"No," Cole repeated, his voice cracking as tears unwillingly fell down his scruffy, bloody face. "No, not Greyson. Please, God, no."

He army crawled to him, digging his elbows into the mud to inch himself forward.

"Blimey," Sol said from somewhere behind him. "I loved that fucker. Was a great friend."

"Greyson." Cole had reached him now, and Grey tilted his head slowly to look at him, his eyes barely moving. "Grey," Cole cried again. "Greyson, I'm here, buddy. I'm right here."

Luna sobbed behind Cole as Grey locked eyes with him.

"I . . . tried," he croaked. "I . . . tried, Colestice."

Pain stabbed Cole's heart. "I know, buddy. You did so good. We almost got 'em. You did good."

Greyson rolled his head back to stare at the sky, and a single tear trickled down his cheek. He took one last staggering breath, and then . . . nothing.

Cole stared at his friend's blank, unmoving eyes, and he knew.

Greyson was dead.

"Dammit!" Cole screamed before laying his forehead against Grey's. His hands were still bound, so Cole couldn't hug him, but he curled inward, wanting nothing more than to hug his friend who sacrificed his life to save them.

Cole wept.

"I guess we're going to have to speed things up," Dani said, her voice somewhere in the distance. "Can't have *that* happening again."

Cole knew he should move, knew he needed to fight against his grief and store it away for later, but for some reason, he simply couldn't. He'd been running on adrenaline and fumes all night—had acted on autopilot as he chopped his poor brother to bits, stood by while he watched Clementine get raped, listened while Luna tried to drown their dog, and then broke out Jaxson when the pup won victoriously.

All night, he'd been able to charge forward, been able to disassociate well enough to stay in survival mode.

But now, seeing Greyson of all people, lying here on the cold, hard earth, dead because he had tried to protect them, something inside him broke.

Cole was once again a helpless dad, except this time, he couldn't even hold the dead child he'd lost.

That's what Greyson had really felt like to him. A cranky nephew who liked to tease him, but whom Cole loved so very much.

He wasn't River, or Jax, or even Clara, but he was family no less.

And these monsters had just killed him in cold blood.

Cole hated them for it.

"I'm gonna get them, Grey," he whispered, attempting to wipe the snot from his nose. "I'm going to get every last one of those Raisin Bran fuckers. Gonna eat 'em for breakfast if that's what it takes."

"Herod, go get the boy. I want him to be here for this. Call it his initiation into the family."

Cole grunted under his breath at Dani's words. He couldn't believe he'd let this woman fool him when, all along, the entire thing had felt off. The delayed publication, inviting Clara to the party, hosting it in a secluded cabin—all of it had been strange to Cole, and still, he'd gone along with it and said nothing. How could he have been so stupid?

He shifted off of Grey's body and rolled to his other side. In doing so, he noticed the tie around his hands had been knocked loose slightly. If he could find something to cut it with, then he could still attack. He just had to wait for Herod to leave so that he could go after Dani, kill her, and then find and kill Herod before the man found Jaxson.

It wasn't a foolproof plan, but it was a plan no less.

It was all he had.

"Wait," Herod said to Dani. "Your wound."

Cole shot his gaze up, remembering Dani had been hit. He sent up a silent thank-you to his friend, then started rummaging through the dirt while they were distracted. He just needed to find a piece of glass big enough. Surely, some pieces had floated to the lake's edge after he shattered the cage.

"Please don't do this," he heard Luna silently begging. "There's still time to stop, to be forgiven and atone for your sins. Please."

Cole heard laughter from the wicked duo as they made fun of Luna. It was no surprise to discover they weren't religious, but the way they mocked her—*their*—belief system sent a new wave of wrath and fury through Cole's bones.

Just need to find a piece of—

There!

Shining in the gleam of the moonlight, Cole spotted a large chunk of glass jutting out from the mud. He shot his eyes over to Dani and Herod, confirming they still weren't paying attention as they attempted to stop the bleeding on her arm, and then Cole moved quickly, grabbing the shard of glass before concealing it between his legs as he sat up, still hovering near Greyson's body. If they looked at him now, they would just think he was mourning his friend.

Which he was, thanks to them.

"The bullet is lodged pretty deeply," Herod said. "You're going to need medical attention."

Cole got to work, sawing the shard of glass against the thin rope, creating more slack on the already-loose tension.

"I'll worry about that later," Dani snapped. "Just give me your shirt. Tie it around the wound and create a sling for now."

Luna and Sol both glanced at Cole, simultaneously acknowledging this may be their only chance. When Herod stood to strip down to his undershirt, Cole held up the piece of glass quickly, then shoved his hands back between his legs.

His heart beat rapidly, and he waited a moment to ensure neither Herod or Dani were going to turn around and catch him.

Then he started again.

A moment later, the strands started to break loose.

Cole did his best to contain himself, but joy shot through him as the rope began to snap. He continued sawing until every fiber was cut in half. When he was finished, he made quick work of undoing the rest of the knot and slipping the rope off his hands.

Cole was ready to attack, just as soon as—

LUNA

ANOTHER SHOT RANG THROUGH the night, and Luna screamed, certain she was going to have hearing damage this time.

Good thing you know sign—

Now's not the time, self!

Luna sank to the ground on instinct, but after processing Dani's scream, she shot her head up and looked around.

And she laughed.

Because standing at the edge of the forest, red hair billowing in the wind and a black velvet dress on full display, was Rose.

Cole's ex-wife, and River's and Clara's mom.

The next few moments happened in a blur, a sequence of flashes Luna would later repeat in slow motion, like a movie projector playing the slides in a final horror scene where the villain dies and the good guys escape.

"Dani!" Herod shouted, dropping his gun and falling to the ground next to her. "Dani! Wake up!"

Luna caught sight of Cole, who held up his piece of glass and then tossed it at her feet before standing, slowly at first, and then storming Herod, unleashing every ounce of Prison Cole that Luna had suspected was still in there.

Luna tried not to look, but she also couldn't look away. Cole was attacking with a vengeance, punching the man right, left, then gripping his hands around his neck, the same way he'd done to Zanella.

"Luna!" Rose hissed, running toward her and crouching down to help.

Luna tore her gaze away from Cole and Herod, blinking rapidly at Rose as she tried to process what was happening. Before she knew it, Rose had ripped through the top rope and was working on the bottom one, helping Luna untie herself.

"Come on! Jax is waiting for you back at the cabin with Clara."

Luna stared at Rose in disbelief. "He's safe?"

Rose paused long enough to squeeze Luna's hand. "Yes. I found him wandering in the woods where we were hiding. We snuck back to the cabin and saw the coast was clear. He wrote on a notebook that everyone was dead or at the lake. Then he started rummaging around until he found a phone and somehow called 911. He's hiding upstairs in a closet with Clara while they wait."

For the first time that night, Luna felt like she could breathe.

"He's okay," she said quietly.

Rose squeezed her hand again. "He's okay."

Luna burst into a fit of laughter, then grabbed Rose in an unexpected hug, almost knocking her off her feet. "Thank you."

Rose pulled away and smiled. "You're welcome. No more of our kids are dying."

A tear slipped out of the corner of Luna's eye, and she nodded, turning her attention back to Cole, who was still squeezing the life out of this demented man while Sol egged him on from the sidelines.

Except, this didn't feel right. Her son was safe, they'd killed Dani, and the cops were on their way. No one else had to die tonight.

"Cole, stop!" she yelled suddenly, lunging to his side, knowing she had to stop him. "Cole, the cops are coming! Jax and Clara are safe—God rescued us! Nobody else needs to die!

A crazed look swept over Cole's eyes. "But River's not safe!" he shouted, spit flying out of his mouth. "David's not safe! Greyson isn't *safe!*" Veins popped out of his forehead, another version of him morphing and taking over. "This fucker deserves to die, Lu!"

"Just, just wait!" Luna begged, her mind racing. She still wanted to punish Herod, even agreed that he deserved to die, but not like this. Not by Cole. Life wasn't theirs to give and take. She needed to think of a way to convince him of this before it was too late.

Jesus—

She started to pray, but then words poured out of her before she even realized what was happening.

"We serve a just God! Please, just trust that the Father will take care of this! This man will rot in hell if he doesn't repent of his sins—let that be enough for you, Cole! Please, let go. You don't have to kill him!"

Cole grunted, but something in her words—Jesus's words—must have clicked because, reluctantly, he released his death grip on the man. Luna sighed with relief.

"Is that all you got?" Herod said through a cracked, hoarse voice as Cole sat backward, heaving and panting. "One little *moment from God* and a plea from your stupid girlfriend, and you call it quits? You're more pathetic than your daughter was. I'm glad she's dead. You'd make a shit father."

Cole threw another punch across Herod's jawline, causing him to spit out a tooth as blood splattered out.

Cheese and rice!

On second thought . . . "Rose, give me your gun!"

She obeyed, and Luna cocked the Glock 19 as soon as it hit her hands, adrenaline coursing through her and taking over. "Cole," she yelled, her voice unsteady at first. "Cole, move!"

Cole swung his head back, a questioning look in his gaze. Luna observed the dark loose curls that hung down over his forehead, the blood and mud that coated his handsome face, and the veins in his forearm that bulged out of his rolled-up shirt.

"I've got this," she whispered. "Trust me."

Cole dropped his eyes back to Herod, assessing the damage he'd done, then climbed off him, but not without kicking him in the ribs.

Herod winced. "Fuck you!"

"You know," Luna said, stepping over Herod's left leg, then his right, before firmly planting her feet on either side of him and aiming the gun right at his core. "King Herod's death is widely debated by biblical scholars."

She paused, pressing her finger gently against the safety on the trigger, her heartbeat pounding in her eardrums.

"But my favorite theory," she continued, "is the one that suggests he died from Fournier's gangrene—"

"No!" Herod yelled, begging for his life.

And Luna would grant him that. She would spare his life, just as she'd begged Cole to do.

She couldn't say the same for all his body parts, though.

"—which is an unusual infection of the male genitalia." She lowered the gun so it was directly aimed at his manhood. "You really should have chosen a different name."

Three, two—

Luna.

She gasped and nearly dropped the gun.

I am just, remember?

Frack. She'd been two seconds away from shooting Herod's balls off. Sweat slicked down her palm as she shakily held onto the weapon and started to argue.

But—

But I am God. I will deal with him in due time.

She felt like groaning. Felt like stomping her foot and protesting.

But, of course, she didn't. Because that wouldn't be pleasing to the Lord.

Can I at least kick him where the sun don't shine?

Luna.

She blew out a breath.

Okay, okay. Sorry.

"Lu?" Cole gently prompted.

And so even though she wanted nothing more than to hurt this man, this evil, foolish man who had caused so much strife tonight, she didn't. Instead, she lowered her gun and spoke directly to Herod.

"You better get right with the Lord before your time comes. Otherwise you'll suffer much worse than any pain I could've inflicted."

Then she stuck out her tongue and signed, "*Stupid.*"

ONE MONTH LATER

I suppose you're wondering where this leaves me now.

And to that, I say, you and me both.

—Cole Sloane, *The Great Chase*

COLE

Cole took a deep breath as the crisp November air filled his chest.

It was Sunday morning, just days after Thanksgiving, and he was sitting on his porch in his grandma's old rocker, drinking coffee and enjoying the quiet morning view.

Dad, Lemon whimpered from the bottom step of the porch, wagging her tail back and forth, just waiting for an invitation.

Cole smiled and set down his mug. "Come here, girl."

He patted his thigh, and Lemon bounded up the stairs and into his lap, licking his face in a sweet, frantic canine fury.

"Easy there, girl," Cole said through a chuckle. "You're gonna make your mom jealous with all those kisses."

Lemon barked, then resumed licking his face as Cole continued to laugh. He'd never been so thankful for a pet in his life. When the police and paramedics had arrived on scene that night at the cabin, he'd rushed Lemon to one of the medics, notifying them of the poison in her system. He had been terrified it was too late, that Lem girl would die, joining River and Emmett, and *David and Greyson*, in Heaven all too soon, but the woman had immediately snatched a bottle of peroxide from the ambulance.

"Here," she'd said, offering Lemon a capful to drink. "This will induce vomiting. Should work, depending how long it's been. I'll notify them we need a vet on standby at the hospital."

Poor Lemmy girl had puked her guts out after that, but thankfully, that was it. Cole was weary for the next twenty-four hours, giving her all the extra love and attention he could, all while preparing his heart for the worst yet again, but she was cleared by the vet and given a clean bill of health.

Lemon had survived, just like he, Luna, Jaxson, and Solstice had.

He wished he could say the same for David and Greyson.

A pang of grief and guilt swelled inside him, the same way it did every time he thought of them. His lost brethren, only gone because Cole had brought them together that night, invited them to his party in a vain attempt to celebrate a stupid fucking book.

A book that, following the aftermath of the launch party, was an instant *New York Times* bestseller.

Cole still had muddled feelings about the irony of it all.

At least Herod and Dani didn't get away. His agent was dead, and although Herod hadn't died that night, he was going to spend the rest of his life in prison. Personally, he still wished Luna had shot off his balls. Would've served him right. But Cole understood why she didn't. It was one of the many reasons why he loved her.

He rubbed the pup's snout as she settled down, then grabbed his cup of coffee and took another sip. It really was a beautiful morning.

The back door creaked open, and Jaxson stepped out.

"Hey, buddy."

"Sup?" Jax nodded, then took a seat beside Cole.

"You ready for today?" Cole could tell something was wrong. Jax chewed the corner of his cheek, looking perplexed. *"You okay?"*

Jax picked at his nails, not answering right away. *"I guess."* He shrugged. *"I was just thinking about Z. How he's my real dad and all . . ."*

He dropped his hands.

"It's still hard to believe, right?" Cole was still wrapping his head around it if he was being honest.

"Yeah!" Jax's expression was animated. *"Like how can I be related to that monster? And what if . . . what if I'm like him, Cole? What if I'm crazy?"*

Cole shook his head. *"You're not crazy, Jax. And even if you were, we'd still love you."*

Jax gave a soft smile, but it didn't quite reach his eyes.

"Hey," Cole tried again, taking his concerns more seriously. *"You're an amazing kid. Regardless of whose DNA you have, you're your own person. Your own man whose identity can be found in Christ alone. Never forget that, especially today."*

Jaxson grinned again, and this time, it was genuine. The kid would still need ample time to process this news, and they would likely have many more conversations like this in the years to come, but Cole was ready for it. Welcomed it even.

Cole sat down his mug. *"Come on. We need to get ready before we're late."*

LUNA

The sunlight glittered against the river as Luna took her place in the water next to Cole and Jax.

It was a glorious, beautiful morning, for more reasons than one.

Her son and her dog were alive, her man was out of prison, and today, she would get to baptize the two people who meant the most to her.

And have a wedding!

She squeezed both of their hands as the preacher waded into the water.

"God is good," Pastor Luke said.

"All the time," Luna repeated with the small crowd of attendees.

"And all the time," he continued.

"God is good."

They recited it like clockwork, and Luna beamed inside and out. She'd dreamt of this day so many times, in so many ways. Each time she dragged Jaxson to church with her on a Sunday morning, every time she visited the prison and answered one of Cole's lingering questions about faith. Every morning and every night when she prayed for their salvation and for God to change their hearts, to help them see the love He has in store for them, and to show them how they could fully, truly live in Christ alone.

She'd prayed for this moment so many times, and today, today she got to help baptize both of them.

Together.

In a *river*.

"Preacher man said God is good all the time, then repeated himself backward." Sol, of course, was in attendance, having finally mastered his ASL skills and offering to interpret today. He still butchered a lot of signs, but Luna didn't have the heart to tell him no, especially when she saw how happy it made Jax.

"God is good all the time," Jax replied, making Luna's heart throb. Then he stuck his tongue out at Sol, making them laugh.

"Boys. Focus."

They both raised their hands in mock defeat, then returned their attention to the pastor, who carried on.

"What an honor it is to be here with you both today."

Luna looked away, scanning the crowd as the pastor made his speech. Aside from her, Jax, Cole, and Solstice, there were a select few they'd invited to join them. Lemon, who was wading and jumping at the shore's edge; a friend of Jax's from school; Cole's old pal, Jayce; Luna's mom, Georgia; Luna's best friend, Nyla; and last, but certainly not least, Rose and Clara.

Luna was delighted to have Clara there, especially after she'd seen her practicing sign language with Jax when they'd invited Rose and Clara over a few weeks ago. Rose, on the other hand, was someone whom Luna would've never imagined herself hanging out with, much less inviting to something as intimate as Cole's and Jax's baptisms, but Rose had saved them, saved them all that night. If she hadn't found Jax, gotten him and Clara to safety, called 911, and then shown back up at the lake and shot Dani, giving her, Cole, and Sol the chance to escape and take down He Who Shall Not Be Named, they might have all died that night.

Rose had earned her right to be here—perhaps more than anyone else. And as for her infidelities with Cole, Luna knew he'd forgiven her. They all had.

Because that's what Jesus would have done.

Besides, however they looked at it, they were now a close-knit group, one that could only be formed by their shared traumas from the horrors of that night at the cabin. They'd survived together, they'd mourned Greyson's and David's lives together, and now, they were celebrating together.

To God be the glory.

Luna only wished Clementine were here. She'd invited her, but her parents had taken her out of town for the Thanksgiving holiday, hoping to get her mind off everything she'd endured.

After the terrors of that night were over, Luna had asked the police what had happened to her. She was surprised, and thankful, to learn the child was receiving care at the same hospital everyone else was and that her parents had been found and notified. Luna had waited for their arrival, then asked for permission to see the girl. They'd declined initially but then contacted her a week later, saying Clementine had asked for her. Luna had been overjoyed at the chance to see her, hold her, cry with her. It was a trauma bond for the ages, and Luna vowed to be there for her whenever she needed, even when they all moved to Columbus after the holidays for Jaxson's first semester at the Ohio School for the Deaf.

She made a mental note to text Clementine some pictures later, then smiled, feeling the presence of the Holy Spirit coming upon her, wrapping all the way down to her ring finger with a glow. She still couldn't believe how blessed she was to get to spend the rest of her life with her two favorite boys.

Lemon barked from the edge of the shore, and Luna smiled. She loved that dog so much. Not only because she was the goodest good girl in the whole world for forgiving Luna, but also because she'd saved them. If Lemon hadn't come up for air that night at just the right moment and escaped, if she hadn't bitten Herod and attacked Dani before scurrying off into the night, then the chain of events that had led to everything else would've never happened. God had heard their cries and sent Lemon in for the rescue.

Luna had always felt like dogs were Jesus's little helpers—a special gift given to show humankind just a fraction of a percentage of His love for us.

"Jaxson," Pastor Luke said. "Are you ready, son?"

Luna flicked her eyes to Sol, biting her lip with glee when he translated correctly.

Jax nodded, then moved to stand by the pastor, who was motioning to the spot beside him.

Luna followed, but not before giving Sol an appreciative arm-around-the-neck hug and whispering, "Thank you, but I got this next part."

He smiled at her when she pulled away, respectfully bowing his head and stepping aside.

"Hey, kiddo," she said and signed, wading through the water. "You cool if Mom helps out here?"

"Of course." He grinned at her, then added, *"Who knows what would've happened to my soul if Sol did this part."*

She chuckled but chose not to comment. "All right, Pastor," she said, still signing in tandem with her voice. "All you."

Try as I might, I still haven't found it in my heart
to fully accept Christ as my Savior, but perhaps by
the time of publication, that will have changed.

—Cole Sloane, *The Great Chase*

COLE

Breathe.

Cole watched with bated breath as Luna and the preacher dunked Jaxson underwater, a swell of emotions rising in him.

His future stepson, redeemed and washed by the blood of Christ.

Cole couldn't wait to go next.

He anxiously awaited his turn, smiling from ear to ear as Jaxson came up out of the water.

Luna immediately wrapped him in her arms.

"Ugh, Mom!" he said, trying to push her away. *"You're embarrassing me."*

Luna laughed, a beautiful, infectious sound that danced in Cole's ears. *"News flash: Moms are supposed to embarrass their kids. Come here!"*

Jax rolled his eyes but allowed his mother to pull him into one last death grip before she released him and turned to Cole, causing the breath in his lungs to hitch. She stood waist-deep in the cold water, her white long-sleeve gown flowing around her. She'd cut her hair short again, and it bobbed on her shoulders, her honey-blonde beach waves adorned with colored daisies throughout.

She was the most beautiful bride.

"Cole, you're next," Pastor Luke said.

He nodded, but his gaze was still locked on Luna. After they made it out of that death trap alive, he couldn't wait one more minute to pop the question.

He was serious when he told Luna he'd wait a lifetime for her, but given the circumstances, who knew how long a lifetime was? As soon as the doctors had finished bandaging his ear from where the bullet grazed it, he'd jogged to the gift shop and bought a plastic ring from the little toy dispenser, ran back upstairs to Luna's room, and then dropped down on one knee.

She said yes immediately.

Cole licked his lips as he waded to her and grabbed her hand. The pastor cleared his throat, reminding them they had an audience. Luna blushed, quickly pulling her lips in and diverting her gaze, and Cole laughed.

"Congrats, buddy." He gave Jax a high five, then pulled him into a quick hug before releasing him.

"Thanks, Dad."

Tears lined Cole's eyes. *"You're welcome, son."*

Jax fist-bumped him, then moved out of the way, motioning for Cole to take his spot. He saddled up between the pastor and Luna, his damned emotions already taking over.

Breathe.

Pastor Luke patted his back gently. "Are you okay?"

Cole sniffed, then wiped his eyes and nodded.

"Okay." The pastor cleared his throat. "Cole, it is my honor and privilege to be here with you today—to have gotten to know you and your story over the past few weeks. Your journey is a unique one, having come to Christ much later in life, and I'm saddened to say you've experienced more loss in your life than any man, any father, should ever have to."

More tears threatened Cole's vision as images of River flashed through his mind.

"However," Pastor Luke continued, "I'm also thrilled to know that *you know* God was still there, still with you in your sufferings. When you cried out to him in pain, he answered you, enveloped you in his everlasting love, and carried you through."

"Amen," Cole said, nodding. Luna quickly grabbed his hand and squeezed it before releasing her grip, and Pastor Luke gestured for Cole to cross his arms over his chest, the same way Jaxson had done only moments ago.

"Are you ready?" he asked.

Was he? Was he ready to allow Jesus to forgive him? To take this next symbolic step, despite what he'd done? Despite his resistance to acknowledge his sins?

Do it, Dad.

River's voice floated into the recesses of his mind, and Cole nearly choked on a sob.

"Yes," he said in a rush. "Let's do it." His heart pounded in his chest.

Pastor Luke smiled and placed one hand on Cole's back and the other over his chest. "Then Cole Sloane, it is my honor and privilege to baptize you today, in the name of the Father, the Son, and the Holy Spirit. Buried with Christ in baptism—"

Cole held his breath, then felt his body sway as the pastor dipped him underwater, under the *river,* and time stood still.

River's face flashed through Cole's mind again, and something urged him to open his eyes, to peek at something meant only for him. He did so slowly, ignoring the slight sting from the water, and then his heart stilled.

River.

An angelic version of his daughter sat there, floating in the river with him as her black hair swayed in the current. Cole's heart throbbed, and she smiled, waving at him through the misty water.

River! he mouthed.

She giggled, and Cole reached his hand out, trying, fighting, to reach her, but she shook her head.

Because it wasn't possible.

He couldn't touch her, no matter how hard he tried.

Cole wanted to cry, an ache intensifying in his chest, but then a sudden peace encompassed him.

And he knew this was enough for now. They would meet again in Heaven.

I love you, he mouthed, bubbles floating up around him.

She made a familiar sign with her hand.

I love you, too, Dad.

"—and raised to walk in a new life."

He broke through the water's surface and cried, fresh air filling his lungs.

"Cole!" Luna screamed, jumping on him and wrapping her arms around his neck before he even had a chance to gather what had just happened, the gift God had just given him. "I'm so *stinking* proud of you!"

The pastor winked, and Cole chuckled, a deep throaty laugh coming out as more tears streamed down his face. He hugged Luna back and held her, overwhelmed by it all. "I couldn't have done this without you."

She squeezed him again, then pulled back slowly, drinking him in and making Cole's body feel alive.

"Are you ready to marry me, Cole Sloane?"

His face stretched into a wide, effervescent grin. "You have no *fracking* idea."

THE END

ACKNOWLEDGEMENTS

As always, thank you to my Lord and Savior Jesus Christ for planting this story in my heart. It truly would not be here without your divine inspiration and guidance, so thank you for watering this seed and allowing it to grow. Navigating something as unique and complex as a horror rom-com with Christian values was challenging, but I don't doubt Your greater plan and purpose for this calling. Thank you, Jesus, for your perfect love, humility, and grace.

To my husband, Seth, thank you for taking time off work so I could finish this dang book! Your love and belief in me and my words means more than you'll ever know. I love you.

To my children, Willow and Ezra, thank you for being so kind and understanding when Mommy had to work, AKA write this wonderfully weird story. You two are the greatest joy in my life, and I thank God for you every day. Just please don't look at me differently when you're old enough to read this. I'm only mildly disturbed.

To my mom, Susie, who's always there to support and cheer me on, thank you so much for your unrelenting love. And to my dad, step dad, and uncle, thank you for your continued love and support as well. Who knew you'd all raise this weird little horror writer?

To my editor, Briana, thank you for everything. This manuscript was a mess when I sent it to you, and as always, you made it shine. Thank you for your keen eye, attention to detail, and caring nature.

To my cover designer, Mel, thank you for creating the cover of my dreams! You came in to an existing project and absolutely blew me away with your ability to create exactly what I was picturing.

To my proofreader, Kristin, thank you for having the final eyes on this thing! (And for your love, encouragement, and friendship throughout the process.)

To my beta readers, Rachel, Haley, David, Shaley, and Danielle, thank you for braving the messy second draft that was this story and pointing out all my ridiculous plot holes. We would probably still have an exorcist if it weren't for you.

To the Deaf community, a special thank-you for letting me share a small sliver of your world in this story. And to Lisa Foster, thank you for answering my reader sensitivity questions and providing insight. As a hearing person, I tried to handle Jaxson's character with the utmost care and respect, and I had a blast while doing it.

And lastly, to my readers, thank you so much for your unwavering support. Whether you've been with Cole and Luna from the start or are just meeting them now, I am so humbled by every person who chooses to read my work. This book was especially weird and unique (and certainly hard to market), but you guys gave it a chance, and that is all I can ever ask. Thank you from the bottom of my heart for lending me your time. God bless!

ABOUT THE AUTHOR

Amy is a thriller author who was born in the heart of Appalachia before later relocating to the Midwest. With a Bachelor's degree in journalism and a professional background in content marketing, she has a passion for storytelling. When Amy's not writing, you can find her playing with her wild (lovable) children, hiding her book purchases from her husband, or rambling way too much on her Instagram stories. You can connect with her here: @authoramytackett.

Also by Amy Tackett

The Gala
(The Art of Deception Book 1)

Secret Santa
The Tides of Our Sins